The Mind Control Telepath

The Worlds Apart Series: Book 4

Evelyn Lederman

Paperback
ISBN-13:9780692556955
ISBN-10: 0692556958

e-book
ISBN-13:978-0-9966298-4-3
ISBN-10:099662984X

Cover Design by Fiona Jayde Media
Editing by Tina's Editing Services

Dedicated to my good friend Sheryldean Fernley. How she would have loved the ride!

Acknowledgements:

~

To Fiona Jayde Media for another incredible cover. Fiona has a way of making the vision in my head come alive on the cover

To Tina Winograd for her wonderful edits. I am now dubbed 'The Comma Queen.'

To Alice Calderonello and Katherine Fibiger for being my grammar police and comma patrol. Alice's commas rhyme still plays in my head. My sister and best friend were at my side at my first Romcon as an author.

To Susan Smith for adopting me.

To my tennis team pals for putting up with my constant travels and supporting my writing.

Prologue

7 Years Ago
Estero, Florida
Earth/Ginkgo Terra

She stared at the package with intensity. It would not have surprised her if it burst into flames. Her hands, which held the accompanying letter, shook with emotion. How could her parents ruin her birthday with the one reminder her life was not perfect?

Sweet sixteen. It would have taken more fingers than the ones on her trembling hands to count the boys she had kissed. Kisses that meant nothing, given by boys who did not elicit any emotion from her. They would call her an ice princess if they ever found out. What did it matter? Girls her age were not supposed to feel passion. Look what happened to poor Juliet. Besides, there was nothing wrong with her that finding the right boy wouldn't cure.

Her sun-kissed fingers opened the letter which accompanied the gift. She tore the envelope in her haste. Living in Florida left her with a year-round golden tan. She stared at the setting sun across the Gulf of Mexico, which gave her another excuse to postpone reading the letter from a woman long dead, the woman who had given birth to her.

Her birth mother left her and failed to provide plans for her care if anything happened to her. She had no memory of her father, the one who contributed the other half of her genetic code. It was a strange way to refer to a man who may have held her at one time with pride and joy. Memories of a black haired woman laughing, flashed before her eyes. How different the woman in her memory was from the blonde who had raised her, the one she had called mom. What little she remembered of her true mother, one thing was clear, there was a strong resemblance between them.

She unfolded the letter and began to read.

My dearest daughter, Jolyn.

Jolyn? Her name was JoAnna, JoAnna Carlson. The girls in the orphanage had called her Jo Jo. Not all the girls, the three who had been her world: Alex, Shirl, and Candy. They had been her family in another life, a sad life. She often wondered what had happened to the girls who dominated her early years. Obviously, her desire to know was not strong enough for her to find out. The ice princess would've had to feel something to take action. They wouldn't have fit into the existence she had carved for herself anyway, so what did it matter?

If you are reading this, I am no longer living. This world is hostile to our brain chemistry. Three of us have already died, including your father.

What a strange way to refer to the world. Well, she now knew what had happened to her birth father. Curious, she brought her attention back to the letter.

Ben and I are the only ones not plagued by the severe headaches. I pretend to suffer along with the others, since I do not want him to know the truth.

Know what? Her birth mother's letter raised more questions than it answered. Who were the others? Would her mother reveal her dark secret? There was only one way to find out.

I am a mind control telepath. The same type of being we left the Troyk universe to escape.

Great, now she knew there was mental illness in her biological family's history. What a birthday present! Her birth mother believed she was from another world. There was no such place as the Troyk universe.

It must have been a world from an episode of *Star Trek* or *Farscape*. She had never seen either show, science fiction was not her thing, but what else could it have been? Romantic comedies, with their happily ever after endings, were her passion. The movies seemed to generate a reaction, something her boyfriends had never managed to do.

My only hope is that you are one of us and will not suffer as the others have. If the headaches start, find Ben Clark in Scottsdale, Arizona. Hopefully, by the time you reach your mid-twenties, he will have access to a crystal telepath and can evacuate you through the portal in Sedona. My clan bracelet will identify you as my daughter.

JoAnna opened the package with hands that still trembled. It contained a copper bracelet with various etchings. It looked like costume jewelry she could purchase at any department store for next to nothing.

The placed the cuff over her left wrist. How different it was from the gold bracelets which graced her other arm. JoAnna would wear the bracelet as a daily reminder of how lucky she was the Carlsons adopted her. It had been the first time she had used her special gift to get what she wanted. Was she a mind control telepath as her mother's letter noted? Suddenly, the letter did not seem so crazy after all.

Chapter 1

⁓

Present Time

Estero, Florida

Ginkgo Terra Universe

His stare penetrated her being, melting the ice that had surrounded her for years. The dampness of her panties was evidence the dam had burst. Sensations she never expected to feel bombarded her.

JoAnna had come to terms with this a long time ago; she would never feel anything for a man. After all, she was engaged to one for whom she felt nothing. Blake was handsome, obnoxiously rich, and seemed unaffected that she had no passion for him. They were the perfect match. JoAnna was the eye candy he needed on his arm and he guaranteed she would continue to live in the style in which she had grown accustomed.

The man's icy blue eyes continued to bore into her. There was a primeval quality to the way he looked at her. A caveman's kind of possession, ownership clear in his gaze. She half expected (and secretly wanted) him to grab her by the hair and drag her away to his lair.

He was tall and powerfully built. His dark blond hair was cut short, too short for her liking. JoAnna would have liked to comb her fingers through his locks. She knew she wanted this handsome stranger and her gift would make it a reality.

Through mutual consent, she and Blake had an open relationship. Since she could not give him passion, he took care of those needs elsewhere. His infidelities did not matter to her. She would have had to care to be hurt by his numerous affairs. JoAnna never imagined she would go to bed with a man and find any type of sexual release. Considering what his stare was doing to her, she knew when they came together, it would be explosive.

Her fiancé brushed her arm, breaking the spell the black-haired man had cast over her. "Neil Hargrove is over there. I need to speak to him. He has some insider information to share and we don't want to be overheard." She watched as Blake walked away, plotting how he could add more wealth to their already overflowing coffers. Her gift was partially the reason for his good fortune.

JoAnna wandered to an unpopulated corner of the hotel's lobby. Her father had managed this five star hotel for over a decade. The establishment hosted various receptions which allowed her to mingle with the rich and famous.

Over the years, her beauty and grace brought her to the attention of the powerful and wealthy. She was now one of them in her own right. JoAnna's investments over the years made her an extremely wealthy woman. Not bad for a twenty-three-year-old non-college graduate. Why go to college when she could get anything she wanted with her gift?

The man prowled across the room toward her. He had transitioned from a caveman to a predatory cat in her mind. There was a grace in how he moved, which further drew her eyes to his incredible body. He was oddly dressed, but his clothing only accented his physique. Unlike most prey, she wanted this animal to pounce. JoAnna longed for his touch, her body tingling in anticipation. It was almost a biological need to touch this man.

For the first time, she noticed the cuff bracelet around his wrist. It was similar to the one she had worn for the past seven years. Her instincts were now screaming for her to escape from her stalker. She felt trapped, outdone by her earlier desire to have a little privacy with the man who had captivated her.

Just short of his arrival, she tried to maneuver past him. He grabbed her arm and she felt as if she had been hit by lightning. She had never experienced anything quite like it. Her body felt like every cell had been fried.

"As I suspected, you are my soul mate." JoAnna heard those words in her head. It would have been so easy to dismiss what had just happened and call for security, but she just stood there, unable to move. The initial impact of his touch had worn off; however, she still longed for his hands to explore her body. She felt paralyzed, his hand gripping her arm.

"I don't know what you are talking about," JoAnna addressed her attacker. "My name is -"

"I know your name," the man interrupted with a growl. "It is time you come home, back to the Troyk universe."

She felt her face drain of blood as her complexion paled. He had referred to the place her mother had mentioned in her letter. JoAnna had searched to find any reference of that world over the years. Although she had never found anything, she never gave up hope one day she would.

She traveled the world exploring texts which had not been uploaded to the Internet. Her father supported her obsession; he planned their vacations around her driving need to find another reference of the world her mother revealed in her letter. Now this man who had mesmerized her, let it slip from his sensual lips.

"Where exactly is the Troyk universe?" JoAnna inquired. Her ears longed to hear information she had sought with a fanatical vigor. She feared it was all a misunderstanding and she would come up short once again.

"A parallel dimension to the world you know," the man answered. "My cousin is a crystal telepath. He can take us home."

Another reference she had read in her mother's letter. "A crystal telepath?"

The man sighed loudly. Apparently he was becoming impatient with all her questions. That was too bad, she had searched in vain for too many years to give up now. This Adonis, who stood before her, held the answers she needed.

Koel Mardroft was frustrated at her response to him. His soul mate had not fallen into his arms or communicated through their private channel. As soon as they had touched, the soul mate pathway opened. The electrical current, which rocked his body, was unmistakable. It appeared he was going to have the same issues his cousins and their friends experienced with their soul mates. It would be best to address her questions for the time being.

"We are a telepathic race living in a dimension parallel to yours. I believe String Theory talks about infinite planes of existence." He could see her eyes glaze over. It was not a dissimilar reaction to his own when Shirl started talking about the science behind parallel worlds. "A crystal telepath can control the frequencies of portals between worlds. Your friend, Shirl, is a crystal telepath. Her soul mate is my cousin Starc."

He felt her waiver on her feet, at the mention of Shirl's name. He tightened his hold on her arm and walked her to two unoccupied chairs not far from where they stood. The black leather of the furniture brought out the red of the dress his soul mate wore. It clung to her like a second skin. He needed to draw his attention back to his soul mate, rather than obsess over her body.

"How do you know Shirl?" his soul mate asked in a weak voice. She was clearly shaken by the name from her past. A need to care and nurture this woman replaced his earlier impatience.

"My name is Koel," he told her. It had been an inexcusable oversight not introducing himself earlier. He had been overwhelmed when he finally laid eyes on her. The tight dress she wore left very little to his imagination. It brought out the beauty of her dark skin and ebony hair. His usually sharp mind shut down when he looked at her.

His cousins and friends had found their soul mates, as each made their way through the portal to the Troyk universe. JoAnna was the last of the four orphaned daughters of Benko Jarlyn's followers. Benko was referred to as Ben Clark in this world.

"Koel, how do you know Shirl?" JoAnna asked again. She had a single focus and it was obvious she wanted answers. There was determination in her glare.

He massaged his forehead. His head was killing him. Literally, Ginkgo Terra's atmosphere was toxic to the telepathic brain. His soul mate was the same age as Shirl, who had suffered from debilitating headaches before she left this world. He had witnessed firsthand the shape Shirl had been in when she first arrived in the Troyk universe. However, JoAnna was the picture of excellent health.

"Shirl suffered from migraines, caused by Earth's polluted air. She stumbled across the portal in Sedona, Arizona. She unknowingly opened an event horizon when she came within its proximity. That is what happens when a crystal telepath comes in contact with a natural portal.

"In the Troyk universe, Shirl's headaches stopped. Figuring her friend, Candy, would soon suffer the same headaches, Shirl brought her to our world. The Troyk universe is their home now. They both have blossomed there." He figured now was not the time to bring up how being with their soul mates had been primarily responsible for the powers both now possessed.

"Headaches," JoAnna repeated automatically. Obviously she was thinking, but nothing leaked through their soul mate channel. "We were all once so close." She had a faraway look in her eyes. His soul mate seemed lost in the past.

"You can be together again in my world. We should go now," Koel said to his soul mate. She could come across worlds with nothing, he would provide her with all she needed.

"I am not going anywhere with you," his soul mate declared.

She was magnificent in her defiance. Her bronzed face was framed with black straight hair, which fell over her bare shoulders. Her green eyes had flecks of yellow, which made them appear amber. JoAnna was absolutely stunning.

"Time to leave, Koel," his cousin Darden said, as he approached from behind. Koel had not even heard Darden approach, that was how engrossed he had been. "She needs time to absorb all she has just learned."

"I have waited, while you have all found your soul mates," Koel replied. He had stood by as the four men he was closest to found their other halves. At one point, he was afraid he would never find his own. Every woman he encountered brought new hope, until he touched them and nothing happened.

"My soul mate still resides with her father in this world," Darden reminded him, with an edge in his voice. His cousin's soul mate was Benko Jarlyn's eighteen-year-old daughter, Cassandra. Although the soul mate channel had opened when Darden accidentally bumped into Cassie when she was a young girl, they had not been intimate. If Darden felt a small fraction of what Koel felt for JoAnna, he was amazed at his cousin's restraint.

"Fine," Koel sighed once again. "I certainly do not want to force JoAnna to go anywhere she does not wish. But that does not mean I cannot give her something to remind her of me."

Koel stood, grabbed JoAnna's arm and brought her to her feet. He wrapped his arm around his soul mate and gave her the most passionate kiss he could deliver in public. He could feel her knees give way, as Koel held her tighter and deepened the kiss. His soul mate groaned into his mouth, as she pulled at his tunic. He could feel her hands on his bare back. She caressed him as she explored his naked flesh. JoAnna pulled one arm from beneath his shirt and wrapped it around his neck. She drew him in closer.

Although it nearly killed him, Koel ended the kiss and released his soul mate.

"What?" JoAnna questioned at the loss of his touch. She seemed lost without him to support her.

Darden handed her a card. "Give this man a call when you are ready to start your true life."

Koel walked away from his soul mate. Now was not the time to force her to come with him. She needed to want to join him, to be with him body and soul. He turned to see JoAnna staring at the card, a frown on her face. Koel knew Benko Jarlyn's contact information was on it.

Koel would give her one week to come to terms with all she had learned this evening. After that time, he would muster his tactical talents in a campaign to win his soul mate.

Chapter 2

~

How do you go back to ground chuck after tasting filet mignon? Enjoy a glass from a four dollar bottle of wine, after you sipped Chateau Margaux? That was what JoAnna thought as her fiancé gyrated above her. As usual, when Blake made love to her, she felt nothing, as if she were dead inside. But tonight she knew what was possible.

Blake rolled off her and onto his back. She was covered in his sweat. JoAnna desperately wanted to shower, to wash him from her skin. Not being able to stand it another minute, she got up and headed for the master bath.

"You can't bother to fake it anymore?" her fiancé sneered at her back. He wasn't altogether wrong. Generally, she attempted to act out some type of passion when he touched her. Most of the time she provided Academy Award worthy reactions to his attempts to bring her to an orgasm.

Not bothering to respond, JoAnna walked into the bathroom and went directly into the shower. Although the water was steaming hot, she did not trouble herself to regulate the temperature. The scalding liquid made her feel alive as it tinted her body red. Images of Koel continued to assault her mind. She imagined he was in the stall with her. Koel touched her places Blake never dared.

By the time she dressed, Blake was in the kitchen working on his second cup of coffee. The man was addicted to the stuff. She always made sure the condo was stocked with his favorite blends. JoAnna walked past him and grabbed a diet soda from the refrigerator. She could use a little caffeine to jump start her fatigued body.

"We have to talk," Blake said. Those were the four words you never wanted to hear. It did not take a genius to figure out what was coming next. "This is not working for me anymore. I figured eventually you would thaw out, but you are as cold as the day we met."

JoAnna continued to drink her beverage, she enjoyed the sensation the carbonation made on the back of her throat. The damn soda gave her more physical pleasure than the man standing before her. How she let this charade continue so long was a mystery to her.

She knew this day would come and a sense of relief washed over her. It was exhausting pretending, continually telling herself there was nothing wrong with her. Now she knew the truth and could move forward with a clear conscience.

"We were always better friends and work associates than lovers," JoAnna admitted. "The first time we had sex should have been the last. It was just not an investment which would have paid dividends in the long run."

A smile crossed his face in response to her words. It had been a while since something she said or did outside of their investment strategies generated such a positive reaction. This was the devastatingly handsome, charming man she had longed to have feelings for.

"I will always wonder why we could not reproduce the high we generate together after a successful investment comes in when we are together in bed. Well, at least we still have that."

JoAnna leaned against the kitchen counter. If she verbalized the plans germinating in her mind, she would be more likely to make them happen. By telling Blake, she would be committed to a new path in life.

"I'm going to take off for a while and travel," Joanna said. "This evening I received a new lead about where my biological parents came from." She had shared her quest to find where she was born with Blake. He always listened intently, as she planned each trip and when she returned home.

This time around, she was not mentioning her destination. If she told him she was going to a parallel universe, it would get her a one-way ticket to the funny farm.

"The man you talked to this evening?" He looked at her with an intensity he had not shown in a very long while. Under different circumstances, she would have thought he was jealous.

"How did you know?"

"There was a vitality about you when you were with him I had not witnessed before. Even across the room, I could feel the heat the two of you generated. That kiss he gave you was scorching hot. Originally, I had not planned to accompany you home from the party, but I finally thought we could generate some heat of our own." There was a sadness to his admission.

JoAnna walked to her former fiancé and placed her arms around his shoulder. "I wish I could have been that woman for you." As she held her friend, JoAnna wondered if she could become the very thing Koel claimed they were.

☙

JoAnna stared at the business card Koel's companion had given her. She had taken it out of her evening bag shortly after Blake departed. For something she had searched for with a vigor on insanity, JoAnna could not understand what was holding her back from calling the phone number.

Had she ever expected to find answers? The prospect of traveling to a parallel dimension was daunting. Honestly, she was not sure what made her more nervous, the journey or seeing Koel again. He disturbed her on so many levels.

"For God sake," JoAnna muttered to herself, "stop being a wuss." She grabbed her cell phone and punched the numbers indicated on the card. She held off hitting the call button, just stared at the digits on the display. If she made the call, her life would never be the same.

Everything money could buy had been at her disposal from the day she discovered her gift. But her existence was empty, filled with objects which held no meaning. To this day, with the exception of her father, the closest bond she ever forged was with the girls she could barely remember from the orphanage. She had been close to her adoptive mother and had been devastated when she died two years ago.

"Screw it," she said to herself as she placed the call.

It seemed an eternity until she finally got a ringtone. Her life was about to change and she was impatient to get started. After just two rings, a female answered.

"Hello," a cheerful voice greeted her.

JoAnna was momentarily stunned, she expected Ben Clark to answer. After all this time, she had to wait for answers a little longer.

"I am trying to reach Ben Clark," JoAnna finally replied.

"I'm his daughter, Cassie," the girl responded. "He is not here right now, can I take a message?"

Why couldn't he be in the other room? There was no telling how long she would have to wait to talk to him, assuming Cassie gave him the message. JoAnna had no idea if the girl was trustworthy.

"Can you tell him JoAnna Carlson called?"

"Holy shit!" Cassie screamed into the phone, cutting JoAnna off. "How quickly can you get to Phoenix, Arizona?"

JoAnna rubbed her forehead, trying to figure out what the girl on the other end of the call wanted. Cassie rattled on about them traveling to Sedona. In the back of her mind the small town held some relevance. She just could not determine how with Cassie continuing to yammer.

"Cassie," JoAnna finally cut her off. "I don't understand why you just can't get a message to your father and have him return my call."

"Dad is off world," Cassie explained. "We need to get you home to the Troyk universe. My soul mate, Darden, is expected to return through the portal tomorrow."

Darden was the name of the man who traveled with Koel. All the nonsense Cassie had said finally made sense.

"I'll be on the next flight," JoAnna replied.

JoAnna massaged her temple, the girl's constant talking had given her a raging headache. She sat back, making contact with the car's headrest, trying to block out the constant chatter. JoAnna was tempted to ask if they could make a restroom stop, just to get a few minutes of peace.

"Those will go away, once you are in the Troyk Universe."

"What?" It amazed JoAnna how Cassie could change from topic to topic, with no transitional sentence to help prepare the poor listener. The girl was overwhelming.

"The headaches," Cassie replied. "Our atmosphere is toxic to the telepathic brain." The girl placed her right hand on JoAnna's arm. "That was how your father died, a brain embolism. Your mother would have met the same fate, had she not died in the car crash."

Although she knew about the headaches from her mother's letter and later from Koel, she had never confirmed how her mother died. She knew her mother was immune to the headaches from reading the letter. How different her life would have been if her mother had not taken that fateful ride.

Thoughts of a woman who only lived in her memories evaporated as they drove into the parking lot for the Boynton Canyon's hiking trails. Although JoAnna had enjoyed the scenery since they had entered the outskirts of Sedona, she thought they would meet Darden in a restaurant or some other public place. JoAnna looked at her high-heeled sandals, she kicked herself for not wearing more practical shoes.

"Let's go," Cassie ordered as soon as she turned off the ignition. "The portal is about a twenty minute hike." The girl bounced out of the car, leaving JoAnna behind, still staring at her sandals. "Come on, he may be on his way down the trail by now."

"Cassie, I am not going anywhere in these shoes." To prove her point, JoAnna pulled off one of her sandals and presented it to her. "How about I pull another pair from my suitcase." She could see the look of frustration on Cassie's face. "The time we lose while I change out of these fashionable torture instruments will be easily made up when I am walking up the trail in more appropriate shoes."

JoAnna got out of the car and pulled her suitcase from the backseat. Noticing only she and Cassie were in the parking lot, JoAnna also changed into a sleeveless cotton top. She was now ready to conquer the mountain. She hoped the physical activity in climbing would shut up her chatty traveling companion.

They gingerly made their way up the trail. JoAnna had one eye on the breathtaking surroundings and with the other she looked for snakes. She wished she had been wearing a pair of boots and heavy denim jeans. Considering how strange the last few days had been, it would not have surprised her if some viper came out and introduced himself.

There was noise farther up the trail and Cassie took off running. When JoAnna caught up, it was to find Cassie in Darden's arms. They were kissing as if they had not seen each other in months. Considering Darden was from a parallel universe, it may have been that long. They brought a whole new meaning to the term "long-distance relationship."

11

"You need to return to the Troyk universe. JoAnna has a headache," Cassie managed to get out between kisses. It never dawned on the girl that she had created the headache. Darden released his grasp on Cassie and glanced at JoAnna.

"Thank the Supreme Being," Darden said. "Koel has been impossible to live with since he returned without you. Are you finally ready to return to your true home?"

Two pairs of eyes fell on her, as they waited for her answer. She had traveled all this way, it would be cowardly to turn back now. JoAnna was many things, but a coward was not one of them.

"Let me just get my suitcase," JoAnna answered, "then we can head out."

A wide smile graced Darden's face. JoAnna could see why Cassie was head over heels in love with the guy. Hell, if they had a fraction of the chemistry she had with Koel, Cassie was one lucky girl.

"Our mode of dress is quite different from what you are used to," Darden responded. JoAnna's eyes ran down his physique. He wore the same tunic and leggings he did the other night.

"Don't tell me women wear the same unattractive outfits?" JoAnna addressed her question to Cassie.

"How would I know?" the girl said impatiently. "I have never left this dimensional realm." From the edge in Cassie's voice and the way she glared at Darden, it was clear the girl was not happy being left behind.

Although silence met Cassie's remarks, from the body language, both displayed, they were involved in quite a telepathic argument. It was awkward standing beside the battling couple. It felt similar to hearing the murmurs of whispers, where you want to get close enough to hear what was being said. Paranoia set in, JoAnna wondered if she was the topic of their discussion.

Ultimately, Darden took Cassie in his arms and gave her a type of kiss that would quiet any girl's mind. JoAnna could almost feel Koel's lips on hers, giving her the same type of treatment if she said something he did not want to hear. A longing she had never experienced descended on her. An invisible force pulled JoAnna forward, as she continued her journey up the mountain.

JoAnna heard footsteps behind her, but continued her trek. She did not know where the portal was, but she could feel the power drive her forward. She came to a dead stop in front of a mass of shimmering air. Although a part of her was ready to walk through the portal, she had enough sense to know

Darden was required to navigate the energy force. She turned to see him standing behind her, the amethyst in the necklace he wore glowed with power.

"A crystal telepath," JoAnna muttered. Once again aspects of her mother's letter were proving true. This man had brought her soul mate to Earth and now would return her to the parallel world of her mother's birth. Without a doubt in her mind, she was ready to enter the event horizon.

She held her breath as she stepped into the unknown, not sure what she would find on the other side.

Chapter 3

~

The Troyk Universe

JoAnna pried her eyes open. She knew in a blink, she would miss the opportunity of seeing within the portal. There was stillness and darkness, but in the distance, she caught electrical currents which created momentary light. Some type of force protected her and Darden from the elements she sensed swirling in the air.

The instant within the portal somehow expanded, as if time stood still. It was said your life flashed before you at the time of death, but this was different. Without knowing how, JoAnna knew her mind had linked with Darden and it was his perception of the portal she picked up.

A slight breeze caught a wisp of hair as JoAnna stepped onto solid ground. Her eyes adjusted to the light as if she only blinked. She felt she would forget the sensations she felt within the portal, as one forgets a dream upon waking. How she wished she could store the incredible experience in her mind.

"Welcome to the Troyk universe," Darden said.

Her eyes shifted to where he stood and saw a city nestled in the valley below. They were on a mountain trail, but she could tell they were no longer outside Sedona. She had to be dreaming; no place like this could exist in reality.

"The sky is purple," JoAnna commented. "How is that possible?" A momentary terror consumed her, as she wondered if the air was safe to breathe. She was afraid to take a breath. On top of everything else, there was a buzzing in her head, which kept getting louder.

Cool hands grabbed her arms, as she placed her hands over her ears. She struggled not to take another breath. How could she be so stupid to enter the portal with no understanding of what was on the other side?

"Pollen has discolored our sky," Darden informed her. "You need to take in air before you pass out. I do not want to carry you off this mountain." Although the noise in her head increased in volume, his words came in loud and clear. JoAnna gasped, as she took in oxygen to feed her deprived cells.

"There is terrible static in my head," JoAnna cried. She could feel perspiration run down her nose. Her hand brushed her upper lip. She was horrified to see her hand covered with blood.

"The communal pathways are trying to connect with your telepathic brain," Darden tried to reason her out of the panic which grew steadily within. "The blood is normal, just try to relax."

JoAnna looked at him as if he were insane. She had entered his mind, then was in a world with a violet sky, and now she was bleeding. Hysterics seemed a normal reaction to what was happening.

"Your friend Candy's boyfriend, Tolfer, will be able to help you manage the impact the telepathic channels have on your brain."

Memories of a ferocious little girl from the orphanage came to her mind. Candy was two years younger than she was, but she wanted to be included in all the games they played. As JoAnna continued to concentrate on remembering Candy, the pressure in her head lessened. She focused on the times they had together years ago, continually reducing the static.

"Good, the color in your cheeks has returned," Darden observed. "Whatever you are doing, keep it up. The closer we get to Aster Province, the more the pathways will try to connect with your mind."

Great, JoAnna thought. She was not sure how long she would be able to bring up memories of a girl she was separated from when she was six. Although JoAnna had thought her time in the children's home as the low point in her life, only positive memories came back to her. The four little girls had created their own family, the strongest ties she had ever formed.

JoAnna carefully followed Darden down the mountain trail. It was steeper than the one in Sedona. Since her shoes had very little traction, she spent more time sliding, rather than walking. Fortunately, Darden did not appear to be in any hurry, so they took the trip down nice and easy. She balanced, concentrating on memories to reduce the pressure in her head, while she watched her step as they traversed the path.

The closer they got to the city, the easier it was to make out the different types of purple foliage. From high on the mountain, Aster Province seemed more like a painting by Monet. She placed more focus on her mind, as the buzzing got worse and the trail started to even out.

JoAnna and Darden finally reached flat land and came to the outskirts of the city. Two women were waiting for them as they came to a paved road. The taller woman looked eerily familiar. They both were dressed in the tunic and leggings combo Darden sported. Surprisingly, the outfit was quite flattering to the female form.

The tall brunette stepped forward and stood before JoAnna. She had an expectant look on her face, as if she waited for her to respond to something she had said. It finally dawned on JoAnna she tried to communicate telepathically.

"Whatever channel you're using, or whatever Darden called it, you have not connected with me." JoAnna held her ground, she figured the woman would eventually connect with her or finally speak.

"I'm Candy," the tall woman stepped forward and embraced her. "I tried to use a telepathic channel which opened when we were kids in the orphanage. It was the first pathway Shirl and I were able to communicate through. It's so nice to finally have you home, Jo Jo."

A warm sensation she had not felt since she left the orphanage came over her when Candy called her by the old nickname. JoAnna placed her arms around Candy and returned her embrace. It was the oddest feeling, almost as if she had returned to the only home she had ever known. Afraid she could lose the warmth she had missed, JoAnna tightened her hold on Candy.

"I hate to break up this reunion," a female voice said, "but Jeryl Jarlyn and Prime Adholm are waiting for us."

"Who?" JoAnna asked as she released her hold on Candy. The other woman was probably ten years older than JoAnna and was stunning. There was something unnerving in the way the woman stared at her. The harpy's piercing blue eyes seemed to see right through her. JoAnna was instantly suspicious of who she was and what she wanted.

"Jeryl Jarlyn is the Prime Ruler of the Troyk people," Candy responded. "Prime Adholm is your uncle. Both men are very anxious to meet you. I went through a similar interview with the Prime Ruler when I first arrived."

JoAnna stared at Candy. For whatever reason, she had never considered she would have family in this universe. It mystified her how they were able to find her relatives so quickly. Her birth parents had played such a small part in her life, she barely gave them a second thought until she received the note and bracelet from her mother. Would her Troyk relatives have the same gift she possessed? Now that she knew she had family, JoAnna wondered if she would be staying with them.

"I will accompany you ladies," Darden shared. "JoAnna, this is Solfa Theffar. She is in charge of Troyk government's central intelligence." JoAnna's initial feelings to be weary of this woman had been right on point. Although she had nothing to hide, the chestnut haired beauty made her nervous.

"It's going to be fine, Jo Jo," Candy reassured her. "We are both children of dissidents from this world. Naturally, we were ignorant of their crimes. You and Shirl were born in this world and were carried through the portal when our parents left. The Prime Ruler and Prime Adholm want to welcome you home.

"When Darden communicated you had accompanied him back to the Troyk universe, I was asked by the Prime Ruler himself to come and greet you. He felt connecting with an old friend would make your initial impressions of your new home favorable."

"What happens to me after the meeting? Can I return to Earth?" JoAnna had no desire at this point to return to her old life, but wanted to keep her options open. Other than her father, she had no reason to return. The opportunity to catch up with Candy and Shirl, as well as get to know her Troyk family was too seductive not to take advantage of. She also had unfinished business with Koel.

"I imagine Prime Adholm will want you to stay with him," Candy responded. "When I first came to this world, I stayed with the family who had sheltered Shirl. The Childers took wonderful care of me. Their son, Tolfer, helped me manage the communal pathways. He is now my boyfriend, so hands off."

JoAnna could not help but laugh at Candy's playfulness and the expression on her face. She walked through the streets of Aster Province as she chatted with her long-lost friend. JoAnna was so absorbed in her conversation with

Candy, she had not truly taken in her surroundings. It finally dawned on her, there were no cars.

"Is there public transportation?" JoAnna inquired. She drove everywhere when she was at home. All her shoes were purchased based on how fashionable they were, not on comfort. Not that it mattered, all her possessions had been left behind.

"Everyone walks, although there are high-speed trams that travel between cities. You have to admit," Candy continued, "it's tranquil without all the noise produced by automobiles, not to mention the lack of air pollution."

It would be wonderful, JoAnna admitted to herself, if the damn static in her head would go away. During the conversation with Candy, she stopped concentrating on the memories, which had lessened the pressure. The last thing JoAnna wanted was to get another nosebleed when she met the ruler of this world and her uncle.

"Good Lord," JoAnna said, as she stopped dead in her tracks. In front of her was the most impressive palace she had ever seen. The building literally sparkled as the sun reflected off flecks embedded in the marble. It was how she envisioned Mount Olympus would look when she studied Greek mythology.

"That is the Aster Province Palace," Darden said. "Our government operates here, and Jeryl Jarlyn lives on the top floor."

"I will accompany JoAnna," Solfa informed the small group. JoAnna would have preferred Candy or Darden to join her, but it did not appear she had a choice in the matter. "Candy, do not wander off, just in case it is determined JoAnna will stay with the Childers."

JoAnna and Solfa walked through the main entrance into The Palace without having to go through security. They walked up four flights of stairs and bypassed the small guard station at the top of the staircase. JoAnna felt she was in some kind of museum surrounded by beautiful pieces of art as they made their way down the hall in the Prime Ruler's living quarters.

Solfa stopped in front of a door and grabbed JoAnna's wrist. "Both men have mind control telepathic abilities. You will feel pressure in your head as they use their powers. Do not be concerned; there is no lasting negative effect on your brain."

For the first time, JoAnna wondered if she had caused any one discomfort as she used her gift over the years. There had been no telltale evidence any of her friends or family had been in pain as she made her requests. JoAnna would not have continued using her powers if she was aware she caused anyone harm.

Her companion opened the door and both women entered. Two older men were seated in an area on the other side of an impressive collection of geodes. The crystals were absolutely breathtaking. A flash of a little blond girl with a purple amethyst around her neck came back to her. Shirl never took off her prize possession, the only thing her dead mother had left behind.

"Jolyn!" the gray-haired man rose in greeting. He was tall, good looking, and amazingly fit for a man his age. "Welcome home. You look so much like your mother, it is quite startling." He came forward to embrace her. JoAnna figured he was her uncle, but stepped back from the physical contact. The old man stopped in his tracks, respecting her non-verbal request. "I am Jeryl Jarlyn. Your mother was like a daughter to me."

JoAnna's gaze left the Prime Ruler and fell on the other man still seated. Her uncle made no attempt to make eye-contact with her. He was heavier than the Prime Ruler, but still maintained a head of dark brown hair. His behavior was odd, considering she was the niece he had not seen since she was a baby. From his profile, JoAnna could see a look of guilt and regret written on his face. Had her uncle's past actions driven his sister through the portal to another world?

Solfa grabbed her upper arm and led her to stand in front of her uncle. "Prime Adholm, I present your niece. Her Ginkgo Terra name is JoAnna." She was grateful Solfa used the name she was accustomed to, regardless of the name these men were familiar with.

Her uncle slowly raised his eyes, until their gazes finally met. A smile graced his face, as he rose to greet his flesh and blood. This time JoAnna did not back away from an embrace.

She felt no warm emotions while being held by her uncle. However, Prime Adholm seemed deeply affected. His hold on her tightened, as his body began to quake. Sobs of grief escaped from him.

"It is all right, my friend." Jeryl Jarlyn pulled her uncle from her and embraced him. "The Supreme Being has been generous by replacing a lost daughter with a beautiful niece now returned to the fold. It is truly a great gift he has bestowed onto you."

"Chartail," her uncle cried, tearing himself from the Prime Ruler. He staggered from the room, as the echoes of his cries were left in his wake. JoAnna stood frozen, not sure what to do. Her uncle was a stranger; she could offer him no comfort.

"What happened to Chartail?" It was the obvious question for JoAnna to ask. Her uncle still grieved for her cousin's loss.

"She was a foolish, misguided girl," Jeryl Jarlyn replied. "Chartail plotted an unsuccessful assassination attempt on my life. For her crimes, she was banished to our off-world penal colony."

JoAnna gasped, unable to control her body's reaction to the startling news. She wanted to know what had driven her cousin to such a drastic act, but knew these people were not the ones to ask. Perhaps Candy would enlighten her on what had transpired.

"I would like to get JoAnna settled." Solfa's voice cut through the silence which followed JoAnna's involuntary reaction to what Chartail had done. "It is clear Prime Adholm is not ready to share his home with JoAnna. The Childers have generously offered their home once again. Candy plans to move in with my mother, so there is room for her in their household."

"Yes," Jeryl Jarlyn answered, "that will work nicely. Little Alexia is still in residence there, so JoAnna will have another companion around her age to help her assimilate to her new home. However, I have a few questions to ask JoAnna before you leave."

Solfa nodded her understanding of The Prime Ruler's wishes. "Let us sit and get comfortable." The woman in charge of Troyk intelligence sat on the couch and indicated for JoAnna to sit next to her. "Have you heard the name Benko Jarlyn before?"

The name Ben Clark instantly came to JoAnna's mind. The first names were similar, but not enough to share Cassie's father's identity with these people. Besides, she was not sure who she could trust in this world.

"I have never met a Benko Jarlyn or heard anyone mention him before. Who is he?"

"Benko is my son," the Prime Ruler answered. "Your mother and father followed him through a portal to Ginkgo Terra after a failed attempt to unseat me from government control. You were just a baby at the time."

"Another plot against you?" The words escaped JoAnna's mouth before her brain could censor what she said. She played with her hair, hoping it made the comment less judgmental. She stared at her knees, unable to make eye contact with the most powerful man in this universe.

Jeryl Jarlyn leaned forward in his chair and reached for JoAnna's hand. This time she did not resist the contact, she did not have a death wish. The Prime Ruler was not someone she wanted to alienate.

"We are a telepathic people, JoAnna," Jarlyn said. "We have a variety of gifts given to us by the Supreme Being. You have already witnessed the power a crystal telepath possesses. They can navigate a portal by adjusting the energy's frequencies while they travel from world to world."

They were interrupted as a servant entered with refreshments. Several beverages were on the tray, as well as pastries that looked scrumptious. Cassie had driven them directly to Sedona once she landed in Phoenix. She had not eaten since the meal she was served in first class on the flight. JoAnna was hungry, but held off grabbing one of the desserts.

As soon as the servant left, Solfa reached for the sole mug on the tray. "This tea will help reduce the static in your head. It contains many herbs which will help as the telepathic channels attempt to connect with your brain. Have you been able to pick-up any conversations?"

"No, it is all incoherent at his point." JoAnna took a tentative sip from the mug. The tea had a pleasant taste and was not too hot. She could feel the static reduce as she continued to drink. No longer able to hold back, JoAnna grabbed the pastry closest to her and took a large bite. It had a sweet, nutty flavor. She finished off the treat, barely breathing between bites.

The Prime Ruler placed his coffee cup on the center table, obviously ready to continue the discussion. "Another gift bestowed upon us is the ability to sway the indecisive. Our world is no longer dragged down by endless debate or the chaos as factions fight to get their dissenting voices heard. All the inefficiencies were eliminated when the mind control government was put in place."

"Harmony rules our communities," Solfa continued. "We work for a common goal, rather than being stymied by a chamber of different ideas which brought everything to a halt. Our governing body was a group of individuals shouting to be heard over the screams of other members."

JoAnna knew firsthand what happened when government was gridlocked. However, with only one voice making decisions, there was no chance for the opposing sides to work together to display statesmanship and reach a compromise. An opposition party was needed to bring moderation to whatever legislation was considered.

"Do you possess this ability, JoAnna?" The Prime Ruler startled her with the question. "The gift runs in your family, although Chartail never developed the power."

Jeryl Jarlyn said those last words in such a condescending tone, JoAnna wondered if Chartail had been driven to her act by being made to feel defective. She could certainly sympathize with her cousin if she had been treated in such a fashion, although there were other avenues she could have taken to deal with her issues. Regardless, JoAnna was not going to reveal her gift, at least, not yet.

"I wouldn't know where to start," JoAnna said. She lied through her teeth. JoAnna said it with as much innocence as she could muster. It was best to appear harmless, until she figured out who were the good guys in this universe.

"How could you, growing up in a non-telepathic world?" Jarlyn spoke to her as if she were a child. She had managed to manipulate him without relying on her gift. "But you have the power; I can feel it. Earlier, I tried to determine if you were lying to me, but your mind was locked to mine. The ability to close your mind to another telepath indicates you have tremendous power. I can only imagine how incredible you will be once you have mated."

"Excuse me," JoAnna squeaked out. How did the conversation drift to sex and what an odd way to refer to it? The Prime Ruler's face reddened, as he realized what he said and her reaction to it.

"Soul mates were considered legendary beings until we had a pairing recently." Solfa's calming voice cut through the awkwardness of the previous moment. It was the only non-threatening part of the woman, her gaze still scared the heck out of JoAnna. "When soul mates make love for the first time, a hormone is excreted and each partner enters the next evolutionary stage of their telepathic abilities."

JoAnna already knew who her soul mate was, although she had not planned on sharing that bit of information. The idea she could gain additional telepathic abilities was exciting. Although she did not know where to find Koel, Darden would. She had already planned to bed him, now she had another reason to do it sooner than later.

"How did you find Darden, or even know about the Troyk universe?" Jeryl Jarlyn inquired.

"When I was sixteen, I was given a note and a gift from my deceased birth mother. Her letter spoke of the Troyk universe and she left me her bracelet." JoAnna raised her arm, as she showed the piece of jewelry that graced her wrist. As she vowed when she first put it on, JoAnna wore it every day. "Koel and Darden tracked me down and gave me a number to call when I was ready to return to the universe of my birth."

"Who did the number belong to?" Jarlyn asked. His excitement in what she had communicated was evident.

"Darden's girlfriend, Cassie," JoAnna responded.

"After Candy came through the portal," Solfa explained, "Darden started to research the girls who had been at the orphanage with Candy and Shirl, searching for the offspring of your son's companions. He tracked down JoAnna and noticed her pronounced resemblance to the Adholm family."

"And the girl?" the Prime Ruler asked.

"Some child Darden must have charmed," Solfa answered. "The girl is so besotted with him, she gathers the ginkgo biloba herb and awaits his return. It is one of the reasons he comes back with so much of the product."

The Prime Ruler seemed satisfied with Solfa's response. "Solfa, take her to the Childers," Jeryl Jarlyn ordered. "I want to see her every afternoon so we can develop her talents. I want only the best for her, make sure my wishes are seen to."

Two guards entered the room. "These men will take you to Candy, who will accompany you to where you will stay for the time being." Solfa had an odd expression on her face, as she explained the guards' presence. The look changed to become unreadable, almost immediately. Something had been communicated to the head of intelligence which obviously had shaken her. JoAnna wished it had nothing to do with her.

Chapter 4

⁓

Alexandra Mann readjusted the pillow for the third time. There was no need to straighten the common room, Leenea Childers was an immaculate housekeeper. With her nerves on edge because of the news Jo Jo had entered the Troyk universe, Alex had to do something to redirect her anxiety.

She had long wanted to reunite with her childhood friend. That desire had soured when Candy had a premonition Jo Jo meant trouble. Her vision had been non-descriptive, more of a feeling of apprehension. Candy had developed the ability to see physical strikes before they occurred, as well as the gift of foresight, after she made love to her soul mate, Tolfer. Her friend had become the Troyk Warrior Woman of legend come to life.

Now she had to present herself as Alexia Montiff from the Starling Province in the Troyk Universe, rather than little Alex from the orphanage. That was the cover story they had created when she was dragged into this parallel world. Shirl and Candy were brought to the attention of the Troyk ruler when they first arrived. So they did not have to present a charade to the world. Alex had a role to play, until they had proof Jo Jo could be trusted. They were opening the Childers's household to a possible mind control telepath of unknown power and motives.

"Relax, baby," Alex said as she patted her abdomen. Her unborn daughter communicated telepathically to her. The communication was more a transfer of emotions Alex's brain translated into some semblance of understanding. "Jo Jo and I played together when we were little girls. In those days, it was the four of us against the world. When she was adopted, I cried myself to sleep for a week. She'll prove herself trustworthy, don't worry."

Alex made her way to the kitchen and prepared herself a hot mug of the herbal beverage she lived on. She was still having issues with the telepathic channels after she suffered from two concussions, courtesy of Raine Narmouth. That psycho was never going to bother her again, her friends made sure of that. After the last time he assaulted and kidnapped her, Candy and Shirl delivered him to the Nightshade universe. It was a terrifying parallel world populated by blood-lusting vampires.

A feeling of euphoria consumed her, which radiated from Star. She named her unborn daughter after her mother, Starta. Her Troyk relatives became emotional every time her mother's name was voiced, so Alex started to call her daughter Star.

When Alex was in the Nightshade universe, a vampire named Drake claimed her unborn child. It freaked her out, but Star already seemed to love the monster. Fortunately, Drake appeared as a handsome man, rather than as a decomposing corpse like the other vampires. A certain peace came over Alex when Star thought of Drake or was in his presence. Alex could only hope something changed in the next eighteen years.

Tarsea, her soul mate, entered the kitchen and embraced her, before he grabbed something to drink. He had just risen from the bed where they had made love. Alex had thought their passion for each other would have waned after time passed, but it only intensified.

"Candy and Jo Jo should be here any time," Alex said between sips. "Unfortunately, Darden was called in for questioning."

"We knew that would happen as soon as JoAnna came through the portal. There are too many loose ends about the past now coming to light. Both Solfa and Darden are communicating the discussion through the warrior channel," her soul mate shared. "Jeryl Jarlyn seems to have accepted the story of half-truths we concocted. But it is only a matter of time before Darden will have to leave us and reside with Benko Jarlyn in the penal colony. Cassie has now been exposed, so it is best for her to leave Ginkgo Terra. Darden will finally be able to be with his soul mate. How he lasted this long without her is beyond my comprehension."

The warrior channel was a telepathic link her soul mate and their friends had access to. It was a closed channel accessible to only those faithful and trustworthy to the true leader of the Troyk universe, Benko Jarlyn. Because of the link still forming between Alex and her daughter, her connection to other pathways had become erratic. When she first found out she was pregnant, she could only connect to Tarsea's familial link. Until Alex could reliably link-in without interruptions, Tarsea shared pertinent information through the familial channel.

"It's for the best, I suppose. I don't like the fact we are forced to live a charade in our own home," Alex complained. "Worse yet, I can't use contractions in Jo Jo's presence. Why you Troyk people have to say every word is very annoying."

Tarsea laughed and pulled her into his arms. "I thought you were going to stop speaking in that manner, even in private." He placed his lips on hers, which distracted her from the excuses she was about to provide to his comment. Tarsea tasted of coffee, mint, and a unique savory essence all his own. When he kissed her, she could not think straight.

Alex deepened the kiss, she wondered if they had time for a mid-afternoon fling before Candy and Jo Jo arrived. They had made love before on the kitchen counter when the house was empty, like it was now. Tarsea started to pull down her leggings when Candy's voice echoed through the house.

"We are here," her friend bellowed. Candy knew she and Tarsea had very little self-control when others were not around, so she loudly announced their presence. Alex and her soul mate quickly separated and adjusted their clothing before their company physically arrived.

Alex's eyes immediately fell on the breathtakingly beautiful woman who entered the kitchen beside Candy. JoAnna could give gorgeous Shirl a run for her money. It took all of Alex's self-control not to run into Jo Jo's arms in greeting.

JoAnna immediately recognized Alex. Although it had been seventeen years since they had last been together, JoAnna would have known her anywhere. Why hadn't Candy said anything on the walk over? They had talked about Shirl, but there had not been a whisper about Alex.

"This is Tarsea Childers and his girlfriend Alexia Montiff." Candy's introduction made it clear for some reason her friend was not going by the name Alexandra Mann. JoAnna had no choice but to play along.

"Nice to meet you both," JoAnna settled on saying. "The Prime Ruler said there would be a woman my age living here. I hope we can be friends." She almost choked on the last word.

"It is nice to meet you, JoAnna," Alex said. "Can I offer you anything to drink? We have a wonderful herbal beverage which will help if you have any static in your head. Candy said it helped her until she finally could manage the different telepathic channels."

"Sounds great," JoAnna replied. She noticed Alex drank the same beverage. "How long have you been here?" When Alex gave her a questioning look, JoAnna tilted her head toward the mug in front of Alex with the herbs.

"Oh, that," Alex said with relief evident in her voice. "I was born and raised in Starling Province, here in the Troyk universe. Recently I was a psychopath's obsession and suffered a couple of concussions. The beverage is helping to lessen the effects of the injuries. Besides, I love the taste."

JoAnna wished she could have asked her old friend more about what had happened to her, but they played the part of strangers. So Alex was the gracious hostess and JoAnna would continue to pretend they had never met. Her head was still bothering her a bit, but she would kill for a carbonated beverage.

"You wouldn't happen to have a diet soda?" JoAnna asked.

"I wish," Alex said too quickly. Panic evident in her eyes after such an obvious slip. "Candy and Shirl talk about those beverages all the time. I would love to try the bubbly orange one that does not have any calories." It was a beautiful recovery. JoAnna was impressed at Alex's ability to lie. It was evident she had the skill, since she was living in this universe under an assumed identity.

"Solfa wants us to purchase JoAnna some Troyk outfits," Candy said. It was a beautiful means to change the subject. What woman does not like to talk about shopping? "Jeryl Jarlyn himself will purchase them for her. I thought you'd like to go with us, Alexia. You could use some new clothes and we both know you can't go shopping with Tarsea along."

A wicked smile crossed Alex's face. JoAnna wondered what happened when Alex went shopping with her boyfriend. She imagined it was X-rated based on the way Alex now blushed. There was a closeness and friendly banter between the two women. JoAnna once again thought what it would have been like had she not been adopted and grew up with them. She had never felt more alone in her life.

"I need to head to The Palace and attend this afternoon's Prime Council session." Tarsea got up and gave Alex a passionate kiss. It was a claiming kiss, an alpha male marking his mate. "Darden and I are playing cards tonight, so do not wait up. I will have to tear your new clothes off you another time."

Tarsea walked to JoAnna and took her hand, gently brought it to his lips, and kissed it. "It was a pleasure to meet you, JoAnna. Welcome home, we are thrilled to have you here." All three women were silent as Tarsea left the kitchen and finally the house.

"Oh my, God!" JoAnna said as soon as she heard the front door shut. "Alex, you lucky girl! I'd cross dimensions for a man like that." Ironically, that was exactly what JoAnna had done.

Alex did not correct JoAnna on the name she just used. She merely gave JoAnna a knowing smile, "I know. As Candy would say, let's go shopping. We will hit the designer racks for JoAnna and the sale ones for me. Tarsea did not exaggerate about what he does with my clothes. On account of that, I only buy the cheapest stuff possible."

JoAnna wondered if Koel would have the same reaction as Alex's Tarsea did to whatever she purchased. It was a new fantasy she added to the others she had stored up for Koel and her to act out. Where the hell was he anyway?

❦

The shopping trip was a blast. On Earth, JoAnna tended to shop alone, with a style consultant on call. Spending time with Alex and Candy brought her back again to the wonderful times she once had with the girls as well as what had been missing in her life.

JoAnna stood before the mirror in one of the outfits she had just purchased. It was the type of outfit Troyk women wore at night when they attended what was referred to as the second seating at any restaurant. The tunic was made of transparent, delicate fabric with beading strategically placed around her breasts. JoAnna had never worn anything this daring and could not wait for Koel to see her in it.

There was a knock on the door and Candy entered. "You look great in that. When Shirl and Starc get back, we will all go out and show it off to the world." Her friend sat in the only chair in the bedroom she had been assigned. While they shopped, Candy decided she would continue to stay with the Childers and JoAnna was moved to the small guest room toward the front of the house.

"I have never had anything quite like this before," JoAnna admitted. "Don't you feel a little self-conscious wearing it in public?" JoAnna carefully pulled the tunic over her head and put on one of the more practical tops she had purchased.

"At first I did, but when I noticed all the other women wore the same type of evening wear, it became less an issue." Candy shifted in her chair, it was obvious she wanted to talk about something other than fashion.

"Spit it out, Candy," JoAnna said, "I can see you are flailing in the chair. What is it you want to know?"

"Are you a mind control telepath?" JoAnna's stomach fell to her knees after Candy's question. She momentarily was not sure how to answer her.

"Well, that was certainly direct," JoAnna finally answered, she struggled to sound as unaffected as possible. "Why do you ask?"

"I saw how you were able to manipulate the salesclerk," Candy replied. "You are living with us for the time being, I have to know what you are capable of. Shirl and I are all new to these powers and it is a little scary."

JoAnna had done what she always did when she went shopping, doing it without thought. She had been caught by her old friend and she would not deny it. It was the first time JoAnna was going to come clean about her ability to influence another person.

"I realized the day I met the Carlsons I had a gift. For the first time I really wanted something, for them to adopt me, and I made it happen. If you have a power, it would be foolish not to use it. Why work so hard for something, if it can be handed to you?"

Candy looked at her for what felt like an eternity. Butterflies swarmed in JoAnna's stomach, waiting for Candy's verdict about the use of her gift. She never really cared what people thought about her before, but for some reason it mattered with Candy.

"Shirl has a gift, I suppose it would be silly for her not to use it to travel from world to world." Candy got up and started to pace. JoAnna figured Candy was still determining what to say. "I struggle with the whole mind control thing. Alexia's aunt went apartment hunting and did not get the cute little garden home she liked because she had an open mind to continue looking. A mind control telepath ended up manipulating her into renting his unit. She did not even realize it had happened until Tolfer pointed it out. It is scary that you have the ability to do that to me."

"I do not do that to people!" JoAnna said defensively. However, one of the words Candy had said kept rolling in her mind, *manipulation*. She could not deny she had done exactly that on many occasions. "Besides, sometimes I cannot help what ends up happening, I can't always control my gift."

"Listen, I am not condemning you, Jo Jo. Shirl and I did not know we were telepathic until we entered this dimension. We both have different powers we are constantly struggling with trying to understand and control. You developed yours early, without knowledge of what it was. I know a mind control telepath you can talk to about your gift."

JoAnna did not want her abilities broadcast to the world, especially Jeryl Jarlyn and her uncle. There were a lot of secrets being kept in this household and she was going to add another. "I don't want the Prime Ruler to know until I am ready. He already has suspicions about my gift. It would be nice to have another person's perspective, if we can keep it between us."

Candy smiled and came over to hug her. "Trust me, Tarah Mardroft will keep your secret. She is the sister of our good friend, Koel."

It was the first time her soul mate's name had been mentioned by one of her old friends. "Koel?"

"Don't play coy with me, Jo Jo," Candy said. "I know he went to Earth to see you. When he returned, Koel was in a foul mood, since his soul mate had not returned with him. Koel told us the soul mate telepathic channel opened between the two of you when you first touched. It's hard to miss the electrical jolt that occurs, even though I was stupid enough to believe it was static electricity when it happened between me and Tolfer."

"The Prime Ruler just mentioned about one couple," JoAnna shared, "I assumed it was Shirl and Starc he had been talking about."

"It was, they are the only outed couple, and we'd like to keep it that way," Candy warned her. "So we both have secrets to keep. I am going out on a limb and will trust you." Her friend's voice shook, which concerned her. Was that why they hid Alex's true identity, they did not have faith in her?

"You can count on me to keep your secrets."

"I hope you can. Our lives depend on it."

Chapter 5

~

The Troyk Penal Colony World

Chartail Adholm sat on the small sandy beach which bordered a pristine lake. The moon was full; its light reflected on the black water. It was a breathtaking sight. The sound of waves rippling to shore was lulling her to sleep.

There was a tranquility sitting here alone in the dark. She had purposely distanced herself from the small settlement nestled near the banks of the large body of water. It had been a week since the Utopia community moved to the camp that had once belonged to the portal guardians. Chartail, like the others, had worked hard relocating the former Troyk freedom fighters. For now, she just wanted the near quiet this spot afforded. Although she could still hear rumblings from the village, it was more like white noise.

She heard footsteps approach from the direction of the settlement. Chartail hoped whoever it was would pass her by. She was not ready to be social just yet. Being strong in front of others was exhausting. If she had fifteen more minutes of peace, she would be ready to return.

"There you are," a male's voice she was familiar with came from the direction of the earlier noise. "I have looked everywhere for you."

Chartail turned to see Tarsea Childers, who stood a stone's throw away. Without an invitation, her former boyfriend sat next to her. At least he was not chattering away. Tarsea tended to be on the quieter side. He wrapped his arm around her shoulder. It was an embrace between friends who were no longer lovers. Murmurs of voices from the village and cricket chirps serenaded them.

"I had to get away from all the sorrow, before it started to weigh me down." Chartail did not have anyone in the village to talk to, so she took advantage of

Tarsea's presence. "If I submerge into depression, I do not know if I will be able to surface again."

Tarsea applied a little pressure to his hold on her shoulder. It was his way to offer support. He was one of the few people who knew what she had suffered in the Nightshade universe, and then been subjected to once she entered the penal colony world.

"There is no disgrace in doing whatever is required to survive, Chartail," Tarsea finally said. "I never realized what an incredibly strong woman you are. If only I had been a better boyfriend, rather than just using you as a cover for my anti-government activities."

Chartail knew Tarsea felt guilty about their former relationship. Ironically, they had both worked to overthrow the government that ruled their world. Where Tarsea took the non-violent approach, Chartail had gone for quick, violent change. It was through Tarsea she had been able to get close to Prime Hosp, certainly not her father. Although her father was one of the most powerful men in the Prime Council, he would never have offered her the opportunity to talk to one of his associates. Prime Hosp represented the change she wanted so desperately to exact.

"Did you ever consider, Tarsea," Chartail said, "I used you, as much as you used me? We both needed to present a certain face to the general public and together we managed it."

"But if I had known," Tarsea reasoned, "I would have stopped you from the assassination plot you concocted with Prime Hosp. Everything that had transpired after you were caught would never have happened. If I had only been a true boyfriend."

"And you would have dumped me as soon as you laid eyes on Alex." Chartail had never believed that soul mates existed until Alexandra Mann had entered their universe. "Speaking of Alex, how is she?"

"Actually, she is with your cousin," Tarsea answered.

Chartail had remembered her father's sister had a baby girl she had taken through the portal when she left the Troyk universe with Benko Jarlyn. For some reason, Chartail had not thought about her cousin, even when Alex, Shirl, and Candy arrived in their dimension. It was not surprising, if you considered the upheaval her life had gone through recently.

"Good Lord, another daughter of a dissident has returned home!" Chartail could not believe it. Mind control telepathic powers ran in her family, although Chartail had not inherited the gift. "What telepathic powers does she possess?"

Tarsea took a hard, long look at Chartail. She figured Tarsea was trying to determine if he should tell her the truth or not bother to answer the question. "We are not sure. Candy had a premonition that your cousin meant trouble, so I imagine she has the power. The only question is, how will she use it? Plus, we have an additional problem."

Chartail laughed. Her life had become one problem after another. "What now?"

"Koel is her soul mate," Tarsea responded. "Darden and I have fought over who is going to tell him he cannot have sex with her until we know she can be trusted."

"That could be a problem," Chartail commented. "Based on everything I have heard about Candy's power, it is not something you want to dismiss. I assume my cousin is staying at your parents'. Does this unseen cousin of mine still go by the name Jolyn?"

"JoAnna," Tarsea answered. "She spent several years in the orphanage with Alex and the girls. They called her Jo Jo. It seems she used her mind control abilities to get herself adopted by a rich couple."

She could not fault her cousin. Chartail had spent her family's money with little restraint. Since she was treated as an ornament, thought to have little brains or telepathic abilities, Chartail milked her father for everything she could. No item was too lavish, once upon a time. Finally, she took more drastic steps to address an injury inflicted by her father and the Prime Ruler.

"We should head back to the settlement," Chartail finally said. "I assume you were here to see Benko."

Benko had entered her life during the battle between the Utopia settlement and portal guardians. They had fought side by side. Although Benko lived in Ginkgo Terra, he decided to stay in the penal colony universe. He was finally ready to start preparations to challenge his father for the right to rule the Troyk universe. The penal colony was the best place to launch such an effort. He already had the support of every man, woman, and child in the village, as well as allies he cultivated from the Terra Nova and the Nightshade universes.

Chartail discovered Benko Jarlyn was her soul mate after they defeated the portal guardians. Everyone around them was aware of their relationship as soon as they touched. However, Chartail was too embarrassed to tell Tarsea she had not developed any new telepathic powers. Her soul mate needed to make love to her for that to happen.

~◦

Benko Jarlyn stood at the perimeter of the settlement and waited for Chartail to return. He knew there were numerous issues plaguing his soul mate. After they concluded their meeting, Tarsea had gone to look for her. Hopefully, Chartail took the opportunity to talk to him about whatever was bothering her. If she was not comfortable talking to Tarsea, Benko would ask him to bring Alex or Shirl with him on his next trip.

Tarsea and Chartail finally entered the outskirts of the village. She walked right past him and entered the shelter they shared. Things were supposed to become easier when one found their soul mate. He had never believed in the legends. Benko had been surprised to find out the girls he had looked after on Earth had found their other halves in the Troyk universe. However, things were not simple when it came to Chartail.

Darden walked over to Benko after Tarsea joined him. He was pleased with the men who aligned their allegiance to him. On top of everything else, Darden was his daughter's soul mate. For eight long years, Darden waited for Cassie to grow up. As far as Benko knew, his daughter and Darden had not had sexual relations. Cassie shared everything with him, much to his horror from time to time.

"I think it is time you brought Cassie to this universe," Benko instructed Darden. "My father's gatherers must be combing every inch of the Earth in their search for me. It is unlikely they would associate Ben Clark and his daughter with Benko Jarlyn, but I do not want to take the chance. Darden, as soon as you feel it is time, you need to join us here permanently."

Benko did not want to push his daughter and Darden into close proximity to each other, but it had been eight years and the young man had been honorable. He also feared what would happen to his mind control telepathic daughter, once she made love with her soul mate. Cassie had been sheltered most of her life and he was concerned too much power and responsibility would be thrown at his naive daughter.

Although Alex and Candy were only twenty-one when they entered the Troyk universe, they had grown up as orphans and had made their way through the world alone. Both girls had handled their transition to living in the Troyk universe and possessing soul mates with a maturity that surprised him. Although he loved his daughter, he did not feel she was ready to take on a revolution, a change in universes, and a soul mate with the same maturity.

Darden smiled at the news. "I had already come to the conclusion I needed to leave the Troyk universe and bring your daughter here. Cassie will be delighted, she has been unhappy being left behind. I could see the disappointment in her eyes when I took JoAnna to the Troyk universe and did not include her."

"Neither of us are ready to return to my father's realm just yet."

Benko had delayed the inevitable during most of his time on Earth, he never bothered to call it Ginkgo Terra. When Shirl's headaches worsened, he knew they were short on time and they had to get the girls to the Troyk Universe. Although he and Darden planned their return, he could not help but think of his own eventual homecoming. He loved his father dearly, always had. Benko just could not stomach how the mind control telepathic government took advantage of their people.

He watched as Tarsea and Darden entered the portal, returning them to the Troyk universe. Since the portal on the other side was monitored, the two men were supposedly returning from explorations of an uncharted world for a new source of crystals. His father had become more and more frantic to possess crystals as he aged, a need Benko mirrored. He would need a wealth of crystals if his next campaign against Jeryl Jarlyn was to be successful.

The camp was quiet, since most of the citizens had retired for the evening. A small group of guards walked the borders of the village, in case any lone marauders decided to attack. He walked the short distance to the shelter he shared with Chartail. When living assignments had been determined, they were matched together since they were soul mates. His clan mates just assumed they would wish to be together.

When he entered the makeshift hut, Chartail sat in front of a small fire. Their dwelling was properly ventilated to allow for one fire in the center of the lodging. She did not look up, as he entered. Sitting there, she looked so young. Regardless of how many times he told himself age did not matter, he could not come to terms with the fact he was forty-four years old and Chartail was twenty-three. Soul mates or not, she was too young for him.

"How did your meeting with Tarsea and Darden go?" Chartail asked. He could hear Chartail's anger under the surface of her disguised interest. "Although I spent some time with Tarsea, he did not mention what you three talked about. It is just like it was before."

He did not have to ask her to clarify what she referred to. Benko knew Chartail wanted to be actively involved in the planning stages of the revolution that would ultimately bring him to power. There were so many reasons he did not include her, but Chartail's lack of intelligence was not one of them. His soul mate was brilliant. The plot she spearheaded to kill his father had almost succeeded. One traitorous coward had warned the palace guard of the attempt and lives were lost on both sides when the plot was finally executed.

"Do not peg me in a category with your father or mine," Benko said. "At no time have I questioned your ability to contribute greatly to our plans. My main concern is for you to heal mind, body, and soul. You have been through so much, you need to mend."

"And the other people in this village have not?" Chartail cried. "A quarter of their friends and families died during the attack. Yet, somehow they managed to make this place their home, even while they mourn."

He was impressed with the villagers' work ethic. Had they banded together earlier, rather than working independently to overthrow his father, Benko did not doubt he would now rule the Troyk universe. They had worked hard to set up the Utopia community, but their struggles did not compare to Chartail's.

"They were not forced to have sexual relations with a psychopath who ran the portal guardians," Benko pointed out, "or raped and fed upon by vampires in the Nightshade universe."

"Why does Tarsea see me as a strong woman, and you only see a broken one?" her voice cracked as she communicated how she felt to him. He could kick himself for fighting with her over this topic once again. "You cannot even bring yourself to touch me!"

If she went to make a fatal shot, she was right on target. He had longed to bury himself inside his soul mate, but knew he would be taking advantage of her. Regardless of her words to the contrary, he could not do something he felt was morally wrong.

"Stop looking at me that way." This time Chartail had an edge to her voice. She had obviously lost patience with him. "I am not taking this any longer. For years I was made to feel I was defective because I was not a mind control telepath. There is no way I am going to have my soul mate treat me as if I am broken. I have more courage in my little finger than you have in your whole body. For twenty two years you were safe on Ginkgo Terra, unscathed from the loss of free will your people in the Troyk universe were without. I am not remaining underneath this roof for another instant."

Chartail got up and started to collect what little she possessed. Shirl had brought a number of things for her during her last trip through the portal. He was helpless to stop her, perhaps because he knew she was right.

"The next time, Darden or Shirl is here, I will ask one of them to take me to Terra Nova," Chartail informed him. "I did not miss the way their leader looked at me. He is young and strong. I am sure he knows how to treat a woman."

What little control he managed to maintain, snapped with those words. Benko Jarlyn sprang to his feet and took his soul mate in his arms. "Over my dead body, are you giving yourself to a barbarian."

Benko kissed his soul mate, as if his life depended on it. The kiss was rough, full of emotion and passion. Chartail deepened the kiss and grabbed his short sable hair. He laid her on the animal pelt before the fire, and tore her clothing in the process. The animal within had finally won out, he was going to claim his mate.

Chartail loved his weight on her. She was tall, but he was taller by a good four inches. Their lips were adhered to each other, with neither coming up for air. Breathing at a time like this was highly overrated. All she could think was to remove the clothing he still wore. Benko had managed to remove hers with a skill she had never encountered before.

Her lovers in the past were considerate partners, even Tarsea. When Alex spoke of her time with Tarsea, Chartail barely recognized the man she referred to. Now Benko seemed to be caught up in the same feral madness Alex described. Chartail knew she would admire every bruise she would possess in the morning.

"Get rid of the clothes you are still wearing," Chartail communicated through their closed channel. Neither had used the pathway they opened as soon as they touched. Although they were a telepathic race, in the Troyk penal colony they rarely used their telepathic gifts. Now she was able to order her soul mate without removing her lips from the all-consuming kiss.

Benko lifted himself from Chartail and made quick work of eliminating his clothing. Although the fire did not generate much light, she could see the shadows of the contours of his muscular physique. She longed to run her fingers across each ridge that constituted his chest. Her digits literally ached to become busy exploring his body.

"Do you have protection?" Benko asked, as he once again lowered himself on top of her.

"I have a couple of knives," she managed to say between kisses. "The sentries should call out if there is any danger."

"No, protection against pregnancy," Benko said, as he stopped the kiss.

Chartail looked at him, confused. People in the Troyk universe did not practice birth control. There was ample land and resources to allow couples to reproduce, if the Supreme Being was generous enough to create a child. Child care was shared by both partners and their extended family. Familial telepathic links allowed for constant communication, related to the health and welfare of each child. In the penal colony, although resources were sparse, each birth was celebrated.

"Never mind," Benko reconsidered, as he brought his lips back on to hers.

Chartail was no blushing virgin, she had experienced her first sexual encounter when she was sixteen years old. At an early age, she figured out how to get the most out of every relationship. She enjoyed sex and the boys she dated were more generous when she had relations with them. The looks of disappointment she was given at home were replaced with puppy-dog-like gazes from the boys.

However, Benko was not a boy, but a full grown man. A soul mate who knew what he wanted. He obviously had not lived the life of a hermit when his daughter's mother passed away. Benko played her body like it was a cherished instrument. His hands caressed every bit of flesh he could reach.

Chartail wrapped her legs around Benko's hips, she invited him to touch her in places he had been avoiding. She was thrilled when his hands reached the inside of her thighs and then ultimately her moist folds. He entered her with two fingers, performing exploratory reconnaissance before he consummated their union. She could have told him she was ready telepathically, but she enjoyed this foreplay.

She deepened the kiss as he entered her with one decisive thrust. The guttural moans she let out were captured by his mouth. He was devouring her mouth, as his member entered and exited her core. His pace was matched by her as they performed a mating dance as old as time. As he ejaculated, Chartail knew it was going to change her life forever. She did not know how, but she was certain they were about to conceive a child.

Chapter 6

~

The Troyk Universe

JoAnna waited in the Prime Ruler's receiving room, she thought of nothing in particular. This was the third session she had with Jeryl Jarlyn and he seemed ready to give up hope she had the gift. After the first two sessions, his temper flared as she failed time and time again to be able to perform tests to prove her to be a mind control telepath. Her uncle attended each session, not participating, but threw her looks of anticipation of a breakthrough. She had the gift, but never used it in the manner they requested.

She had to determine whether someone was lying or not. Who cared, as long as she was able to get what she wanted in the long-run? The idea of spending countless hours listening to someone being interrogated, determining whether or not they were telling the truth, seemed duller than watching paint dry. Although she had not met with Koel's sister yet, JoAnna understood that was what Tarah did.

Secondly, she had to telepathically sway someone to her way of thinking. In the past, she would make eye contact and merely suggest verbally what she wanted. That was how she managed to get the Carlson's to adopt her. She had never used her gift through the means Jeryl Jarlyn required until this point. As far as she was concerned, her powers here were just a lot of static and headaches. Even though Tolfer tried to work with her, she had no desire to communicate telepathically. If she could control her headaches with the herbal tea, that was good enough for her. Candy and Alex seemed relieved she was not interested in expanding her telepathic abilities. Both girls were accustomed to verbal communication and it was still their preferred means of communication.

Jeryl Jarlyn finally entered the room and joined her. A rather short man accompanied him, he took the seat next to the Prime Ruler. No introductions were made, which was odd, since Jeryl was obsessive about social etiquette.

The stranger addressed her, with no greeting whatsoever. "I have been informed the Childers have decided that you will no longer be lodging with them. They are used to living alone and now both sons have brought girlfriends into their home. They thought they had room, but they re-evaluated their situation."

The man's words did not ring true. There was a nuance she had picked up, it almost sounded like a bad note sung by a singer. She had similar reactions in the past, but disregarded how she felt because the topic had been unimportant to her.

"He's lying," JoAnna said.

"How do you know?" the Prime Ruler asked. He seemed genuinely interested in her answer. Jeryl Jarlyn leaned forward in his chair, focusing on her. He barely hid his excitement.

She momentarily struggled with how to answer. How do you translate something that just sounds off in your mind? "The pitch my brain heard was off," she simply said. There really was no other way to describe it.

"Excellent," Jeryl stated, while clapping his hands. "You may retire from my presence." The little man rose and left the room. It had been a test and it appeared she passed with flying colors.

Her uncle got up, placed her favorite pastry on a plate, and then passed it to her. "Precisely," he said, as she accepted the plate. JoAnna felt like one of Pavlov's dogs. Actually, she was too hungry to be insulted, she bit into the buttery goodness with relish.

"It is that anomaly of sound that tells you someone is lying," the Prime Ruler continued. "Only a lie can generate that type of sound. The more you use your telepathic gifts, the faster you will pick up on them. Unfortunately, a half-truth is undetectable. That is why one asks the same question in different ways so they can catch someone in a lie."

"Does it work on a mind control telepath?" she asked. The whole lying thing made her uneasy, especially since she generally was so good at it.

"Absolutely," Jeryl answered. "There are rare exceptions, where someone can close their mind to a telepath, as you did the first day we met. I continue to try and connect with you and have been unsuccessful each time."

JoAnna did her best to hide her emotions from both men. "What about you, uncle, can you enter my mind?"

"It seemed unlikely I could, if Jeryl could not," her uncle replied. "I tried regardless and was unsuccessful. You have a powerful gift, my girl."

JoAnna did not like when the Prime Ruler or her uncle referred to her in that manner. Although the term was an endearment between an older gentleman and a younger female, she felt no warmth from either man when they addressed her in that fashion. When Zane Childers, Tarsea's father, called her 'my girl,' JoAnna felt genuine feelings from the man. She did not know if it was an aspect of her telepathic gift or instinct.

"Perhaps you should reside here in The Palace, so we can spend more time together honing your skills," Jeryl Jarlyn commented. JoAnna had an inkling how the creature from *Frankenstein* felt. The offer was not made related to her comfort, but as a means to manipulate the power she would ultimately possess.

"That is a very generous offer, sir," JoAnna finally responded to Jeryl's suggestion. "But, it has been so nice becoming re-acquainted with Candy again and Shirl is expected back this evening. I would like to continue living with the Childers for the time being." JoAnna held her breath, she hoped the Prime Ruler would honor her request. The prospect of staying behind these walls seemed more like a death sentence.

"Yes, yes," Jeryl Jarlyn responded. "I am glad you have reconnected with your old friends. Besides, we should give your mind time to rest, as you start to enhance your skills."

The Prime Ruler seemed to be hatching something else in his devious mind. All signs indicated to her he had just one agenda, whatever would give him more power. For some reason, JoAnna could see past the charismatic exterior to the evil man who resided within his soul.

"I have been unable to spend time with your friend Shirl. If you could find out how her powers have evolved since she mated, I would be extremely grateful." JoAnna must have gotten a funny look on her face, since the Prime Ruler quickly tried to temper his words. "She has traveled so much, I fear she may be overtaxing her brain using her abilities."

JoAnna's uncle continued to sit beside her, mute. He perked up a bit when Shirl's name was mentioned. In what little JoAnna had been able to discover, Shirl had been with her cousin in the Nightshade universe and had returned Chartail temporarily back to the Troyk universe. Prime Adholm had met briefly with his daughter before she was sent to the Troyk penal colony.

"It is time to work on your persuasion capabilities," the Prime Ruler stated. "This is a skill you must master. Three people will join us and I want you to convince them to support Prime Adholm in his quest to be re-elected."

"I am sure my uncle does not need to use mind control to get people to vote for him." JoAnna felt it was obscene manipulating her power in such a manner. It was obvious Jarlyn did not like her response. "Besides, since Shirl returns shortly, I am so excited, I am having difficulty concentrating."

"Let her go, Jeryl," her uncle finally spoke up. Turns out her uncle had a backbone after all. "Perhaps we can sanction a trip for JoAnna and me to visit Chartail in the penal colony. Shirl managed to liberate Candy and the Childers' boy without any prisoners escaping."

"I told you, old friend, I will consider your request." There was a crispness in the Prime Ruler's voice she had not heard before when he addressed her uncle.

"You should run home," Jeryl Jarlyn finally said, excusing her from his presence. JoAnna left the room immediately, before he could change his mind.

She had witnessed firsthand how quickly Jeryl Jarlyn turned on his oldest friend. It was clear he did not like Prime Adholm sticking up for her or desiring something that was not on his agenda. What would happen if JoAnna pushed him too far?

JoAnna decided to do a little shopping on her way back to the Childers's residence. She had worn the clothing she had purchased with Candy and Alex, but was dissatisfied with their quality. There were some upper-end stores she had passed numerous times as she walked to The Palace, but had not the opportunity to stop in and check out what was available.

As she continued to walk, she had a strange sensation she was being followed. JoAnna casually glanced behind her, but did not notice anyone who stood out. She listened to the communal pathways, in case someone commented on anything suspicious.

The first store JoAnna came across had a porter at its entrance, a positive sign she would find exactly what she was looking for. JoAnna entered the store and could tell immediately they would have more suitable clothing for her needs. She headed to the women's clothing department, located on the second floor. She walked up the marble stairway, taking in the elegance of the store. There was a large crystal chandelier which hung from the center ceiling that she admired as she continued up the stairs. JoAnna wondered if Shirl had seen the lovely piece of art.

She had not noticed anyone as she entered the store or someone loitering outside. It was possible she had imagined the whole thing. Perhaps she spent too much time in The Palace, honing her telepathic gift. She was seeing intrigue, where none existed.

As she reached the landing on the second floor, a woman approached her. She presented her card and asked her if she could be of service. JoAnna was used to working with personal shoppers at home and decided to take advantage of what appeared to be the same service in this world.

"I am the protégé of our Prime Ruler and am looking for clothing suitable to reflect my status." JoAnna knew she sounded snobbish, but she did not want any misunderstandings about the quality of the clothing she desired to purchase. She had become accustomed to having the very best.

The sales associate perked up. JoAnna was not sure if it was because of her status or the commission the clerk thought she would make on the sale. People tended to work harder when there was something in it for them.

"There are some lovely outfits in our backroom, reserved for our upper-tiered customers. However, I can tell you do not want something you can purchase off the rack. I can take your measurements and we can design a textile, unique to your personality."

"That is exactly what I am looking for." JoAnna followed the woman to a private lounge where they spent the next thirty minutes selecting various designs. The clerk checked the fabric availability, and she created several outfits of her own designs. She could not remember the last time she had so much fun. If the mind control gig did not work out, she might consider becoming a personal shopper herself.

Although she spent a small ransom, JoAnna did not have any packages which weighed her down as she arrived at the Childers. The clothes she purchased would be created and delivered in several batches. This time, she had not felt she was followed. As she entered the home, JoAnna heard voices coming from the kitchen. It did not take a rocket scientist to determine who she would find there.

"Hi," Alex greeted her. "Where have you been? Solfa communicated ninety minutes ago that you had left the Palace."

JoAnna was taken aback by the tone in Alex's voice. There was definite concern and anxiety laced in her speech. Her old friend must have been worried sick.

"I am sorry, Alex," JoAnna said. "I am not used to communicating telepathically, so I was not actively involved in the conversations taking place. Guess you can say, I traveled under the radar. Jeryl gave me money for more appropriate clothing, so I went shopping."

Alex unconsciously looked down at her own clothing. "Candy and I are not exactly fashion icons. We should have waited for Shirl to come back to take you to buy clothing."

No one mentioned where Koel had been, since he had not made an appearance since she arrived. JoAnna hoped he had been traveling with Shirl and would return with her tonight. Although Alex and Candy had been more than welcoming, their lack of trust in her created a gulf between them. JoAnna hoped that once she was reunited with Koel, she would finally have a confidant to unburden all her doubts and fears about her new home. It was clear Jeryl Jarlyn had plans for her and without Koel's assistance, JoAnna feared she would fall prey to the manipulations of the Prime Ruler.

Chapter 7

~

Koel once again stepped onto the soil of the mountain trail, just west of the capital city of the Troyk universe. After spending time in the Nightshade world, he was relieved to be home. He had rarely traveled to parallel dimensions, he preferred his own world. Even with the mind control telepathic rule, his home was superior to any other universe he had seen.

"I still do not like having left Afton in that terrible place," Shirl commented. She was the mated crystal telepath, who could now navigate natural portals with just her mind. With the crystals that hung around her neck, she could create a portal to anywhere, requiring little energy from her stones.

Portal travel was monitored, so they needed to lie when they reported back to crystal telepathic headquarters. With Jeryl Jarlyn's orders to find dissidents who escaped into other worlds, it was easy to say they had explored other dimensions to determine if they were likely locations to discover these traitors.

The Troyk government had cut off relations with the Nightshade universe. The general populace of the Troyk universe were horrified to discover that world was populated by vampires. Worse, Troyk convicted prisoners sentenced to die, had been sent there to be slaughtered. It was unclear how much the Prime Ruler knew of what happened when their people were condemned to that world, but he had little choice but to cease the practice.

"It was her choice, love," his cousin Starc replied. Starc was Shirl's soul mate. Their coming together made Shirl one of the most powerful beings in any world. "We should head back to town and see what has happened in our absence."

"I am going to head home to shower and then find Darden. The two of you can provide our report to the authorities. It is time I bring my soul mate home." Koel had thought of little else while he was in the Nightshade universe on their rescue mission. The fact Afton had chosen her vampire soul mate over returning to Ginkgo Terra gave him fleeting hope about his own relationship.

They were nearly to the location on the trail where he would be able to communicate through the warrior pathway. He wanted to spend as little time as possible here before he headed back to Ginkgo Terra and claimed his soul mate. The doubt JoAnna would accept him this time around had plagued his mind.

"*Darden,*" Koel pushed communication through the warrior channel. "*I want to return for JoAnna. Meet me on the mountain trail in two hours.*"

It was not long before Darden replied. "*There has been a development. Meet me at the safe house.*"

Koel, Shirl, and Starc exchanged glances. It was a rare occurrence for them to meet at the safe house, rather than the Childers's residence. The safe house was used to temporarily hold dissidents before they were taken to the portal if their immediate escape was not possible. It was also used for the occasional tryst. When they rescued Chartail from the Nightshade universe, it had been her temporary home until she was discovered and arrested.

"*What has happened?*" Koel inquired.

"*Just meet me there,*" Darden answered. "*Shirl and Starc should accompany you.*"

"This can't be good," Shirl commented under her breath. "I checked with Alex and Candy, through our closed channel, to see what was going on. They would not provide any information. Candy is at crystal telepathic headquarters training, but Alex will join us."

A number of scenarios ran through Koel's mind. They were all unwanted distractions from his number one mission. One thing after another had prevented him from claiming JoAnna, including his own soul mate.

It did not take long to reach the safe house. The dwelling was strategically placed not far from the mountain trail head. He had surfed various communal channels, attempting to pick-up chatter that would give him a clue about what Darden wanted to discuss.

Alex and Darden were already in the common room when they entered. Tolfer entered from the kitchen, he carried a platter loaded with sandwiches. Before he placed the tray on the center table, Alex grabbed one.

"I thought you might be hungry," Alex said, as she bit into a sandwich. "Tolfer had just finished preparing lunch, so I told him to bring himself and the food with him."

Koel could not help but smile. The young woman in front of him was probably more likely to have thought of her own hunger than be concerned that they had returned from their mission hungry. Alex continually ate and had not gained an ounce. Now that she was pregnant, he imagined she would start filling out.

"That was very considerate of you, Alex," Starc said, as he grabbed a sandwich. He consumed it in two bites and reached for a second.

Growing impatient, Koel finally said, "What has happened?" He did not want to eat, he wanted answers.

Alex gazed in Darden's direction. He did not like the expression on her face. Koel knew this was not about some future mission, it was personal.

"Jo Jo is in the Troyk universe," Alex chirped out. "She is a mind control telepath and has been training with Jeryl Jarlyn. Candy had a premonition about her. We are not sure she can be trusted." Alex fell back in her chair as she completed sharing the information.

There was momentary silence after Alex finished. Koel's usual tactical brain had momentarily shut down. His soul mate was home and embedded in the enemy camp. Would she have fallen prey to the Prime Ruler had he been here to protect her, rather than rescuing another woman?

Darden leaned forward, noticeably ready to share some tidbit of information about what had transpired in Koel's absence. He knew his cousin well enough to know he was not going to like what he had to say. "She is staying with the Childers, but has spent most of her time at The Palace."

"Has she said or done anything to indicate she cannot be trusted?" Shirl chimed in.

"Not so far," Alex responded. "We have been walking on eggshells since she arrived. Officially, I was introduced to her as Alexia Montiff, but I think she knows who I really am. The looks she gives me breaks my heart. I want to tell her the truth, but I know I can't. Even before I fell through the portal, I often thought of Jo Jo and now I'm afraid to acknowledge who I am."

"We have no idea what powers she will possess once she is mated. Until we know what side of the war she is on, you cannot have sex with her." Darden verbalized exactly what Koel had thought. His soul mate was finally home, and Koel knew he could not touch her.

Koel did not bother to tell Darden he did not know what he asked of him. No one but Darden could have delivered those orders. His cousin had known his soul mate since she was ten years old and had maintained a platonic relationship with her for eight years. Even once she turned eighteen, Darden had held off having sexual relations with his soul mate. Things were still unstable related to Benko and Cassandra Jarlyn's place in this or any other world. His cousin did not want to complicate matters or place Cassie in any more danger.

"Koel, I can take you to the penal colony world," Shirl offered. "You can spend time with Benko Jarlyn, planning our revolution. Plus, they could use your help to rebuild after their battle with the portal guardians."

Koel was grateful Shirl made the offer, but could not consider it. He was not about to run away from his soul mate. Darden had shown restraint all these years, Koel could do the same. Besides, maybe with her soul mate beside her, JoAnna would make better choices. She was alone in this world, not sure who *she* could trust.

"Although I appreciate the offer," he told Shirl, "my place is beside my soul mate. How can she prove to be trustworthy, if we have already branded her a traitor?"

"What about Candy's premonition?" Alex asked. Her tone indicated she wanted Koel to come up with words that would give Alex hope her friend was salvageable.

"Feelings of an ensuing danger," Koel answered, "is not a particular action. Candy sensed you were in danger, Alex. It was not until Candy saw in her mind Chanz plunged the dagger into your back that the premonition came to light. Had Tarsea or Tolfer been better positioned, Chanz would not have gotten close to you with that knife."

Alex frowned, "That did not help! He still had the knife and his intent was clear."

"But a number of factors could have swayed him from that action. A boyfriend from one of his former victims could have been waiting for him or he could have been called into work. He may have had the courage at that given moment to attack you, but would possibly not been able to do it another time."

"I suppose you are right," Alex said, she did not sound convinced. "Either way, I am glad you are standing by her."

"Things would have been so much easier if you had been my soul mate," Koel said. He had not meant it, but each pairing since Alex came over seemed to be more complicated than the next.

Alex laughed, "I already told you, you're too much of a goof for me."

It seemed like a lifetime ago when he purposely said things to get a rise out of people. He loved watching their reactions to the outrageous comments he made. He learned a lot about people from how they reacted to the unexpected. When Koel went on missions, he needed to know how people were going to behave when faced with an unplanned occurrence.

JoAnna had been exactly that. He was surprised by the independence of the sultry beauty. Although she spent time with Jeryl Jarlyn, he doubted she had given him her loyalty.

Darden rose and approached Koel. "I will be heading out to reside in the penal colony. Although Jarlyn has swallowed the half-truths we have told him, it is too dangerous for me to remain. Cassie will be joining me there."

Koel knew this day would come. His cousin had postponed his final departure from the Troyk universe until JoAnna arrived. Darden had been their only crystal telepath to help save the dissidents they would send through the portal. Now all the women were in the Troyk universe and Shirl could take over as their crystal telepath.

"You will be sorely missed," Koel rose and hugged his cousin. "I will see you in the penal colony world when we travel to meet with Benko Jarlyn. It is time you are united with your soul mate and for me to head to the Childers to be with mine."

Koel could see the apprehensive look depicted on Alex's face. He wished his gut feeling did not mirror her look.

Koel stopped dead in his tracks when he saw JoAnna in the Childers's common room. His reaction to his soul mate had not lessened upon second sight. It was hard to dismiss his body's reaction to her, as violent as it had been in Ginkgo Terra.

Shirl shoved him in the back, she wanted to fully enter the room and reunite with her childhood friend. *"Get control of yourself,"* Shirl warned him through the warrior channel. *"You are dead meat if you show any weakness."* Half the time he had no idea what Candy, Shirl, or Alex talked about. Although he did not like the analogy, Koel got the gist of what she said.

"JoAnna," Koel said. Although he had rehearsed what he would say when he was once again in his soul mate's presence, Koel could not find the words to continue. He stood back, paralyzed, as Shirl stepped around him.

The crystal telepath hugged his soul mate. "It is so good to see you again," Shirl said. "We should have stayed in touch after you were adopted."

Koel continued to watch the two women embrace, cemented in place with indecision. His instinct was to move forward and pull JoAnna out of Shirl's arms, into his own. The practical part of him held him back, clearly aware of the danger she represented.

"We have so much to make up for," Shirl cried. "I can't believe you are here. When Koel came back without you, I feared you would remain on Earth. The thought we had lost you again was overwhelming."

His soul mate's glance returned to him. There was so much heat in her cat-like eyes, Koel's internal temperature started to rise in response. How was he ever going to maintain a non-sexual relationship with JoAnna?

Shirl released his soul mate and JoAnna walked to where Koel stood, still frozen in place. She wrapped her arms around his neck and brought her body into his. Without a word, JoAnna placed her lips against his. This was no sweet, welcoming kiss! As he opened his mouth, her tongue entered to meet his. She tasted incredible.

Everything around him faded. JoAnna became his reality, nothing else mattered. All he desired was to possess the woman in his arms. Koel grabbed the hem of JoAnna's tunic and started to pull it up her torso. He had never felt a softer material, although he knew her bared flesh would be finer than the most expensive silk.

"Whoa, cowboy, slow down." Shirl's voice cut through the trance he had been in.

Koel had lost control. It felt as if he had been directed by a force outside of his own mind. There was not a doubt, Koel would have had JoAnna on the floor and he would have plunged into her with an audience present.

"The two of you were as frantic as Shirl and I were the first time we had sex," Starc commented. "We had no control as the soul mate link attempted to right itself after that damned vampire Drake corrupted it." Koel was as confused about what had just happened as his baffled cousin was.

"I guess we'll have to pick up where we left off later," JoAnna said. "My uncle just called me to The Palace. Jeryl Jarlyn wishes to see me. Koel, can you accompany me?"

"Shirl, can you walk with JoAnna?" Koel asked through the warrior channel. *"I have some things I need to figure out."* He had never lost his faculties as he just had. All of a sudden, spending time in the penal colony did not seem like such a bad idea.

"Jo Jo, I have to report to crystal telepath headquarters. Starc and I have not been debriefed on our last mission. The Palace is on the way, let me go with you. It will give me a chance for us to catch-up. Candy had her turn, now it's mine. I am sure Koel will understand."

Although JoAnna looked momentarily disappointed, she nodded her approval. Koel took a step back, he broadened the space between him and his soul mate. He needed to figure out what had just happened before he came within close proximity to her again.

As soon as JoAnna, Shirl, and Starc left, Koel headed to the common room and poured himself a drink. He downed it in a single gulp and poured himself another glass. With the drink in his hand, he sat in the overstuffed chair, he needed to think.

"There is not enough alcohol to dull the ache you are feeling, my friend." Tarsea pulled out a glass and joined Koel. "My relationship with Alex has had its peaks and valleys. I woke up one morning too often with a hangover. Trust me when I tell you it does not work."

"If you weren't so bossy and controlling, we would not have fought," Alex said as she sat in Tarsea's lap.

"What was JoAnna like when you all lived in the orphanage?" Koel knew it had been a lifetime ago, but he yearned to learn as much as he could about his soul mate.

"Jo Jo was so full of life," Alex responded. "She was always up for a challenge. If she was told not to do something, she found a way around the rule or warning. Actually, she reminds me a lot of you. Jo Jo always looked at all the possibilities and took the best path. She was only six when she left, I can only imagine what she is capable of now."

"That is what I am afraid of." Koel had not planned to voice his doubts. Nature would not be so cruel as to tie him to a woman he could never have. He took another sip from his drink. There had to be a way to rescue JoAnna from Jeryl Jarlyn's clutches.

Chapter 8

~

JoAnna only half-listened to Shirl, as they made their way to The Palace. The kiss she shared with Koel was nothing like the one he gave her on Earth. That kiss had been the knee weakening kind. What had just occurred was mind-shattering explosive. He reacted exactly how she had wanted, almost as if she had directed his actions. She had been so caught up in the moment, she forgot Shirl and Starc had been present.

"Earth to JoAnna," Shirl screamed in her ear. "I can imagine what you are thinking about, but we are here. If you are going to meet with Jeryl Jarlyn, you need all your mental faculties." It felt like Shirl wanted to say more, but she did not continue. Once again, her friends were guarded about the information they shared with her.

"I'll find my way back when I am done with the Prime Ruler," JoAnna said. It was hard to mask her disappointment in Shirl. "You must be exhausted after your mission."

"Yes, I am. We'll go out to *Gerard's* for their second seating of dinner tomorrow night. I understand you have some awesome outfits. I can't wait to see them."

"Shirl?"

"Yes?"

Confronting her friend on the street in front of The Palace did not seem like the appropriate place. "Nothing," she replied. "We'll talk tomorrow." She desperately needed a sounding board, but did not know if Shirl was the one she could confide in. JoAnna was the outsider, the one who had abandoned them.

Shirl gave her a long assessing look. Her expressive eyes showed she still struggled over what to say to JoAnna. "How much do you know about the legend of the mated female crystal telepath?"

"Next to nothing," JoAnna admitted. "Jeryl Jarlyn has mentioned it several times, but not to the extent I understand the stories shared or what you are capable of." She was on a cliff and decided to jump into the mix of all the intrigue in this world. "The Prime Ruler mentioned I should watch you and report back to him."

Shirl did not seem surprised by JoAnna's confession. "There is not a whole lot to tell him. Tread carefully where he is concerned. Everything he does is about garnering more power. You seem like a smart woman, JoAnna. Do not be taken in by his charm."

This had been the most honest conversation JoAnna had had since she arrived. Unfortunately, Shirl had to report in and Jeryl Jarlyn waited for her. They embraced and Shirl was on her way. JoAnna momentarily stared at the majestic beauty of The Palace. Once again, beauty provided a facade for the corruption of the mind control telepathic government.

Unable to delay her meeting with Jeryl Jarlyn any longer, JoAnna made her way into The Palace. She was now known to all the palace guards, who waved her on. Her trip up the stairs was uneventful, with nothing to temporarily distract her from making the meeting. When she entered The Prime Ruler's receiving room, he was alone. Her uncle, who always attended their meetings, was not present.

"JoAnna, my girl," Jeryl Jarlyn greeted her. "We have a lot to discuss today, let us get straight to business."

She sat in her usual chair. There was a cup of coffee and a pastry laid out in front of her. Everything seemed normal, with the exception of her uncle's absence. JoAnna felt Jeryl Jarlyn was finally going to get to his real agenda. She picked up the cup with the black brew and started to sip.

"Have you been able to enter another's mind?" Jeryl Jarlyn asked.

It took a tremendous amount of self-control to swallow the coffee and not spit it out. Her mind immediately flashed to the time in the portal and what had happened with Darden. It had been an odd sensation, nothing she had experienced before.

Jeryl sat forward in his chair, aware of her reaction to his question. She could not deny anything had happened. Her usual poker face had abandoned her.

"When I entered the portal with Darden, I had a strange cerebral moment. Did I enter his mind, I don't know. It felt like I saw the workings of the space oddity through his eyes. There was nothing intentional in what occurred and I doubt if I could reproduce it."

"It is indeed a rare talent a mind control telepath possesses," The Prime Ruler admitted. "However, through the use of crystals, you can hone your skill and control another person."

The ability to sway indecisiveness was one thing, what Jeryl admitted was quite another. The idea of making another person a puppet to be controlled was a scary and atrocious proposition. Suddenly, JoAnna thought of the kiss she had just shared with Koel. He had been holding back and her desire for him to become more aggressive plagued her thoughts. Had she been responsible for the loss of control Koel had experienced?

"There was another occurrence, was there not?"

"I'm not sure," JoAnna answered truthfully. She was full of doubt over whether she had driven Koel to crave her as much as she wanted him. How could she start to understand the extent of her power and how to control it, if she was not honest with Jeryl Jarlyn?

"Tell me," Jarlyn commanded.

"I kissed someone and it turned into a frenzied affair."

"Was there a discharge of electrical current and the ability to communicate through a new telepathic channel?" The Prime Ruler could barely contain his excitement.

JoAnna's face reddened, through no fault of her own. She could not control her body's reaction to Jarlyn's words. "Yes, it happened on Earth when Koel touched me." Jeryl Jarlyn knew of the soul mate relationship between Shirl and Starc. JoAnna just hoped The Prime Ruler would give her and Koel the space he had provided the other couple.

"Excellent," Jeryl Jarlyn answered, "when you are ready to be with him, your power will become intensified. But first, you need to harness the gift you have barely touched the surface of." The Prime Ruler rose and walked over to a display case of crystals. He picked up a gold stone and returned to JoAnna, handing her his treasure. "This is herderite. It will help to awaken the power you have dormant in your brain."

JoAnna could feel the power emanating from the gem. She had never believed in hocus pocus or the power of crystals, but the sensation she felt as she held the stone was hard to deny. "How does it work?"

"In the beginning you will have to concentrate, get into a meditative state. Eventually, you will just need to grasp it in your hand to harness its power. I had called you here to tell you I wanted you to start to travel with Shirl and Starc in order to exercise your power with non-telepathic people. However, I think we need to have you and the team travel to Terra Flora to retrieve more herderite."

JoAnna had not considered she could journey from world to world, as Shirl and Starc did. Shirl had been so tight lipped related to her travels, JoAnna questioned whether she would be welcome. Ultimately, it appeared they would have little choice if the Prime Ruler so decreed it. Jeryl Jarlyn did not delay in executing his latest plan. The communal pathway was already abuzz with news that the Prime Ruler's protégée would be traveling with the female crystal telepath.

"You should report to crystal telepath headquarters and prepare to leave with Shirl and Starc immediately," Jeryl Jarlyn ordered. JoAnna doubted Jarlyn took into consideration Shirl's present state of exhaustion.

"Is it not true a crystal telepath gets power primarily from the brain?" JoAnna asked. "Shirl just returned from a mission that lasted almost a week. Wouldn't it be wise to have her rest a day or two before you send her out again?" Besides, JoAnna was also concerned about traveling through an unstable portal with a crystal telepath who was not at one hundred percent of her capabilities.

"I suppose you are correct; Shirl should rest for a day. It is hard not to be excited about what power you will possess. Grasp the crystal and concentrate on absorbing its essence."

JoAnna fisted the herderite, until its rough edges dug into her palm. She was not sure how one went about gathering energy from stones, but she had nothing to lose in making an attempt. Rather than pushing through telepathic communication the way Tolfer had shown her, JoAnna concentrated her gift on the object in her hand. She felt a sharp pain in her head and she started to bleed from her nose.

"Careful," Jeryl Jarden warned, "you have collected too much energy with one telepathic pull. Imagine you are sipping wine, rather than gulping down water."

JoAnna rose to collect some tissues to clean herself up. Wouldn't it be convenient if she had the gift of telekinesis? All she would have done was concentrate on the box of tissues and it would have come to her. She stopped in her tracks and tried to manipulate her power to move objects. Having no success, she continued her short trip to the tissues.

"Take the stone home and practice with it," Jeryl Jarlyn instructed. "Although the bleeding will have no lasting effect, it is a sign you are overtaxing your brain. Too much of that carelessness could result in you damaging the part of your brain that contains your gifts."

The warning was duly noted by JoAnna. For the first time, the occurrence of a nosebleed resulted in a warning that permanent damage would result if her behavior was not modified. JoAnna wondered how many of the Prime Ruler's protégées ended up destroying their brains.

JoAnna was escorted to crystal telepath headquarters by one of the palace guards. Although she had not felt the sensation that someone followed her, she thought it wise to have someone accompany her. In addition, she had not visited this building in the short time she had been in the Troyk universe.

As she entered the establishment, JoAnna was bowled over by the sight of good-looking men who populated the main hall. It did not take long to establish none of them seemed to attract her the way Koel did. There certainly was no harm in enjoying the amazing sight before her. The room was initially quiet as she entered, but the hum of conversations between the men increased as they noticed her.

A tall blond man approached. He looked so much like Shirl, he could only be the brother JoAnna had heard so much about. Although Shirl had not mentioned him, Candy had clued her into the problems that existed between the two siblings. Over time, Cianan had gotten over blaming his sister for his parents' abandonment of him when they left for Earth.

"You must be JoAnna," Shirl's brother said. "My name is Cianan, although I suspect you already know that."

"Yes, Candy's stories have been very amusing," JoAnna responded. "I understand you will lead the party going to Terra Flora tomorrow to gather more crystals."

"Yes," Cianan grunted. The last time Cianan had been to Terra Flora, one of the native animals almost took off his leg. They barely got him back to the Troyk universe before he bled to death. "It is a miserable place, so you will need to get a lot of rest tonight. Also make sure you are properly hydrated as well. Let me take you to Shirl. She will tell you more about tomorrow's trip."

JoAnna followed Cianan through the hall and into an area where a number of gymnasiums were located. They entered one on the far end, where Candy was giving Shirl self-defense lessons. When they entered, Shirl's attention was diverted and Candy took advantage of the distraction and brought down her lifelong friend.

"No fair, Candy," Shirl cried. "Get off me, we need to brief Jo Jo on tomorrow's trip to Terra Flora." Candy immediately complied with Shirl's request and sprang to her feet. It took longer for Shirl to get up from the mat after she had been nailed by Candy. As she rose, Jo Jo could not help but catch the dirty look Shirl gave Candy.

"Anyone who takes it easy on you during training is not doing you any favors," Candy informed Shirl. "Anytime you want some pointers, Jo Jo, I will be happy to work with you." The grown Candy was just as fierce as the little girl she remembered. JoAnna imagined she would be black and blue after working with her, but she would be better prepared if anyone attacked her.

"I will take you up on the offer," JoAnna replied. "Perhaps after we get back from Terra Flora. I have never taken self-defense lessons, but I think it is a good idea considering what Jeryl Jarlyn has in store for me."

Candy and Shirl looked at each other and then at JoAnna. They both had questioning looks on their faces. "What exactly does he have planned for you?" Shirl asked.

"Nothing specific, it's just a feeling I have," JoAnna responded.

"Listen to your intuition, it will save your life," Candy said in a deadly serious tone. "You never know what is on the other side of a portal, let alone around the corner in this universe. Your gut should tell you who you can trust and who you need to be leery of."

This conversation had gotten too serious and contained too much innuendo for her taste. JoAnna already knew she could not trust Jeryl Jarlyn, but not who she could count on. Her gut told her nothing, other than giving her indigestion.

"Enough of talking in circles," Shirl said. "We have a mission to plan for. Koel will be here in about ten minutes, so let's head to a conference room and get comfortable."

"Koel is going with us?" JoAnna inquired. She hoped that would be the case. JoAnna had seen so little of Koel, it would be nice to spend more time with him.

"Solfa requires Koel to be involved in the planning stages of each mission we go on. We had an incident on Terra Nova which caused Solfa to go ballistic. From that point on, Koel has reviewed the tactical aspect of each trip, although he normally does not accompany us through the portal."

JoAnna was equally intrigued to find out what had occurred on Terra Nova and disappointed Koel would not be going with them to Terra Flora. It sounded like such a lovely universe and it would only help to bring them closer romantically.

They had reached the conference room where they were to meet with Koel. JoAnna sat in what looked to be a very comfortable armchair. She was not disappointed as her body molded into the cozy soft leather. It supported her back perfectly and was the appropriate height in order to properly plant her feet. Too many chairs she sat on in the past felt like torture devices if she was in them for any amount of time.

"What can you tell me about Terra Flora?" JoAnna asked.

"Think of Florida in the summer, add twenty more degrees and more humidity," Shirl said. "You will want to wear clothes that will breathe. They have mosquitoes the size of automobiles, but we will take insect repellent with us. They also have very aggressive animal life on the planet."

"You are not exaggerating, are you?" JoAnna asked. She had heard about the attack on Cianan, but not all the other issues related to the parallel universe. So much for a romantic get-away with Koel.

"I really wish I were," Shirl responded. "Terra Flora is rich in crystals and minerals, so it makes the dangers and the miserable climate worth the trip. We just have to be diligent and not dally. It is best to be off the planet before the sun sets and the nocturnal animals run rampant."

JoAnna started to rethink her involvement in tomorrow's mission, regardless of Jeryl Jarlyn's wishes. She was no good to him if she died on the planet or developed malaria and ultimately perished in the Troyk universe. JoAnna hated the taste of tonic water, so the idea of drinking the quinine enriched beverage did not thrill her. She thought of drinking straight gin, when Koel entered the room.

As JoAnna looked up at her soul mate, she could feel her pulse quicken. His rich blue eyes were mesmerizing. This man was created just for her and she wanted him beyond anything she had ever experienced. She grabbed on to the arm rest with both hands, controlling her need to get up and engulf Koel in her arms.

Once Koel's eyes came to her, he continued to stare. She could tell he was as affected by her presence, as she was to his. Unfortunately, she could also feel him try to hold back his emotions. Although she knew she shouldn't, JoAnna concentrated on entering Koel's mind. She could see herself through his eyes.

JoAnna was surprised because she was surrounded by a brilliant red aura, looking through Koel's eyes. Koel definitely had sex on his mind. She saw him shake his head, as if he knew she was playing around in his mind. JoAnna pulled herself out and diverted her glance to Shirl.

"We will leave for Terra Flora tomorrow, let us meet at the Childers's at seven in the morning. After breakfast, we will head to the portal. I plan to accompany the team." JoAnna could hear the thoughts Koel was not communicating about the mission, thoughts about her involvement. When she returned her gaze to Koel, he still looked at her. In fact, glaring would have been a better term. She wondered if he felt her presence in his mind.

"Candy," Cianan added, "I want you along as well. Koel and I will concentrate on JoAnna's safety and you and Starc will be responsible for Shirl's. Get a good night's sleep and drink a lot of water tonight. Coffee is dehydrating, so there will be no caffeine in the morning. I do not want any mishaps this time around."

Koel was the first one to leave the room. JoAnna figured she would not see him again until tomorrow morning. It startled her when he grabbed her arm as she exited. He pushed her against a nearby wall while everyone else hurried away.

"Never enter my brain in that manner again," he growled at her. "I do not know how you did it and I do not care to know the particulars. Soul mates or not, you ever do that again, we are over. Have I made myself clear on the subject?"

All she could do was nod her understanding. JoAnna had a lump in her throat, making it difficult to swallow. For the first time when she looked into Koel's eyes, she had not seen lust. This time it was pure fury. He left her standing, ashamed and fearful. Had she gone too far?

Chapter 9

◡

Koel had not slept the night before, his brain would not shut off. He kept thinking about what JoAnna had done to him. He had heard stories of strong mind control telepathic individuals who could enter another's brain, he just had never met one. It had not been an unpleasant experience, just unexpected. Under different circumstances, he would not have minded, if she had bothered to ask.

There was also the question of what other powers she possessed, which scared him beyond reason. All of it just reinforced the fact they could not have sexual relations. If she was this powerful now, what would the next stage of her telepathic powers consist of?

He reached the Childers's home and proceeded straight to the kitchen. Tolfer was cooking, while Shirl drank orange juice. She had taken her brother's warning about caffeine to heart. For the first time since she had arrived in the Troyk universe, Alex was not in the kitchen.

After what had happened with JoAnna, Koel had warned Tarsea to evacuate them from his parents' home. Alex lived a lie and was pregnant. No one wanted to risk JoAnna purposely or accidentally entering her mind.

"I do not like not having Alex here," Shirl complained through the warrior channel. It was the only safe means of communication in the house, now that JoAnna's presence had been raised to a higher threat level. *"When we get back from Terra Flora, we are going to have to re-evaluate what to do about JoAnna."* It was clear she was shaken by the latest developments regarding their old friend.

"We need you to concentrate on today's mission, not obsess over Alex and the situation here." Koel had not meant to reprimand Shirl, but he needed her mind to be focused on the task at hand.

Shirl merely nodded her understanding. The girls had been so hopeful about bringing their friend to the Troyk universe. Everything that had transpired since JoAnna arrived only added fuel to Candy's premonition concerning her. For his own sanity, Koel had to focus on his desire to somehow be able to reach and convince JoAnna the powers she was born with should not be fully utilized. What happened yesterday, only added more doubt related to him ultimately being successful.

He met briefly with his sister, Tarah, and asked if she would spend time with his soul mate when they returned from Terra Flora. Tarah had struggled most of her life with the moral and practical usage of her gift. His sister had the support of family and friends, JoAnna had neither. Tarah had been assigned to travel off world; it was questionable when she would have the ability to meet with JoAnna.

"How are you doing?" Shirl asked.

Koel could not answer her. He did not want the concern embedded in his heart to adversely impact Shirl. He needed to redirect her and his thoughts. "What is for breakfast, Tolfer?" Koel asked orally.

"A Parmesan and chive egg soufflé, with a side of fruit. I did not want to make anything too heavy. The melon will also help to hydrate you." Tolfer proceeded to pull his masterpiece out of the oven. It was a sight to behold and smelled absolutely wonderful.

"Wow, you could get a job in any five-star restaurant on Earth, Tolfer," JoAnna said as she walked into the kitchen. She wore a sleeveless tunic and skin tight leggings. Immediately Koel's hunger shifted from breakfast to his soul mate. The outfit was practical for the mission, but left very little to the imagination.

When Cianan arrived, the group sat and made quick work of consuming Tolfer's soufflé. The banter between Shirl and her brother helped to keep his mind off his mounting concerns related to JoAnna. Although their sibling relationship was much improved, Shirl and Cianan seemed to enjoy throwing jabs at one another. He did not have that type of relationship with Tarah. Where Koel had enjoyed practical jokes, his sister had always been painfully serious. Although he dearly loved Tarah, he just could not relate to her.

All that was left was to head out to the portal. Although Shirl could have taken them directly to the crystal caves on Terra Flora, with JoAnna present that was impossible. They would have to enter the world through the natural portal and walk for several hours to reach their destination.

As they readied to leave, JoAnna planted herself next to Koel. There was little he had to say to his soul mate. Between his lack of sleep, concern about the mission, and JoAnna's incredible powers, Koel was in no mood to spend time making idle chit chat with her. In the end, Candy solved the issue, by cutting next to JoAnna as they left the house.

Koel walked behind Candy and his soul mate. He listened to their conversation as they made their way to the mountain trail. Although JoAnna could navigate a number of the communal channels, she chose to speak aloud with Candy.

Neither woman had been to Terra Flora. Candy told his soul mate the stories she heard about the parallel dimension. His interest piqued when Candy talked about the world's animal life. He had seen the terrifying giant larma beast at the Aster Province zoo. They were properly armed in case they had an encounter with any of those animals. Candy's description of a hot, humid world worked to further sour his mood.

They quickly made their way up the trail to the natural portal. As soon as Cianan came within several yards of the gateway, his crystal started to glow. Almost immediately the air in front of him started to shimmer. Koel could only hope Candy had been exaggerating about how miserable Terra Flora was.

The Terra Flora Universe

The heat was stifling. JoAnna wondered if it was possible to build a biodome around the part of the world that contained the crystals and the portal. If she thought about impossible tasks, she would be better able to deal with how incredibly hot it was. Well, at least they were out of the pouring rain. The thick jungle vegetation they traversed was taking the brunt of the storm.

When they first arrived in Terra Flora, they were welcomed with an incredibly hard rain. It had been so unexpected, she had actually lost her footing when she had walked out of the portal into the typhoon. They wasted valuable time trudging through the meadow toward the jungle, as their feet sank into the saturated ground. Every minute they lost due to weather, was less time to spend in the crystal caves. JoAnna had to find the crystals Jeryl Jarlyn requested. She did not want to think about what failure would mean.

"*How are you holding up?*" Koel asked her through their soul mate channel. The telepathic communication initially surprised her, since he had not used the channel since it opened on Earth. She imagined he leveraged it now because of the howling wind and the sound of the rain as it hammered the vegetation.

After a moment's hesitation, JoAnna answered honestly. "*I'm miserable. It's hard to determine why I am wet now, the downpour or the fact I am sweating like a pig. At least the insect repellent is doing its job. Thank goodness we sprayed it on before we left the Troyk universe.*" JoAnna shuttered at the thought of dealing with the natural elements of this world, as well as its insect population.

"*Starc said we should gather as many crystals as we can, so we do not have to come back here anytime soon. This is my first trip here and hopefully my last.*" JoAnna could not agree more with those words.

It seemed like they had walked for an eternity. After Koel stopped communicating with her, each minute which passed seemed like an hour. Were they ever going to reach their destination? Candy and Shirl did not seem to be in any better shape. She hated the sensation of feeling sweat run down the small of her back. In addition, she had to keep pushing her wet hair out of her face. With all the water falling from the trees, JoAnna had problems seeing clearly.

"Finally," Shirl muttered, as they left the jungle and entered a small clearing. There were two caves visible on the other side of the meadow. "Welcome to crystal nirvana. I assume Jeryl Jarlyn schooled you in what you need to pick up. He generally has a specific stone he wishes to have collected, as well as the covert mission's stone. JoAnna, you can look for it on your own, or we can assist you."

She did not miss the critical look Shirl gave her brother. There must have been more to the stories related to what had occurred during the last trip. Not confiding in Shirl at this point would signal JoAnna did not trust her old friend. Plus, if she did not volunteer the information, her friends would know she kept information from them. JoAnna was at a crossroads. She could trust the people who surrounded her, or continue alone. It was time to make a leap of faith.

"Our mission is to find herderite." JoAnna felt a ton lifted from her shoulders after she admitted the truth to the group. She pulled out the crystal Jeryl

Jarlyn had given her and displayed it. "It supposedly will intensify my mind control capabilities."

"Are you aware of the stone's properties?" Starc asked Koel. Since his sister was a mind control telepath, if usage of the crystal was common, he would have noticed Tarah using it.

Koel shook his head, as he answered Starc's question. She watched the facial expressions of those around her for any evidence they communicated telepathically through a channel she did not have access to. If they were having a private conversation, it was not obvious.

Shirl extended her arm, with her palm open, indicating she wanted to look at the crystal. Without hesitation, JoAnna handed the piece of herderite to the crystal telepath. Shirl closed her hand around the stone and shut her eyes. Although JoAnna knew it was her imagination, she could have sworn she heard a low intensity hum underneath the other frequencies that played in her head.

"Fascinating, it is almost as if the crystal focuses my telepathic gift. I'm going to have to grab a crystal or two for my own usage." Shirl handed the stone back to JoAnna, a genuine smile on her face. A microcosm of trust had been built between them with JoAnna's confession.

"Let us get on with it," Starc said, "we are burning daylight. I want to be back at the portal well before sunset." He reached for one of the crystals around Shirl's neck and pulled out a black stone. "If you see a rock like this one, pick it up, and give it to Shirl for further examination."

JoAnna nodded she understood and headed toward the cave on her right. Prior to entering it, JoAnna took off her nap sack and pulled out a flashlight. Unlike the ones on Earth, this one was powered by crystals. She grabbed her canteen and took a generous sip of water.

"I understand there is a small waterfall in the cave. They tested the water the last time they were here and it is safe to drink. Let us refill our water supply before we get to the task at hand." Koel placed his arm around her waist and guided her into the cave. Although she was miserable, his touch sparked a fire within her. Unfortunately, Koel was all business and they had work to do.

As soon as she stepped into the cave, JoAnna understood why Koel assisted her. The bare cave floor was wet with condensation, which made it extremely slippery. She looked for areas where rocks covered the floor, which added some traction. Either way, she needed to be careful as she made her way through the cave.

Crystals were embedded in the walls, as well as scattered on the ground. JoAnna realized why Shirl felt this was a crystal lover's paradise. She had not expected the pure volume of the rocks that surrounded her. It made the task of finding one particular stone seem impossible. If she focused on looking for gold and black colors, it was possible she would be successful.

An hour flew by, with little success. JoAnna picked up several amethysts she planned to give Shirl. However, she had been unsuccessful finding any herderite.

"Over here," Koel shouted from deeper in the cave. They had earlier decided to explore different parts of the cavern, while their friends checked out others in the area. If communication was necessary, they would use one of the communal pathways. JoAnna had not missed the excitement radiating from her soul mate's voice. She crossed her fingers as she made her way deeper into the cave.

"What have you got?" JoAnna asked as she approached Koel. She directed her flashlight to the objects she could barely make out that sat in the palm of his hand.

As the beam of her flashlight hit the rocks, she let out a sigh of relief. JoAnna focused on the herderite sparkling in front of her. The stones were larger than the specimens Jeryl Jarlyn had in his collection. What a find!

"Are there any more?" JoAnna asked as she accepted the herderite from Koel. She didn't want to appear greedy, but the more stones they harvested, the less likely they would have to return to Terra Flora any time soon.

With a gleeful smile on his face, Koel directed his flashlight to an area at his feet. JoAnna's flashlight and eyes took in the beauty of her soul mate for another precious moment before she refocused on the spot Koel illuminated. She let out a gasp as her eyes beheld a wealth of the golden crystal.

"I will take half to pacify Jeryl Jarlyn," JoAnna said. "You gather the rest for everyone else's use."

She did not miss the look of surprise on Koel's face. His features were shadowed outside the flashlight's direct radius, but it was clear enough for her to see. As her gaze lit on his face, his expression changed to one she could only describe as pride. Pride in her. It resembled the expression on her father's face when she shared her latest accomplishment with him. Until that moment, she had not realized how much she missed the man who had adopted her all those years ago.

"Do you think Darden or Shirl could take me back to Earth to see my father?"

⁓⊙

His soul mate's question was so unexpected, it took Koel a couple of seconds to internalize her question. He felt no pull on his brain or her presence in his mind, she merely made a request. Koel had been discouraged about whether they had a future together, but once again in this hostile world, he had another glimmer of hope they would overcome the obstacles her power presented.

"We can make arrangements for you to see him," Koel finally responded. "Shirl's headaches were so severe when she left Ginkgo Terra, it would not be wise for her to take you. However, I would imagine Jeryl Jarlyn's gatherers made regular trips there in search of Benko. We would be able to accompany one of them to that world." He had not bothered to mention that Darden would be unavailable, since he now resided in the Troyk penal colony.

JoAnna looked up from her task of gathering the crystals and gifted him with a smile. He leaned over and placed his lips on hers. They both forgot the herderite, as their kiss deepened and he took his soul mate into his arms. He gingerly brought them to their feet, preventing them from falling onto the sharp crystals. The area was not conducive to making love, so Koel felt no concerns about kissing her with the pent up passion he struggled to control.

There was no need to direct his soul mate telepathically related to the mechanics of their kiss. Her response mirrored his thoughts before he realized what he would do next. The power of how in sync they were was amazing. Although Tarsea, Starc, and Tolfer did not flaunt their relationships with their soul mates, Koel deduced what he experienced was the tip of the iceberg of what would eventually be possible with his soul mate.

"I thought I would check on how you two were doing." Candy's voice echoed through the cave as she interrupted their all-consuming kiss. Darkness shrouded them from Candy's probing eyes. Regardless, Koel reluctantly released JoAnna and then squatted to retrieve his flashlight.

"Over here," Koel directed Candy to their location. "We found a wealth of herderite." He started to gather the remaining stones, as well as recover from kissing JoAnna.

"Holy Toledo!" Candy exclaimed, as she saw what Koel had referred to. "Thank God, now we don't have to come back to this scorching hell hole. Why didn't you let us know through the communal channel what you had found?"

Koel had not realized how greedy he had been to spend time alone with this soul mate. He had not thought about letting the others know about their find. Koel imagined they would have joined them if they had been unsuccessful in finding worthy crystals where they were. "Frankly, we were so captivated by the stash of herderite, I did not think about it. We did not find any of the black stones Starc requested."

Candy looked between the two of them. Koel felt like he had when his parents caught him necking with a girl when he was a teenager. JoAnna seemed unaffected by almost being caught in a compromising position. It was a ridiculous way to feel considering they were both adults and soul mates.

"Cianan wants to head back to the portal in an hour," Candy informed them. "Make sure you fill your canteens. I thought I would come and tell you, since JoAnna does not like to communicate telepathically."

"I suppose it is time I started to communicate in that manner," JoAnna admitted, "since I plan to stay in the Troyk universe. Anyway, we are ahead of the game. Koel took care of replenishing our water supply as soon as we got here."

"Super," Candy responded. "That gives you a little extra time to gather more specimens. Shirl, Cianan, and Starc were also successful in finding a variety of crystals, although not herderite. You guys hit the mother lode."

"What about the black stone?" Koel inquired. Koel was grateful his soul mate had been focused on the herderite and had not asked regarding the powers the black stone possessed. He should have asked Candy that question telepathically, but Koel wanted to be able to move past guarded conversations.

"Yup," Candy responded, "as well as a variety of other stones. Shirl rambled on about the characteristics of each crystal. Some things don't change, including me tuning her out."

Koel laughed at Candy's last statement, and was appreciative of her guiding the conversation away from the black stone. If their luck held out, JoAnna would never find out about the power Shirl was able to pull from that crystal.

JoAnna finished securing her treasures into her pack. Between the water she carried and the weight of the crystals, it was significantly heavier than when they arrived. She wasn't used to carrying things, particularly heavy items. Even when she had gone camping, she was able to get others to carry her load. With Candy and Shirl bearing their own burdens, JoAnna could not consider asking any of the men to help her out.

After one unsuccessful attempt at mounting her nap sack on her back, Koel aided her in getting the pack properly situated. With the weight evenly balanced over her shoulders, JoAnna was surprised at how light the pack was. She felt a sort of satisfaction being able to carry her fair share for a change.

"You did not do much camping, did you?" Candy asked, as she untwisted the front straps of JoAnna's pack. "A couple of years after you left, we went on a yearly weekend camping trip at the orphanage. I always had a blast and Shirl was miserable. The two of you would have made quite a pair."

Once again, JoAnna wondered what her life would have been like if she had grown up in the orphanage. Alex would not have to pretend to be her own cousin and Koel would have accepted her immediately. But instead, she drove Alex and Tarsea out of their home, plus Koel walked on eggshells around her.

Her thoughts were interrupted by the sound of thunder, followed by a roar of wind and pouring rain. JoAnna imagined the haul back to the portal was going to be worse than the trip to the caves. She had not imagined such a thing was possible.

"Can we delay our trip back and wait for the storm to pass?" Shirl asked. They had all reunited in the cave JoAnna and Koel had explored since it had the best water source.

"I will check," Cianan said before he headed out. He probably volunteered to examine the weather before Shirl bullied him into it. JoAnna had noticed Cianan's eyes were on his sister when he agreed to determine the magnitude of the storm outside.

JoAnna followed Cianan to the entrance of the cave to see firsthand how bad weather conditions were. She stopped just short of where the cave sheltered them from the brunt of the storm. The wind assaulted Cianan from the east when he had barely left the confines of nature's natural barrier. Within seconds, Cianan was drenched. She noted him survey the sky and quickly ran into the cave.

"It is all around us," Cianan informed the group. "I did not see any blue sky. The weather is not going to clear anytime soon."

Colorful language was muttered around her in response to Cianan's report. JoAnna imagined they all had the same thoughts floating in their minds. It was going to be a long, miserable walk back to the portal.

"We might as well follow the same formation we had on the way here," Koel recommended. Although Cianan was the leader of the group, Koel was in charge of the tactical aspects of the mission. "Let us head out. Delaying will not buy us anything, but increase the likelihood we are not going to get off this parallel world before sunset."

"Agreed," Cianan said. "Everyone perform one last check on your gear and follow me." One by one they followed him into the raging storm.

They were halfway through the meadow when three of the most frightening animals JoAnna had ever seen exited the jungle in front of them. Based on the descriptions given to her, they had to be larma beasts. Unfortunately, they were between the beasts and the shelter they were seeking.

JoAnna pulled out her gun, the same instant Cianan telepathically gave the order. However, she was not going to wait for him to order them to fire. JoAnna had no idea how fast these animals could run. Each weapon was charged with a crystal that would generate three laser blasts.

She fired the gun and stood horrified as the pouring rain extinguished the laser fire. Several other streams fired by other weapons were also made harmless from the violent storm. The sound of the weapons discharging spooked the animals, sending them charging toward the group.

Koel grabbed her by the hips and tackled her to the ground. He rolled just prior to hitting the surface, absorbing most of the impact. JoAnna watched as the animals surged forward, ready to trample them. Rather than closing her eyes, she kept them glued to the giant larma beasts.

Behind her, a blast of energy shot forth, incinerating the animals in an instant. JoAnna shifted her head and glanced up at Shirl standing alone, grasping the black crystal she wore around her neck.

Chapter 10

~

The Troyk Penal Colony World

Chartail woke from her short afternoon nap, to find her soul mate's legs entangled with her own. One of Benko's arms was draped over her upper chest. Their urgency for each other had been so great, they had only undressed from the waist down.

Captivated, Chartail gazed at his slumbering face. When he slept, the tension normally evident on his forehead was gone. Benko was at peace, unlike the nightmares that continued to plague her sleep. Chartail wondered if the night terrors would diminish with time. She knew her soul mate worried about her, which added more stress to the mountain of issues he had to deal with.

They had made love during the short time they had to rest, unable to get enough of each other. Regardless of how often or how long they made love, their desire to be together did not diminish. At least her brain did not fizzle, as it did the first time they had sex. Her brain had excreted the hormone which would bring about her next evolutionary stage in her telepathic abilities. To date, Chartail had not noticed any differences in her lack of powers. She had always been a weak telepath and that did not seem to change.

In the penal colony, telepathic abilities were not celebrated as they were in the Troyk universe. The majority of the people who lived in the displaced Utopia community were there because they fought the mind control telepathic government. Only the crystal telepathic ability was sought out among them. When Shirl was present, she used her crystals to try to find one among them who could open a natural portal. Unfortunately, they had not found one. With Darden, now living in the colony, he would be able to travel between dimensions and bring back supplies. He also continued to search for a crystal telepath within the village.

Benko stirred next to her and slowly opened his eyes. A smile graced his face when he realized who was beside him. Her soul mate had a foggy brain whenever he woke. Fortunately, the latest supply shipment from the Troyk universe included coffee.

"Afternoon, beautiful," Benko murmured. Although his speech was slurred, those words came into her mind as clear as a bell. She brushed his hair from his forehead and gently kissed his lips. "I love waking next to you."

Chartail did not get all excited or bent out of shape by his use of the *L* word. They were little more than strangers at this point, although they knew they were soul mates. The bond between them opened a telepathic channel; it did not manufacture feelings. There was no denying the strong sexual chemistry between them, which only seemed to continue to grow. Over time, general affection would develop to fortify their relationship.

"I should get up," Chartail moaned. "Clarke has agreed to meet with me to talk about the women who want to take a more active role in the defense of the village. He is terrible; I know he will dismiss everything I have to say." Chartail put her signature pout on her face. She had used that expression on her father to get whatever she wanted.

Benko raised his left eyebrow and stared at her. The helpless female was not the persona Chartail presented in this world. That facade was abandoned shortly after it was discovered she had plotted Jeryl Jarlyn's assassination. There was such a very small line between murder and a revolutionary action.

"Fine," Chartail complained, as she got out of bed. "If he gives me attitude, I am not responsible for what I may do to him." She knew her soul mate knew she exaggerated what she would end up doing to Clarke. Chartail pulled up her leggings, still glaring at her soul mate.

"I have faith you will present your case in a logical manner, which he will not be able to counter. Just use that brilliant mind of yours and the charm that always disarms me."

Chartail left their hut, without a single glance back at her soul mate. She knew she projected her frustrations about dealing with Clarke onto Benko. Fortunately, he did not seem to mind. Relocating the Utopia settlement to the portal guardian's village had taken most of their energy. The people around them accepted her as one of their leaders, the woman who led the contingent from the Troyk, Nightshade, and Terra Nova universes to turn the tides of the battle they were close to losing. Only Clarke viewed Chartail strictly as the woman who slept with their leader.

The community came alive after their afternoon rest period. When Candy was here, she called it a siesta. Children were usually the first to emerge, ready to let loose their recharged energy. If anyone overslept, the noise the kids made while they played would rouse them.

Chartail had never related to children, even when she was one. They were too loud and unruly. After arriving in the penal world and the aftermath of the battle, she had a new appreciation for the kids. Their ability to snap back after tragedy struck her as nothing short of amazing. The children gave the villagers a reason to keep going.

A ball rolled in her direction. Chartail picked it up and threw it to a blond little boy. He caught it, as he wrapped his little arms around the ball and held it to his chest. For the first time in her life, she actually considered having children of her own. Had she not had to meet with Clarke, Chartail would have stayed and played with the children.

Clark was exactly where Chartail knew she would find him. Their armory was depleted after the battle with the portal guardians. Both sides had exhausted the weapons they possessed. New spears had to be made for both hunting and defensive purposes.

Chartail sat across from him, she positioned herself so they were eye level with each other. She would give him no other option, but to look her in the face. Chartail was determined to get through his thick skull.

"There are several women who have requested to be placed on defensive watches and you have ignored their requests." Chartail worked to control the anger in her voice. She was not letting emotions overwhelm her and lose any leverage she had with Clarke. "These same women fought bravely beside the men when the portal guardians attacked. With our diminished army, it only makes sense to have women share in protecting the children."

Clarke continued to stare at her, not breaking eye contact once. He finally blinked and said, "With our diminished army, it only makes sense to have women share in protecting the children. I will add them to the shifts starting tonight."

Initially, Chartail had thought Clark was mimicking her. However, that was not part of his personality. Something was wrong, Clarke agreed too easily. In the past, if Chartail said the sun rose in the east, he would argue with her. His expression reflected his commitment to what he just said.

"I have work to do," Clarke growled. "Is there anything else you want?"

"No," Chartail replied in a tone that sounded more like a question, than a statement. A bit dazed Chartail rose to leave, glancing at Clarke once more. He had returned to creating new spears. Deciding to declare victory, Chartail continued to make her late afternoon rounds.

Her next stop was to check on the preparation of dinner. The women of the village had decreed Chartail would have final approval over the daily menus. How her involvement in the short battle brought about this responsibility was beyond her understanding. It seemed irrelevant to these women she could not cook.

The village hunters had a successful day since there were a variety of meats being roasted. They rarely went hungry, but there were days when their diet consisted mostly of vegetables and fruits. It looked like they would eat well tonight. Tolfer must have talked to Troyk officials on his return, since the last portal shipment of supplies included goods that would allow them to cure meat. They would now be able to store protein when they had excess.

"Chartail," a small dark haired woman approached. "These women will not listen to reason. We should not waste the cherries by putting them in the sauce, which will be served with the pork. The children love those cherries as snacks."

Beverlee was one of the first women who had been sentenced to the penal colony. She had known periods of extreme hunger and still pushed for them to be frugal, regardless of the abundance around them. Chartail knew they had so many cherries they started to rot.

"The children love the recipe Tolfer created," Chartail addressed the older woman. "It only requires a small amount of the cherries. Why do we not discuss ways we can use the fruit we will lose if they are not consumed in the next day or two?"

"Chartail," Beverlee said, "why do we not discuss ways we can use the cherries we will lose if they are not consumed in the next day or two?"

Hearing her words uttered back to her for the second time deeply disturbed Chartail. She had seen mind control telepathic people manipulate those around her in the same fashion her whole life. Had the hormone that was created after she made love to Benko brought about latent mind control powers? She needed to find her soul mate immediately.

⌒◯

The communal pathways were unusually busy with tales about his soul mate. It was odd using the telepathic power he had barely used for decades. The villagers rarely used this talent, so something must have occurred to force them to communicate in this manner. He needed to finish his meeting with the architecture committee on the improvements needed to defensively reinforce the portal guardians' village. They needed to rename their new home, leaving behind the horror of what brought them here.

Chartail stormed into the center hut, her eyes filled with tears. The men and women he had met with saw the state she was in and quickly evacuated the premises. He imagined they had listened to all the ridiculous tales being communicated through the pathways. She was probably here because of what she heard.

"I think I have developed mind control capabilities," Chartail cried. He brought her into his arms, he held her as her body shook. "It is a power that should not exist. People should have their free will."

"Chartail, relax," Benko tried to calm his soul mate. "We do not know that is the case. I am not an expert about the legend of soul mates, but based on my understanding, the hormone enhances abilities you already possess."

"Manipulating others is a talent that runs in my family," Chartail replied. "It may have been so weak in me that I had not been able to use it until the hormone intensified the ability. Please, I do not want this power!"

Chartail broke down as she sobbed in his arms. He had never seen her like this before. She was the strongest woman he had ever known. The mind control ability in her opinion was an illness. Everyone knew he was a mind control telepath, they just did not know the extent of the power he possessed. It was a secret he would continue to keep, including from his soul mate.

"My daughter and I both have the power, Chartail. Just because you possess an ability, does not mean you have to use it in a way to take away another's freedom. It can be used to stop a criminal from hurting another human being, help someone who struggled over something they have not been able to come to terms with, or assist a child who cannot remember a crucial fact. I taught Cassie to use it for self-defense purposes, in case one of my father's gatherers caught up with us. A power is not evil, it is how you use it or choose not to."

The tremors stopped, as Chartail considered what he shared with her. She stepped out of his arms and started to pace. From the expressions on her face, he knew she debated the pros and cons of a telepathic power she might or might not have. Based on the chatter, something had happened.

"If I have the power, what had occurred this afternoon was not intentional on my part. How can I control something I do not even know I am doing?" He could hear the frustration laced in her voice. Her pace increased as Chartail continued to struggle with what she had done. Benko realized she looked for him to explain what had occurred and teach her to control her latent talent.

"We do not even know you used mind control against Clarke or Beverlee," Benko reasoned. "It is possible they both just acquiesced to your way of thinking." Chartail's grunt communicated she was not going to fall for that explanation. Although he had not been in this parallel dimension long, he knew both Clarke and Beverlee well enough not to swallow this particular scenario either. "Come here and let me try to connect with your mind."

Chartail came back into his arms, without a moment's hesitation. It humbled him how much his soul mate trusted him. He pulled out a gold crystal he had in his pocket and clasped it in his hand. Benko opened his mind and projected his consciousness to Chartail. The last time he had attempted to enter another's mind was when he lived in the Troyk universe.

He grasped the crystal tighter and concentrated on the woman in his arms. Although it would not have made any difference, he leaned his head against his soul mate's forehead. Images of his own persona started to assault his mind, she thought about him. Benko needed to move past his desire to learn how Chartail felt about him, to the items that caused her distress. Although it had been decades since he attempted this procedure, something redirected his focus.

When Benko realized what her body communicated to him, he held Chartail tighter. He let out a sigh of relief, "It is not your ability you have leveraged, but that of the unborn child your body is preparing for."

Chartail leaned her head back and looked at him with such shock depicted on her face, he almost laughed. Her intelligent eyes finally got a little larger, as what he told her sunk in. Benko had never heard of a situation where an expectant mother's telepathic abilities changed to mimic the talents the unborn child would possess. He figured it was related to the soul mate link that had opened.

"Alex had mentioned she first knew she was pregnant when she lost all but the familial channels. She said nothing about inheriting temporary powers from her child."

"I would imagine each pregnancy is unique based on the abilities each child will possess. As your body prepares to carry the embryo, I imagine your telepathic talents will become erratic, until the link between you and our baby stabilizes."

Chartail once again left his arms and walked to a nearby chair and sat. He watched as she placed her hands on her abdomen and closed her eyes. Tension appeared to leave her body, as Benko watched Chartail commune with her changing body and the child she would one day deliver.

Benko's feelings of joy were slowly replaced with concern regarding how powerful his new son or daughter would be. His father had often commented how very powerful Benko was, so he imagined that the child Chartail carried could have talents that eclipsed his own. Such talent could possibly place Chartail in danger and ultimately the baby, as his or her powers grew. How would his followers deal with another powerful mind control telepath among them?

Chapter 11

～

The Troyk Universe

JoAnna punched her pillow in frustration. After the physically challenging day, she had thought she would sleep like the dead. Rather than falling into a deep coma-like sleep, she found herself staring at the ceiling. How she wished Koel was beside her.

Her mind kept racing, imagining the energy blast Shirl had generated. They had not communicated orally or telepathically on the journey back to the portal. All their strength was used to forage through the jungle, weighed down by the crystals they had collected. Although her body had been overburdened, her mind dealt with what she had seen, with no avenue to ask questions. Shirl had temporarily shut down any means to talk to her.

Frustrated by her inability to sleep, JoAnna rolled out of bed and headed for the kitchen. Even after all the rain that pelted them on their way back to the portal, JoAnna was parched. A glass of ice cold water would quench her thirst.

As she entered the kitchen, she noted someone sat in the dark. Not wanting to disturb the woman shrouded in the shadows, JoAnna went to the sink and filled a glass from the tap, without turning on the light. JoAnna sat next to Shirl and maintained the silence between them.

"You couldn't sleep either?" Shirl asked. Her voice was weighed down by exhaustion. JoAnna could not imagine the amount of energy Shirl had to generate to create the blast. It had surprised her Shirl had been able to walk back to the portal on her own steam.

"No," JoAnna answered. She had so many questions to ask Shirl, but did not know where to begin. Things between them had been awkward from the moment she had entered the Troyk universe. JoAnna knew Shirl had to direct any topic they talked about, as well as what would continue to linger between them in silence.

"Koel said you had the ability to enter someone's mind. I want you to enter mine."

JoAnna was surprised by Shirl's request. She had assumed the other woman would consider such an act a violation. However, JoAnna had been invited to do so. Perhaps Shirl felt it was the quickest way to get to what she needed to share, without struggling to put things into words.

JoAnna closed her eyes and concentrated on the blonde in front of her. The other woman's mind offered no resistance to her entry. She was overwhelmed by feelings of guilt, struggling with a power that terrified her. JoAnna did not know if her concern about her own telepathic gifts intensified Shirl's feelings in JoAnna's mind. No wonder they both sat in the dark.

Almost equal to Shirl's issues related to her powers were concerns about JoAnna and the threat she represented. JoAnna could feel Shirl's greatest hope, the desire she could trust JoAnna. It humbled her how much Shirl craved that.

"You left me to care for Candy and Alex alone." Shirl's confession floored her, as well as finally admitting who Alex really was. "They were our responsibility and you abandoned me."

The scars of the past had been just as powerful as Shirl's concerns about the present. JoAnna was not sure how to respond to what she heard and felt within Shirl's mind. Feelings were overwhelming her and she was not sure she could hold on to her own emotions.

Tears rolled down JoAnna's cheeks. She was not sure how long it had been since she had cried. Even when her mother passed, JoAnna knew she had to be strong for her father and did not shed a single tear.

"I had not realized," JoAnna shared with Shirl. "Even though we were only six, you seemed so self-contained in your protection of Alex and Candy. They followed you like chicks ran after a mother hen." Maybe it was jealousy of Shirl's relationship with the two younger girls that drove her to use her powers to get adopted, not that she would ever admit it to Shirl. JoAnna wanted something all her own.

"Now you know how I feel," Shirl said. "There are no more secrets between us. You hold all our lives in your hands. Jeryl Jarlyn merely has to ask you questions and your inability to shield lies from the Prime Ruler will sink us all."

"That won't be a problem," JoAnna informed Shirl. "For whatever reason, my mind is blocked to him, as well as from my uncle. They feel it was my telepathic abilities that created the barrier. It is the reason they figured I was a powerful mind control telepath."

"The guys are unaware of any legends related to mind control telepathic soul mates, unlike a mated female crystal telepath or the Troyk Warrior Woman."

"Candy?" JoAnna asked.

"I think enough secrets have been revealed today," Shirl answered.

"What can I do to garner your trust?" That was the question JoAnna came back to. Shirl had risked a great deal, while JoAnna had nothing she could offer to reciprocate. She kept wracking her brain to come up with something, but came up short.

"Let Alex try to read your mind," Shirl responded. "She is not a mind control telepath, but she can read your thoughts if she concentrates. Her abilities have become temporarily diminished because of the baby, but we can try."

"I agree to that," JoAnna immediately answered. It would be so nice to spend time with Alex when she was not pretending to be someone she was not.

Living in a world of telepathic beings resulted in quicker communication than JoAnna was used to. Cell phones and texting provided rapid communication, which assumed someone had their phone handy. Once Shirl contacted Alex telepathically, the fiery redhead was there in what JoAnna considered record time.

As Shirl brought Alex up to speed on JoAnna's abilities, she watched the small woman's facial expressions. Alex was able to control her reactions to the information. JoAnna made a mental note not to play poker with Alex.

"How do you go about reading my thoughts?" JoAnna asked. She imagined it would be similar to the process she went through when she entered another's mind.

"I need to concentrate on the person's brain," Alex explained. "Then I just have to fight through the static. Between my pregnancy and the concussions, I'm not sure I will be able to pick up anything."

"Try sipping this," Shirl said, as she handed Alex a mug of the herbal blend.

Alex drank from the mug, while she seemed to concentrate on JoAnna. A number of thoughts were cycling through her mind, now JoAnna knew Alex was trying to read them. She wanted to focus on thoughts that would make everyone comfortable with her, but the memories of the orphanage kept invading her mind.

A tear ran down Alex's cheek, which the redhead absent-mindedly brushed away. Alex did not share with JoAnna what she was picking up, as Alex did not break eye-contact with her. JoAnna finally stopped forcing thoughts and just opened herself to Alex. Since she had no idea how the whole thing worked, it seemed ridiculous to try to manufacture what Alex might or might not be picking up.

"Star likes you," Alex finally said. She took a gulp of her drink and rubbed her forehead. "I managed that without a nose bleed!"

"Who is Star?" JoAnna asked. That remark had been so out of left-field, she was not sure what to make of it. JoAnna knew Alex read her mind and waited to find out if she passed the exam. This was worse than waiting for her chemistry grade when she was in high school.

"My unborn daughter has connected with my telepathic abilities," Alex responded. "I was able to pick up some of your thoughts, but Star picked up your emotions. Don't ask me how any of this works, it's just as likely to give me a bigger headache as the one I already have."

"What did Star pick up?" Shirl inquired. It appeared the crystal telepath was as anxious as JoAnna was to get the verdict. Would they be able to move forward or would they still be locked in place with doubt and distrust?

"Genuine feelings of love," Alex answered. "You struggled with your thoughts, since you knew I tried to read them. However, you can't manufacture emotions. That's what Star picked up."

"We are going to the second seating tonight," Shirl said, "now we have something to celebrate. The Four Musketeers are finally back together again!"

"I will have Norri come and do Candy and my makeup," Alex informed them. "Funny how you and Shirl are always so put together, while Candy and I are messes."

The little redhead looked fine, as far as JoAnna was concerned. Candy and Alex were natural beauties. Makeup on them was just not part of their personalities. For some reason, she and Shirl seemed to need to impress those around them with their looks. Perhaps Candy and Alex had been more comfortable in their skins.

"I need to run to headquarters before I get ready," Shirl said. "Warn me if Pattrice is with Norri, I'll delay my return until the last minute." Shirl hugged both women and then headed out.

The fact Norri and possibly Pattrice were coming over, was proof JoAnna had passed with flying colors. Norri was Alex's aunt, her late mother's twin sister. While Pattrice was their cousin and Solfa's mother. JoAnna wondered if the head of Troyk intelligence had kept both women away from the household because of JoAnna's presence. Norri had adopted Shirl and Candy, as a member of their family, but had not met JoAnna. JoAnna would not have minded all the crying Pattrice did in response to having her cousin's daughter and friends in her life. It would have been a sign she was accepted, which she finally was now.

"I would have liked to have grown up as Alexandra Carlson," Alex confessed. "Although, I do not know if I could have left Shirl and Candy behind. After you left, we dedicated ourselves to not being adopted. I faded into the shadows, Shirl came across as a self-absorbed beauty, and Candy was always filthy. Well, with Candy that was not an act, she was a real tomboy."

"You got all those thoughts?" JoAnna was embarrassed Alex had picked up her memories and dreams from when she was in the orphanage. It had been a fleeting thought she wanted Alex adopted alongside her. JoAnna was afraid Alex had discovered why she really used her gift to get adopted.

Alex sighed, obviously still being able to pick up some of JoAnna's thoughts. "The past is irrelevant now, Jo Jo. What is important is the here and now, and the future we build together. We are in a parallel dimension, with telepathic beings we had never encountered before. Some of us have developed abilities that are quite frightening. The one certainty is we need to be able to depend on each other."

"How did you get so smart?" JoAnna knew Alex indirectly had told her she would keep her secrets.

"It's amazing what you learn hanging in the background," Alex said. "There are benefits to being a chameleon."

"I envy little Star," JoAnna admitted.

"Why for goodness sake?"

"You, Shirl, Candy, and I will make sure her childhood is one full of laughter and family."

Alex paled for a moment, but quickly recovered. There was something she hid from JoAnna about the baby. There had been such an intimacy shared between them; JoAnna was exhausted. If Alex wanted to share what troubled her, JoAnna would listen. However, she was not going to pry to get the information from Alex, not now anyway.

"Let's check out your closet and select something for you to wear tonight. Shirl also brought a couple of additional outfits you can wear." Alex was obviously done with the serious discussion, which relieved JoAnna. There had been enough emotions exposed and secrets revealed for one day. She imagined they barely touched the surface related to the dangers they were exposed to in this universe.

Koel made his way to the Childers's residence. He and his friends were taking their soul mates to dinner. It was the first time he participated in a soul mate couple activity. In the past when the others went out with their women, he and Darden would get drunk. Koel had been alone, while Darden's soul mate was still on Ginkgo Terra.

He had been relieved when he heard Shirl and Alexandra cleared JoAnna as being trustworthy. The news had been communicated through the warrior channel by Shirl. Unfortunately, until JoAnna could link into that particular telepathic stream, there were aspects of his life with JoAnna he still had to guard against. The premonition Candy had related to JoAnna still troubled Koel. He had the ability to unleash an indeterminable amount of telepathic power in his soul mate once he took her to his bed.

Leenea Childers opened the front door as he approached. Tarsea's parents had become his surrogate parents when his mother and father moved to the Starling Province. As the mind control telepathic government grew in strength, his parents decided to relocate to a smaller city where governmental influences on the general populace was less powerful. His cousin Darden's close friendship with the Childers guaranteed he had a home.

Starc, Tarsea, and Tolfer waited for their soul mates in the common room. He heard laughter in the back of the house and he was tempted to continue on his way to see what had amused his soul mate and her friends. But there were traditions to maintain, so Koel joined the rest of the men and awaited JoAnna's entrance.

Tarsea was at the bar and pulled out another glass when he saw Koel. Spending as much time as they did with the women from Ginkgo Terra, they tended to communicate more orally than telepathically. In the past, Tarsea would have already been alerted to Koel's presence through the pathways. After he took the drink from Tarsea, Koel wandered to the couch and joined his cousin.

"If the girls are not here in the next five minutes, we are going to be late for our reservations again," Starc complained. "What are they doing back there anyway? It has been over an hour."

Starc's soul mate had him wrapped around her little finger. Although Starc complained, he was totally besotted with Shirl. Koel imagined he would be in the same state in the very near future, if his current feelings for JoAnna were any indication. Rather than dreading the prospect of being so dependent on another for his happiness, Koel was looking forward to it. The others had fallen across their women, Koel actively sought her out.

"Do not question," Tolfer recommended, "just be grateful for the final result. If you are smart, you will compliment all the girls on how beautiful they are." Although Tolfer had hid the true nature of their relationship from Candy, theirs was the least complicated pairing. Tarsea's brother was a nurturer and it turned out that was exactly what Candy needed. Once again, Koel wondered about the dynamics of his own relationship with JoAnna.

The sound of heels tapping against the tiled floor caused Koel to look up from his drink. The women they had waited for stood before them. However, Koel only had eyes for his soul mate. He barely registered her elaborately coiffed hair or the dramatic makeup job, it was her nearly exposed body that caused havoc to rage rampant in his mind. Now he understood Tarsea's reaction whenever Alex wanted to leave the house wearing such a revealing outfit.

JoAnna must have noticed his reaction, since she started to leave the common room. Her friends stopped her, while throwing lethal looks in his direction. Koel's throat became dry, as his soul mate came to stand before him. Koel tried to adjust the expression on his face that had caused her initial reaction.

An awkward silence continued, as Koel and JoAnna stared at each other. There had been too many occasions when his soul mate left him mute, where he struggled for the right thing to say. He needed to get control of himself and take steps to make JoAnna feel comfortable.

"You look beautiful," he finally said. "There is a chill in the air tonight, you may wish to grab a sweater." The weather outside was quite temperate, he just wanted JoAnna to cover herself.

A sly grin crossed her face. He was not as clever as he thought. Obviously, JoAnna saw right through his ruse. She walked over to Norri and took a black wrap, which she placed around her shoulders and pulled across her chest. The sheer black material with the small black beading, which barely covered her breasts, was no longer visible. Tarsea grabbed another shawl and assisted Alexandra in the same fashion, which shielded her from prying eyes. Koel needed to talk with Tarsea concerning all the strategies he had in place to shroud his soul mate from the gaze of other men.

"We are going to be late again," Starc informed the group. His cousin grabbed his soul mate's hand and headed out of the house. Shirl turned her head and winked at his soul mate. Koel glanced at JoAnna, who laughed to herself, shaking her head. What had those girls discussed?

They walked through the crowded streets of Aster Province. Couples made their way to second seatings, while families headed home from their early evening activities. Women wore outfits that exposed their bodies to the gaze of anyone who chose to look in their direction. Koel's eyes were glued to JoAnna's face.

"It's a beautiful night," JoAnna returned his gaze. Koel saw a small drop of perspiration roll down the side of her hairline, as JoAnna tightened the shawl across her chest. He was not sure if she did it for his benefit or due to her own modesty.

"Get down!" Candy yelled.

Out of the corner of his eye, he saw movement, as Candy tackled his soul mate to the ground. Koel was about to ask what was going on, when a laser blast fired and laid a path crossing where JoAnna would have been standing.

Chapter 12

JoAnna spat grass and dirt out of her mouth. She had been about to say something else to Koel, when she was pushed from behind. Her scream had been muffled as the lower part of her face made contact with the ground. Thank goodness they had just entered a park. She could have possibly broken her jaw if she had come down on concrete.

"Stay down," Candy shouted. "The shot came from the alley next to the jewelry store. Do you see anything?" JoAnna tried to shift her position to see what was going on. Candy had her well pinned to the ground and was not letting up.

"Whoever it was, he is gone." JoAnna heard Koel yell from a short distance away. "It is a closed alley. Tarsea, head east and see if anyone looks suspicious. Starc, head west and do the same thing. Tolfer and I will check around the park. Whoever fired the weapon could have easily blended in with the crowd created in response to the blast."

JoAnna had not witnessed the aftermath of the attempt on her life, but she had heard the shouts and cries. Since Candy was still on top of her, it was evident she felt JoAnna had been the target. Her friend had reacted before JoAnna heard the weapon discharge.

"Candy, do you sense anymore danger?" Alex asked. Alex's voice sounded like she was on the ground as well. JoAnna imagined Tarsea must have reacted shortly after Candy had, or in response to the weapon being fired.

Candy finally rolled off her and back onto her feet. Shirl provided JoAnna a hand, as she slowly lifted herself off the ground. The front of her body was covered with dirt and grass stains.

"I think we are all right," Candy finally said. "We should head back home, just in case." JoAnna couldn't agree more, whatever appetite she had was gone. All she wanted was to clean herself up and have a drink to calm her nerves, not necessarily in that order. After what JoAnna witnessed on Terra Flora, she felt perfectly safe in Shirl's company. It was also obvious there was more to Candy's powers, than to communicate telepathically.

As soon as they returned to the Childers's home, JoAnna headed for the shower. The shawl she had worn had been soiled and her sheer tunic was ripped beyond repair. She quickly redressed and joined her friends in the common room. The men had not returned as of yet.

For a change, JoAnna purposely listened to the chatter within the communal pathways. All the conversations focused on the attempt on her life. She was viewed as Jeryl Jarlyn's successor, since Benko had not returned to the Troyk universe. The Prime Ruler also had a close relationship with the Adholm family. From this point on, it seemed she was as much of a target as Jeryl Jarlyn was. The conversations about the multiple attacks on his life replayed in her mind.

"I must have misread my initial premonition," Candy admitted. "It should have been interpreted as JoAnna was in trouble, not JoAnna was trouble."

"What are you talking about?" JoAnna snapped. She officially had it with all the secrets which were being kept from her. Someone had tried to kill her and her friends held back information because of something Candy saw or felt. "Full exposure from this moment on!"

"I have the gift of foresight," Candy admitted. "Before you arrived, I had felt anxious when I thought of you. When we discovered you were Prime Adholm's niece, I didn't give you the benefit of the doubt. For that, I am so sorry." Although part of JoAnna wanted to rail on Candy, she knew she could not make her friend feel any worse than she already felt. Besides, Candy had saved her life today.

JoAnna needed Candy at her best and she knew she needed to forgive her. "I probably would have done the same thing. Are you picking up any vibes, or whatever you call it?"

Alex brought over three shots, one for each of them. Due to her pregnancy, she only had water. If there had been a time when a drink was called for, it was certainly now.

JoAnna swallowed the liquor in one gulp. It burned on the way down, which caused her to cough. The drink immediately caused a warm sensation to spread through her body and she relaxed a bit.

"I sense danger ahead, but nothing more specific." Candy sounded like one of those charlatan fortune tellers who read Tarot cards at most of the fairs she attended as a girl. The big difference was Candy was the real thing. Tonight she saw firsthand proof Candy's powers were legitimate, talents she was not questioning.

The men returned, defeat depicted in their posture. They all grabbed a drink, with the exception of Tolfer, who headed for the kitchen. Since they had not eaten, he had gone to whip something together. No one wanted hunger to cloud their thoughts, although the alcohol they were consuming needed to be cut off quickly. She noted Koel had only taken one shot and started to drink water from the pitcher Alex had brought in.

"We did not see anything," Koel reported to the women. "Our team members are on alert. If anyone finds anything, they will communicate through the warrior link." Before she had the opportunity to ask him what he was talking about, Koel turned and addressed her directly. "A number of us can communicate through a closed communal channel, reserved for only those loyal to the true ruler of the Troyk universe."

Since she had never heard of this telepathic link before, JoAnna imagined Koel had not referred to Jeryl Jarlyn. She looked at Tarsea, who seemed to be the leader of this group. He certainly had the leadership skills this world needed desperately.

"Not me!" Tarsea exclaimed. He looked like a deer caught in someone's headlights. "Benko Jarlyn is the true leader of the Troyk universe."

"Oh, God," JoAnna said. How was she going to be in the same room with Jeryl, now knowing the truth about his son? "Don't tell me anything more about Benko Jarlyn. His father cannot enter my mind, but that does not mean he won't be able to in the future, or I say something unconsciously. With all the herderite we provided him, he may become powerful enough to break through whatever barrier I created."

Koel sat next to her and placed his arm across her shoulders. She figured it was his way of offering support. She placed her head back and used his shoulder as a pillow. With the attempt on her life and all the information she had been provided, JoAnna just wanted a brief second of peace. She would close her eyes for only a moment.

With all the chatter still taking place in the communal pathways, JoAnna was surprised to hear communication from The Palace ordering her and Koel's attendance. She opened her eyes to see everyone on their feet and Koel still as a corpse.

"What else has happened?" JoAnna asked. She looked at her soul mate and waited for an answer.

"My sister Tarah was just arrested," Koel said, his voice shook with anger.

Koel did not think it was a coincidence he and JoAnna were summoned to The Palace just as he received the news about his sister. Solfa still telepathically advised them of Tarah's arrest, although there was little information to be shared. His sister had always been at the peripheral of their anti-government activities. She could link into the warrior channel, but was only used occasionally because of her mind control capabilities. Whatever game Jeryl Jarlyn was playing, Koel did not like it.

"You need to calm down," Tarsea said. "Treat this like any other mission your tactical brain has to deal with. They cannot possibly have anything on Tarah, she is being held as leverage. Unfortunately, you will not know what is going on until you meet with Jarlyn."

He agreed with everything Tarsea said, but being objective when his sister's life was in danger was easier said than done. They had never been close, as Tarsea and Tolfer were, but Koel loved and respected Tarah. He knew she was loyal to a fault. Koel had nothing to fear personally related to her arrest, she was the one at risk. Tarah would never give Koel or his friends up. She also knew how to manipulate another mind control telepath, should one come to interrogate her.

"I want to grab some herderite before we head to The Palace," JoAnna said. "We need every advantage going into that meeting." He watched his soul mate leave the room, Shirl followed close behind her.

Koel could not agree more with JoAnna's assessment. They had directly and indirectly stifled JoAnna's mind control telepathic abilities. Now, they needed her to be as powerful as they feared she was. If JoAnna was forced to use her powers in Jarlyn's presence, she would be rusty from lack of practice.

"She may still be in mortal danger." Candy's statement pulled him out of his thoughts about his soul mate's abilities and back to the risks before them. "I doubt the attack on her life is related to why the Prime Ruler wishes to see you both. Either way, we should accompany you to The Palace."

Koel knew Candy's premonitions allowed her to see a violent act before it occurred, which eased his anxiety a small amount. Unfortunately, there was nothing any of them could do to protect themselves against the Prime Ruler. It would be a waiting game until they were physically in Jarlyn's presence.

"Do not forget," Tarsea said, "if he uses his mind control powers, half-truths are undetectable." Koel had known this most of his life, his older sister was one after all. Koel knew it was Tarsea's way of contributing support where it was definitely needed. He nodded, acknowledging the information as if he had never heard it before.

A second summons was broadcast through the communal channels. Koel did not like the public announcement of where JoAnna would be headed so soon after the attempt on her life. He noted when JoAnna returned with the herderite, Shirl had added the black crystal to the collection of stones she already wore around her neck. The last thing any of them wanted was Shirl generating an energy blast in the Troyk universe. It spoke volumes in regards to what the crystal telepath would do to protect her friend."

"Let us go then," Koel finally announced. "After the failed attack, Solfa has sent a squad of the Palace guards to accompany us. They are already outside, waiting for our departure." Koel grabbed JoAnna's hand and headed toward the front door. He squeezed it, signaling everything would be all right.

They headed toward The Palace, surrounded by their friends and two Palace Guard squads. Jeryl Jarlyn himself had dispatched the second group immediately after Solfa arranged for the first set. The streets were littered with spectators. It felt like the parade, which occurred each year to celebrate the Prime Ruler's birthday. Koel kept looking behind him at Candy he had strategically placed behind his soul mate. The Warrior Woman of Troyk legend did not seem overly concerned, which provided Koel momentary relief. At least there was no immediate danger when Candy looked relaxed.

It felt like the trip to The Palace took longer than usual. They were totally exposed if anyone wanted to take another shot at JoAnna. Whoever had fired the first blast could easily strike at any moment. Even though they were to meet with Jeryl Jarlyn, The Palace at this point was a safe haven.

Solfa provided an update through the warrior channel. She had been unable to discover any more about the arrest, not even what the charges were. All she had been able to find out was the arrest warrant came from Jeryl Jarlyn, with no details. Nothing as of yet had been communicated through the communal pathways. All the chatter was still about JoAnna, with a larger number of negative comments being broadcast.

He was not the only one who let out a deep sigh of relief when they finally reached The Palace. It was almost as if they had stopped breathing as a collective. The group was able to accompany them all the way to the fourth floor, to Jeryl Jarlyn's living quarters.

A small commotion occurred when Shirl and Candy demanded to be included in the audience with The Prime Ruler. They argued JoAnna was new to the Troyk universe and needed an advocate to look out for her interests. His soul mate joined the argument, while he leaned back and watched. He almost felt sorry for the two guards who were present to escort them the small distance to Jarlyn's study.

Koel had never been on the fourth floor before and was surprised how many pieces of art populated the hallway. As the women continued to argue with the guard, Koel took in the variety of items on display from various parallel worlds. Jeryl Jarlyn's gatherers brought back pieces from each world they visited. It was a moment's relief from the stress he was under worrying about his sister.

When three additional guards arrived, Alexandra approached her friends and communicated through a communal pathway, the women needed to back down. Alex played her role perfectly. A native from the Troyk universe would naturally communicate telepathically. Whether they agreed with Alex or were surprised by her intervention, Candy and Shirl stepped back.

JoAnna and Koel were led to the end of the hallway. One of the guards knocked and then opened the door, he motioned for them to enter. The room was substantially darker than the hallway. It took a moment for Koel's eyes to adjust. He placed his hand on the small of JoAnna's back and guided her into the room.

Jeryl Jarlyn was behind a massive wooden desk and did not stand as they entered. "I know JoAnna does not like to communicate telepathically, so we will speak. Besides, there are certain subjects we do not wish to broadcast through the pathways."

"Why has my sister been arrested?" Koel asked, he modulated his voice to strip his delivery of the hatred he felt. He wanted answers about his sister, but also needed to safeguard his soul mate. The sooner they talked about why they were here, the sooner he could come up with a strategy to make the best of the situation before him.

"Solfa speaks highly of you, Koel," the Prime Ruler addressed him. "I was surprised when she started using you to review the logistics of Shirl's off-world trips. Funny, I never realized how a commodity dealer could develop tactical skills. How Solfa discovered your gift is a topic for another evening."

"What is it you wish, Jeryl?" JoAnna asked. Koel had never heard anyone refer to the Prime Ruler by his first name. Maybe some of the rumors related to JoAnna being his heir were not so outlandish. All of this still did not explain why his sister had been arrested.

"We have talked in the past about Troyk soul mates and the power a mated telepath can possess. You let it slip that Koel was your soul mate." Jeryl Jarlyn picked up a key and dragged it across the desk until it sat in front of JoAnna. "It is time you had a place of your own and the privacy it accords. This is to a house not far from the Childers's, allowing you to maintain your relationships with the young ladies residing there. I taught you all I can, it is time you go through the evolutionary change that will enhance your telepathic abilities."

Koel could not believe his ears. The Prime Ruler was ordering them to have sex. Suddenly it made sense why the only member of his family in the Aster Province was being held by Jeryl Jarlyn.

"Why was Tarah Mardroft arrested?" JoAnna chimed in. She probably suspected the same thing Koel did, but wanted confirmation that was the case. It did surprise him she was asking after his sister, rather than reacting to Jarlyn ordering them to have sex.

"I cannot imagine why the two of you have not coupled," Jarlyn replied. "However, I thought I would offer an incentive to one of you. Claim your soul mate and your sister will be released."

"You son of a bitch!" JoAnna screamed. "What kind of freak orders people to have sex before they are ready? Do you realize the position you are placing Koel in?"

"I know the exact position, right on top of your lovely body." Koel could not believe how crass the Prime Ruler was or the hostility he felt wash over JoAnna. He had never felt so much negative emotion coming from his soul mate.

JoAnna reached inside the pocket Koel had seen her place the herderite. He imagined she had it tightly in her grip. "You will release Tarah Mardroft immediately and allow our relationship to grow organically."

Jeryl Jarlyn fell back in his chair, laughing. "You think you can use your mind control powers on me, little girl? I have the ability to force Koel to take you here, right in front of me."

Koel leapt from his chair and was about to attack the Prime Ruler when JoAnna yelled at him to stop. For a brief second, Koel calculated the chance of him being able to kill the Prime Ruler with his bare hands before the guards stormed through the door. The odds were not in his favor, so he acquiesced to JoAnna's cries.

"You have until tomorrow morning to start the change and we escalate your training. If you disappoint me, Tarah will nourish my friend Yorik in the Nightshade universe." There was such venom in Jeryl Jarlyn's voice, Koel believed he would send an innocent woman to a violent death at the hands of a vampire without batting an eye. The Prime Ruler had a number of his gatherers who were loyal to a fault and would follow Jarlyn's order without questioning the moral aspects of what was being asked.

Koel had built an alliance with the vampire Drake. However, he had no hope of contacting Drake and soliciting his help before Tarah's time was up. Shirl was able to travel to the Nightshade universe by creating her own portals, but they had to know where Drake could be found. Using Drake to save Tarah once she was delivered was not an option. They had no choice but to honor Jarlyn's request.

"You know how I feel about you, Koel," JoAnna communicated through their soul mate channel. *"I wanted you from the first moment I saw you. It is no secret you have held back your lust for me because you were afraid of what you would create. You would not be taking me against my will."*

A drop of blood ran down from Jeryl Jarlyn's left nostril. "Get out," the Prime Ruler yelled after he realized he was bleeding. Koel had never seen an uninjured adult telepath bleed in that manner. It was even more of a surprise, since The Prime Ruler was one of the most powerful mind control telepaths in creation. What was going on with Jeryl Jarlyn? How could he have the first time with his soul mate be more about his sister's life than what he hoped to one day share with JoAnna?

Chapter 13

JoAnna pulled out the black lace lingerie she had purchased the first time she had gone shopping with Candy and Alex. The three of them had laughed and cracked jokes, as they looked at the barely there seductive garments. She had envisioned her first time with Koel a million ways, but never shrouded in intrigue, as part of a blackmail scheme. Her stomach rolled, just thinking about their meeting with Jeryl Jarlyn.

They had exited the fourth floor of The Palace through the back way. Neither of them wanted to face their friends with what had transpired with the Prime Ruler. JoAnna could barely believe Jeryl Jarlyn could be so monstrous. Throughout their acquaintance, she had sensed what was behind his caring façade. Nevertheless, she hardly recognized the man she had been meeting with these past weeks. The nose bleed he had toward the end of his meeting was probably not the first he had suffered. He was not the man she had originally met.

The idea of having sex in the house Jeryl Jarlyn provided was offensive. It felt too much like she was prostituting herself or Koel, depending on the perspective of the real victim. For her own sanity, she decided they both needed to look beyond the circumstances of what drove them to finally come together.

She had vetoed going to Koel's apartment, since they would end up eventually living there. Neither wanted the stain of their first time together to pollute their future home. They also could not have intercourse in the Childers's residence. True lovemaking was performed in that home and JoAnna did not know if she could face her friends immediately after the deed was done. She cursed Jeryl Jarlyn for putting them in the untenable position they were in now.

They finally decided on the safe house Koel and his friends maintained, not too far from the mountain portal. Koel had been willing to explain why they had the residence, but JoAnna did not want to know. As it was, she had Koel explain to the others what had happened at their meeting with Jeryl Jarlyn. He used the closed channeled warrior link to communicate with them. JoAnna was relieved she did not share a closed channel with any of her friends. It would have been too humiliating having to explain what had occurred.

There was a light knock on the bedroom door. "Just a minute," JoAnna yelled. Once again, she had forgotten she could have communicated telepathically to her soul mate, rather than screaming through the closed door. With all the pressure she was under, falling back into old habits was not a surprising result. JoAnna quickly put on the delicate black lace teddy and walked to the foot of the bed. She took a deep, cleansing breath and said, "Come in."

Koel entered, shutting the door behind him with the back of his foot. She expected to see anger depicted in his face and was taken aback by his passionate gaze. For half a breath, they stood, drinking in each other's beauty.

As she let out the air in her lungs, Koel was upon her. He placed his lips on hers, giving her a kiss similar to the one he planted on her in the crystal cave. That had been the last time he had kissed her. Regardless of what had brought them together tonight, JoAnna wanted a lifetime of these kisses. She had searched her whole life for something she could not conceptualize, but she knew at this moment, this man was her other half.

Koel embraced her, his fingers gathered the lace in his large, capable hands. She expected him to tear the lingerie from her body, instead he treated it with reverence, as if it was a part of her. Carefully, he lifted the material, only breaking the kiss long enough to pass the lace over her head. She figured he let the lingerie fall from his fingers to the floor. Within an instant, one of his hands was caressing her back, while the other fingered the waistline of the barely there panties she wore. When she had put them on, she had wondered why she had bothered. Now she knew. The way he touched her was so damn sexy, she could barely stand it.

"You are so much more than I expected," Koel communicated telepathically. *"I want to savor every second we are together. How I held off making you mine is a mystery to me."* JoAnna knew exactly why he had delayed making love to her and what was

driving them together now. It was all irrelevant, she was taking Alex's advice to only look forward.

Her soul mate tugged on her panties, bringing them past her hips. She stepped out of the last shred of clothing she had worn. Koel continued to explore her waist and lower back, as JoAnna grabbed the bottom of his shirt. It appeared Koel was just as anxious to remove his clothes as she was, since he stepped back and lifted the material off his incredible body. He made short work of pulling down his leggings, along with his undergarments.

Koel stood before her in all his magnificence. Any Renaissance artist would have fought over the opportunity to capture him in marble. JoAnna had seen the statue of *David* on many occasions, but that masterpiece paled against the man who stood before her. If she could, JoAnna would have frozen this moment in time. There were no disappointments at this point, only appreciation and longing between them.

As Koel moved, JoAnna matched his forward progress, by moving backwards until her calves brushed against the bed's mattress. She stood paralyzed in place, as Koel took her into his arms. He returned his lips to hers, giving her another mind-numbing kiss.

"You taste of strawberries," Koel communicated, *"ripe and ready to harvest."* He shifted slightly and took one of her breasts in his hands.

JoAnna groaned into Koel's mouth, in reaction to what he was doing to her nipple. Men had fumbled touching her in the past, this was something totally new. Sensations rocked her body, the likes of which she had never experienced. If he could do this to her with just his touch, what would happen when Koel entered her?

She was momentarily disappointed when Koel released his lips, until his mouth clasped around her other breast. This time there was nothing to muffle the moan that escaped her. Her legs gave out, which caused her to tumble backwards. Koel wrapped his free arm around her waist and followed her down to the bed. He released his claim to her breast, as he landed on top of her.

Once again, JoAnna was disappointed at the loss of his lips around a part of her anatomy. She did not care where he placed his mouth, as long as it was somewhere on her. He was an addictive drug she could not get enough of. *"Do not worry, I am not done,"* Koel shared through their soul mate link. JoAnna was not sure if her thoughts leaked through their channel or Koel had been able to sense how she was feeling. Either way, he was quick to correct her misconception of his intent. She pulled back her head and let out a cry, as he brought her breast deeper into his mouth. Never before had they been so sensitive. JoAnna nearly bucked him off when his tongue assaulted her hardened nipple.

Koel released his hold on her other breast and brought his hand down her torso, lightly exploring her body as he made his way down to her hips. His touch had a feather light quality, which drove her insane. The more he touched her, the more she wanted.

JoAnna held her breath as his talented fingers changed course and finally reached the tender folds between her legs. He was not going to torture her by taunting touches along her inner thigh, he went right for the bull's eye. She slightly spread her legs, providing him a silent invitation.

Koel abandoned her breast and slid up her slick body, realigning his face to be in front of hers. He brushed away the wet hair, which had started to encroach on her face. "You are perfect, JoAnna. We fit perfectly together. I never believed in soul mates until Tarsea and Alexandra came together. Even then, I did not think I would have someone created just for me. The Supreme Being brought us together and I should have had faith our joining would result in nothing but wondrous by-products. My words are clumsy, but I hope you understand what I am trying to tell you." Rather than communicating telepathically, Koel had spoken the words to her.

JoAnna was so overcome with emotion, all she could do was nod. If her brain was close to overload, her body skyrocketed, as Koel entered her with a single finger. She was not sure how much more she could stand before she shattered into a million pieces.

Koel quickly entered her with a second finger, preparing her for his final penetration. It was not really necessary, she was slick and ready for him. He placed his forehead on hers, as he brought his engorged rod into her body. She had always dreaded this part in the past, never really prepared for the invasion her body had to withstand. With Koel, her body was prepared for him, like it had never before. This was the man she was meant to be with.

He massaged, tantalized, and frankly drove her crazy, as he entered and exited her body. As he sped up his pace, she matched his urgency with a fury of her own. If bodies were to spontaneously combust, she was getting damn close. Her breathing became erratic as she reached the cusp of her first orgasm.

She did not know how much longer she could hold on. Without understanding why, she knew she had to climax at the same time as her soul mate.

Koel let out a shout as he came into her body and JoAnna reached a zenith she had never thought possible. There was something unworldly about what had just occurred. Her soul mate fell on top of her, JoAnna happily bearing his weight. She ran her hands up and down his sweat drenched back.

"If I ask really nicely, Tolfer will prepare us a meal and leave it at the front door." Koel once again cleared her face of the drenched wisps of hair. "I want to make love to you again, but if I do not eat something soon, I may just devour you."

JoAnna nearly choked, she figured Koel was unaware of how a statement like that would be interpreted on Earth. Her face began to blush, as Koel gave her a questioning look. She was about to tell him to disregard her reaction, when JoAnna felt a funny sensation in the vicinity of her brain.

"Koel, what exactly causes the next stage of telepathic evolutionary change?"

Koel could not understand why JoAnna had such a funny response to his suggestion they have dinner. He was about to inquire why, when his brain excreted the hormone that would enhance his telepathic abilities. Before he had a chance to tell JoAnna what was probably happening to her, she asked about the process. Once again, she approached something new with a calm demeanor and a sharp mind.

"What feels like your head sizzling is the hormone being generated and saturating your brain." It was important to Koel not to frighten his soul mate. "The change is gradual."

JoAnna sat up in bed, wrapping the sheets around her body. He would have liked to have admired it a little longer, but he understood she probably felt exposed. "I think we should clean up and then head to The Palace. The thought of Tarah being imprisoned there for another minute is abhorrent to me."

Koel could not believe he had momentarily forgotten his sister, he had been so wrapped up in his soul mate and what they had just shared. It spoke volumes to him that JoAnna had not dismissed his sister's plight as he had. "I am yet again humbled by the gift that has been bestowed upon me. Use the shower in the master bath, I will use the guest bathroom." Before he got up he took her hand, kissed it, and said, "Thank you."

Considering how long it had taken the women to prepare for the aborted dinner tonight, Koel was surprised when JoAnna exited the master bedroom dressed and ready to go. He had contacted Tarsea while he showered and requested a small army be prepared to escort them to The Palace. Too much had happened tonight to walk unguarded in the streets of Aster Province.

He had barely time to kiss his soul mate, when there was a knock on the door and a parade of his friends and their soul mates entered. Everyone was there with the exception of Alex. With her pregnancy, Tarsea would have demanded she stay home, regardless of how much resistance Alex initially provided. When it came to the health and safety of the baby, Alex gave in to Tarsea every time. Koel hoped his friend did not get too comfortable winning arguments with his soul mate. As soon as the baby was born, Koel imagined Alex would once again have the upper hand.

"Koel?" he heard Tarah in their familial link. The whole time she had been held captive, something had blocked him from communicating with her. He imagined she had been unconscious, although Solfa had not said anything about the condition she was in when she was held.

"Are you all right?" Koel held his breath, as he waited for her reply.

"Yes, I believe so. I was brought before Jeryl Jarlyn and he did something to me which disrupted my telepathic abilities. After I met with him I was brought to some rooms and was told to wait. No one would answer any of my questions."

"Tarah, I am sending Starc and Shirl to escort you to me. Are you still in The Palace?" While Koel communicated with Tarah through their familial channel, he asked Starc and Shirl to escort his sister to their present location. Starc and his soul mate left the safe house without uttering a word. No one would feel they were out of the woods until Tarah was safely delivered.

"I am in Solfa's office on the third floor." This time his sister communicated through the warrior channel, which allowed Starc to have the information he needed once they arrived at The Palace.

As Koel finished communicating with his sister, he noticed JoAnna had a strange look on her face. Since she was not volunteering what the issue was, he was going to ask her directly through their closed channel. *"You look confused, JoAnna. What is wrong?"*

"I heard some woman, whose voice I did not recognize, communicate telepathically with me that she was in Solfa's office. Alex's cousin is frightening, but I do not understand why the woman reached out to me." JoAnna's confession proved to Koel his soul mate had finally linked in the warrior channel.

Koel was happy to announce to the whole room his soul mate had passed the last test to prove she was one of them, someone they could trust without a thread of doubt. "JoAnna, the woman was my sister who communicated through the warrior channel. You were finally able to link in and more of the chatter within that telepathic pathway will connect with you in the future."

"Thank goodness!" Candy cried, as she went to give her friend a hug. "See if you can pick this up."

Koel waited while Candy telepathically communicated to Shirl and Alex in their own private channel. It was the channel they also shared with Chartail Adholm. No one was sure what exactly that channel was, but they imagined it had something to do with Chartail being Benko Jarlyn's soul mate.

A radiant smile replaced JoAnna's earlier befuddled look. "Wow, that channel opened in the orphanage and we never knew it? No wonder we thought there was a special bond between us."

"Can someone help me set the table?" Tolfer shouted from the kitchen. "Dinner is almost ready. I do not think I have ever started a meal one place and finished it in another. If the quality is not up to my normal standards, we can blame it on my mother. She actually helped me in the kitchen when we returned from the attack on JoAnna."

Koel could not believe everything had occurred in a single day. His soul mate had been attacked, they had been blackmailed with his sister's life, and he had the most amazing sex of his life. He figured nothing more could happen tonight.

It was with that thought that JoAnna was telepathically called to The Palace through one of the communal pathways.

Chapter 14

⌒

The Troyk Penal Colony World

Chartail sat back and drank her wine as the fawners around Benko talked about their value and what they envisioned life in the Troyk universe would be like once Benko was in charge. Most of the people who now resided in the former portal guardian village were freedom fighters who had been sentenced to this world. They placed unrealistic expectations on her soul mate's shoulders.

"Fowler, you should take your girlfriend out for a moonlight stroll around the lake," Chartail suggested. "It is such a beautiful night. Harvor, you should do the same."

Both men broke eye contact with her and left to take their significant others on a romantic interlude. Chartail took another sip, thrilled she was once again alone with her soul mate.

"You may have thought that was a suggestion," Benko commented. "In fact, you used mind control against each of those men."

"I did not," Chartail claimed. To be truthful, she was not sure if she had. The power was so subtle, she was never sure when she used it and when she was merely communicating. "They did not repeat back my recommendation."

Benko shook his head. "Mind control does not always manifest itself in that manner."

Chartail was so frustrated, she wanted to scream. Her body had not changed at all this early in the pregnancy, yet telepathic abilities she abhorred were messing up her life. "How can you tell if I was using telepathic control over those two sycophants?"

"First of all, I can tell from the frequency you are emitting when you use your borrowed power," Benko answered. "Secondly, where in the world did you learn that word?"

"Candy once used it to describe someone in the Utopia settlement," Chartail admitted. "I felt it beautifully described that person and I like the dynamics of the word."

"The dynamics of the word?" Benko chuckled.

Chartail decided to ignore his question and ask one of her own. "What type of frequency are you referring to? Would I be able to hear it and know I am using the power? If I am aware I was doing it, I would then be able to back off."

"All telepathic communication is done through frequencies, just as a crystal telepath can leverage frequencies within the multi-dimensional portal." Her soul mate took a sip of his wine and leaned back on his elbow. "If you concentrate on the pitch, rather than the words you want to communicate, you should be able to pick up on it"

Chartail had never considered all the static in her mind as frequencies. Troyk children were taught to disregard all the noise and concentrate on the substance of the communication. A child who could not control the frequencies would get terrible headaches and nosebleeds. The same was true of adults who had some kind of brain trauma, like a concussion.

Their time alone together near the village center fire was once again interrupted, this time by Benko's daughter Cassie. Chartail had been impressed by the maturity shown by the three orphaned Ginkgo Terra women she had met in the Troyk universe and later befriended. Cassie did not show the maturity Alex, Shirl, and Candy possessed. Benko's daughter was a spoiled brat.

"Daddy," Cassie whined. "I want my own living quarters. The women I am staying with are like policewomen, they watch me every minute of the day. Darden and I cannot get any time alone. If it weren't for the headaches Darden suffers on Earth, I'd say we should go back to Ginkgo Terra."

"Cassie," Benko answered his daughter. "These people have just had their lives ripped apart by a group of violent men. Their homes have been destroyed and they have lost many of their friends and family. This encampment is much smaller than their former settlement and we are all doubling and tripling up until more huts can be built."

"Why can't I just stay with Darden?"

Chartail was tired of this discussion, since it normally occurred at least twice a day. The girl was eighteen years old and had a soul mate, so Chartail could not present an argument to Cassie against her living with Darden. It had been Benko's decision and he had provided no ammunition to properly answer his daughter's request.

"Cassandra," Benko used his authoritarian father's voice to address his daughter. "I have had a long day and do not have the energy to discuss this again with you. Why don't you help the team that is erecting the new hut on the outskirts of the village?"

Cassie looked between her father and Chartail, shrugged, and took off.

"Thanks for the support, Chartail."

"Benko, how can I argue a point with your daughter, when you will not tell me what the issue is? She is eighteen years old and Darden is an honorable man. Why do you want to keep them apart? I do not understand."

Her soul mate got up and poured himself another glass of wine. If he had any more to drink, they would not make love again tonight. She had come very close to suggesting Cassie move in with her father and she would move in with the single women Cassie currently boarded with. If Chartail did not take Benko in hand soon, she knew she was going to lose him. She did not care about who ruled the Troyk universe, Chartail only wanted her soul mate.

"Each generation of like telepathic abilities grows in power. Generally, a given power skips a generation or multiple generations. That is nature's way to control the power bestowed on any given person. My father is a third-generation mind control telepath and he has an indecent amount of power. One of the reasons I left the Troyk universe after my failed attempt to unseat my father, was to live in a world where telepathic powers were not used. If my father has enormous power, mine would be greater. I saw a fraction of what he was capable of and it scared me. Cassie's power will eclipse my own. She has only learned enough about her skills to protect herself. Once she makes love with Darden and goes through the evolutionary change, I am afraid of what she will become."

Chartail slowly took in the magnitude of what Benko was telling her. "Is Darden aware of all of this?"

Benko nodded. "Cassie was ten years old when they discovered they were soul mates. When she was so young, it was reassuring to know Darden would not lay a hand on her. As she grew up, I became more and more concerned. Aspects of her talent would come to light from time to time, as well as her natural ability to control the mind of others.

"When she was sixteen, I told Darden about my fears related to Cassie. He has continued to maintain a brother sister relationship with Cassie, I just do not know how long they will be able to resist coming together. For years I purposely spoiled her rotten, to make her a handful and less attractive to Darden. Now I have created a monster and Darden can unleash a creature I may not be able to control."

Her soul mate's frankness, once again startled Chartail. No wonder he drank. When Benko unloaded, he did not hold anything back. Another thought came to her related to another newly discovered multi-generational mind control telepath. She could feel the color drain from her face.

"JoAnna is a fifth generation mind control telepath."

Chapter 15

~

The Troyk Universe

"I am going to ignore the summons," JoAnna announced to anyone who cared to listen. "They have no idea where I am and I have not eaten since lunch. Tolfer, even if the dishes you prepared taste like crap, I will enjoy every bite."

Her announcement was met with silence. She ignored the reactions around her and grabbed a plate to prepare herself a dish. Because of Tolfer's warning, she took a tentative bite and was relieved the food tasted great. She closed her eyes and savored the flavor. It was not long before Koel, Tarsea, Tolfer, and Candy squeezed in at the small table, joining her.

"If Mom helped prepare this," Tarsea said, "there is still hope in the world for every conceivable good thing to happen." JoAnna had heard numerous times Leenea and Zane Childers were the worse cooks across infinite parallel dimensions.

"Being a grandmother changes things," Candy added between bites. "Leenea wants to help raise the baby and has started taking cooking lessons."

Both brothers exchanged glances, sharing looks of utter astonishment. "By the Supreme Being, I am going to have to taste everything that woman cooks to make sure she does not poison my little girl." JoAnna was not sure if Tarsea was exaggerating or truly meant what he said. Could Leenea's food be that bad?

"This may sound like a strange request," JoAnna said. "Tarsea, can I enter your mind and see if I can taste how bad your mother's food was?"

JoAnna was not sure what got a bigger reaction, Leenea Childers taking food preparation lessons or JoAnna asking to enter Tarsea's mind.

"She needs to start to grow her telepathic abilities," Koel added. "This seems like a harmless test. We will need JoAnna as powerful as she can be when it is time for Benko to make his move."

Her soul mate had provided the one argument, it appeared Tarsea could not dispute. "Give it a try. But I warn you, it is the most atrocious food you have ever experienced."

JoAnna could not help but smile in response to Tarsea's comment. She concentrated on Tarsea, looking him straight in the eyes. Her mind projected in an attempt to connect with the brain she wished to penetrate.

The first thing JoAnna picked up was Tarsea's all-consuming love for Alexandra. It was overwhelming to take in such intense feelings. JoAnna pulled out and closed her mind for a moment, trying to clear her head.

"Tarsea, I know it may be impossible," JoAnna continued. "Can you try not to think of Alex? You don't have to worry about mind control telepaths entering your mind to pull out sensitive information. They would not be able to get past your feelings for your soul mate." JoAnna would have to see if Koel had the same obsessive emotions about her, now that they were mated.

"Sorry," Tarsea said, turning a deep shade of red. It was unfortunate Alex was not present to witness Tarsea's reaction. JoAnna and Candy were going to have to share this tidbit with Alex the next time they were together.

JoAnna concentrated once again on Tarsea. This time she was able to get through the multiple layers of thoughts pertaining to Alex. She concentrated on not stumbling over any of the very personal feelings he had for his soul mate. A memory of his mother was within her grasp. JoAnna could see a much younger version of Leenea depicted in her mind. A plate of food was being placed in front of a boy, who she assumed was Tarsea. She could feel the boy's apprehension as he picked up his fork and moved the food on his plate from side to side. After being chastised for playing with his food, the smaller version of Tarsea shoveled a fork full of food into his mouth.

"Oh good Lord," JoAnna cried. She tried to spit out non-existent food from her mouth. "How did you two grow up to be so big and strong? That was horrible! I thought you were exaggerating."

"That was quite impressive," her soul mate said. "Do you have a headache? You are not bleeding, which is a good sign. I have never seen anything like that before. You could actually taste the food from Tarsea's memory. Incredible."

Her soul mate examined her visually to determine if there were any adverse effects to her usage of the enhanced telepathic abilities.

"Jeryl Jarlyn will probably have a list of things he will want JoAnna to try," Candy commented. "We should make a list of our own. The next time we venture to the Troyk penal colony, we should talk to Benko and see what else he would recommend. With Shirl, it was trial and error, although Cianan secretly knew what Jarlyn was looking for."

"That is why those two have issues, her brother was the Prime Ruler's spy?" Shirl must have been devastated by his duplicity. JoAnna could not imagine finding out she had a brother, only to be betrayed by him. "No wonder you did not trust me at first, visions or not." JoAnna had not picked up that gem of information when she had entered Shirl's brain earlier. It was mind blowing how much information was stored in someone's brain, not to mention the privacy issues. The powers also presented a danger to her health. She had been warned about nose bleeds, now she was taking them to heart. No wonder Koel continued to look in her direction with a critical eye.

"We have all had to come to grips with the powers we possess and the moral dilemmas they represent. The problem is everyone has their own scale of what is acceptable and when you cross the line. With Jeryl Jarlyn, after tonight, it does not appear he has one." Candy was being too profound after the day JoAnna had.

Another summons came through a communal pathway. This time JoAnna did not ignore it. She communicated she had a long day and suffered with a migraine. Jeryl Jarlyn would have no idea what type of side effects she would have after the hormone was produced. He had only been exposed to one set of soul mates and Shirl had been in questionable shape after having spent time in the Nightshade universe. JoAnna promised to arrive first thing in the morning, assuming her headache had passed.

The Prime Ruler communicated she should take care of herself and he would see her in the morning. She was off the hook for this evening and could spend some quality time with Koel. The questions were how long would she be able to hold off Jeryl Jarlyn and what did he want from her?

⚬〜◯

Koel felt a tremendous sense of relief when Tarah walked through the door. If anything had happened to his sister, he was not sure he would have ever forgiven himself. His soul mate had been blameless, but he feared he would have one day blamed her for Tarah's loss. It was all irrelevant. He needed to concentrate on the danger Jeryl Jarlyn presented here and now, rather than suffer over what could have occurred.

JoAnna tentatively moved closer to Tarah, waiting to be introduced. He imagined the same thoughts which had plagued him ran rampant through his soul mate's mind. To his relief, a genuine smile crossed his sister's face when she met JoAnna.

"Thank the Supreme Being, you joined us in the Troyk universe," his sister said. "Koel assaulted every woman he had contact with looking for his soul mate." Tarah laughed at the look of horror on JoAnna's face. "He did not literally assault them, just made skin to skin contact. Koel had become impossible to live with."

"Actually, the girls did not seem to mind," Candy added. Koel remember the first thing he did when he met Candy was to touch her. He hoped Candy did not share that piece of news with JoAnna. "Although, by the time I entered the Troyk universe, Koel was no longer the smart mouthed character I had been warned against."

Koel did not miss the questioning look his soul mate sent his direction. "All right, enough dumping on me. I want to know what happened at The Palace." Fortunately, that did the trick, all eyes were now on his sister.

"Jeryl Jarlyn had assigned me to off-world teams who looked for dissidents," his sister started to answer his question. "That was why I had not come by to meet JoAnna. I barely had time to breathe between missions. When I returned yesterday, palace guards were present to escort me to The Palace for questioning. I was brought to a lovely set of rooms. Other than a quick visit from Jeryl Jarlyn, I was left alone."

Koel felt there had to be more to the story. "When you finally communicated to me, you mentioned Jarlyn had somehow turned off your telepathic abilities. How did he do that?"

"I have no idea," Tarah answered. "He held a gold crystal in his hands and merely stared at me. I can only assume he managed to shut off my ability to respond through any channel. During my time there, I was able to pick up chatter, but not respond." His sister got up and put her hand on JoAnna's shoulder. "I was aware of what Jarlyn demanded of you and how I played a role in what occurred."

"The Prime Ruler merely advanced the timing of what we would have done eventually. We have acted like idiots, not soul mates." JoAnna had no reason to bear part of the blame for what had happened to his sister. Koel should have had faith in JoAnna from the minute the soul mate channel had opened.

"There is one more thing," his sister added. "Whatever power Jeryl Jarlyn leveraged, it caused him to bleed through his right ear, as well as his nose. I have never witnessed anything like it."

"He was overtaxing his brain," JoAnna commented. "Jarlyn had a nosebleed when he met with me and Koel."

Was Jeryl Jarlyn abusing his power to such an extent that he had created irreparable damage to his mind? His latest actions were not those of a charismatic ruler who felt it was the Supreme Being's gifts that made him the guardian of his people. Koel did not believe in what he was doing, but until recently, he never considered him an evil man.

"I believe we need to see Benko Jarlyn and get his opinion about what is occurring with his father," Tarsea said. "All of this may be signs of the Prime Ruler losing his grip on his powers and his mind. Our time for action may be coming sooner than we planned."

Koel could not disagree with his friend's assessment. Jeryl Jarlyn was a ruthless politician, not an amoral man. "I need to stay here for the time being with JoAnna. Tarsea, you should head out with Starc, Shirl, and Candy. If any more of us go, it would look suspicious." Tarsea nodded his agreement.

The group made quick work to clean the dining room and kitchen. Tarah would spend the night in the safe house's second bedroom. Koel felt more comfortable with his sister under the same roof. It was doubtful she would be used as a pawn again, but Koel knew he would rest easier, knowing she was in the other room.

His soul mate could barely keep her eyes open. As much as he would have liked to make love to JoAnna, she needed sleep. Koel would hold her close and treasure every moment he had with her. She needed all her strength to deal with whatever Jeryl Jarlyn had planned for her.

Chapter 16

JoAnna slept like the dead. It was debatable whether it was because of the action-packed day she had or being held in her soul mate's arms. Whenever she had sex in the past, she wanted the man to leave as soon as they finished. Waking in Koel's arms was life affirming. With all the chaos thrown at her, she felt at peace lying next to her soul mate. JoAnna reluctantly rose, aware she had to meet with Jeryl Jarlyn.

They walked hand in hand to the Childers's residence in order for her to change into fresh clothing. JoAnna had been so preoccupied with preparing to be with Koel and the threat to his sister, she had not thought to bring an additional set of clothes.

Tolfer had left them breakfast. It was clear the rest of the household had evacuated to places unknown, to give them privacy. The atrocious taste her telepathic abilities conjured up last night had finally left her memory and JoAnna was hungry.

"What do you think Jeryl Jarlyn has up his sleeve?" JoAnna asked between bites.

"After last night, I would not know where to begin. He was ruthless to us, but did not harm Tarah physically. Jarlyn had no idea about the warrior channel we communicate through and Tarah's ability to link in. To the best of his knowledge, she was merely frustrated because she could not communicate telepathically. He would have been ignorant of her knowing he threatened her life. I do not believe there is anyone Jarlyn treasures more than a mind control telepathic subject."

"I guess we won't know until I meet with him." Although she was hungry, the food was not settling easy in her stomach. JoAnna placed her fork on the plate and pushed it away. Koel had barely touched his breakfast as well. "Let me take care of the dishes and then we'll head out."

"Do not worry, JoAnna," Koel reassured her. "I will be by your side the whole time."

"I doubt Jarlyn will agree to that."

"Very little of what Shirl and Starc have together has been leaked to the Prime Ruler," Koel admitted. "The one thing they shared was that Shirl's abilities are greater when her soul mate is beside her. That does not seem to be the case with Tolfer and Candy, but Jarlyn does not know they are soul mates. We merely have to inform Jarlyn we are stronger together. He wants you at your most powerful and I doubt he views me as a threat."

"That may be true," JoAnna reasoned. "Who knows if I could have picked up that taste from Tarsea's mind had you not been there." She turned off the water from the faucet and turned to face him. "May I enter yours to see if I can pick up how you felt when you first saw me? I figure that would be a strong emotion."

JoAnna sucked in her breath in response to the steamy look Koel threw at her. She was really going to enjoy seeing and feeling what her soul mate felt about her. JoAnna concentrated on Koel's beautiful blue eyes. They were normally an icy blue, but now they were lighter with the heat Koel generated.

For the first time since she tried to enter another's mind, JoAnna came up with nothing. Had her powers diminished as the hormone made its way slowly through her brain? She always counted on her gift, what would she do if she had lost it?

"What is wrong?" Koel asked. Panic must have been written all over her face.

"I am not picking up anything from you."

Koel seemed to consider what she said. He never reacted without first considering all the possibilities. Her soul mate did not have a compulsive bone in his body. His calm demeanor helped to reduce her panic.

"Can you hear all the channels, including the warrior pathway?" JoAnna concentrated and nodded as she was deluged with noise from the various channels she had access to. "This is only conjecture," Koel continued, "but I believe the evolutionary change I have gone through has erected a barrier to prevent you from penetrating my mind. I suppose it was created to provide equal footing in our relationship."

That explanation made sense. Shirl had told her Starc was able to hear the portal frequencies through their soul mate connection. Their coming together had provided Koel a similar, but different enhancement.

"Let's head out and see what we can discover at the Palace," JoAnna suggested. "We can test out my powers, as well as your own."

JoAnna really hoped Koel was right with his deduction and that she had not lost her abilities. She was not sure what Jeryl Jarlyn would do if she had. Frankly, just the thought terrified her.

Her world had been turned upside down, but the walk to The Palace seemed so ordinary. People were going about their business, they did not suffer the doubt that plagued her mind. Even Koel seemed unreasonably calm. She once again projected into his mind, yet again unsuccessful.

The Palace guards greeted her, as they always did. JoAnna and Koel made their way to the fourth floor and led to Jeryl Jarlyn's sitting room, rather than the study they had been directed to the night before. A tea service and pastries greeted her, as was the practice in the past. It was as if last night had not occurred.

Jeryl Jarlyn and her uncle entered, they joined her as they always did, except for the one occasion. The Prime Ruler seemed surprised to see Koel. No one must have communicated his presence.

JoAnna decided to immediately go on the offensive. "You forced us to come together as soul mates. We discovered Koel amplifies my telepathic abilities. I guess it makes sense, considering what we are to each other. In the future, he will be by my side whenever I have an assignment, as well as whatever training I am required to take."

Jeryl Jarlyn glanced in Koel's direction, then returned his gaze to JoAnna. He rose and took a piece of herderite from the display case. The Prime Ruler sat once more and appeared to concentrate on her soul mate.

"Impossible," Jarlyn muttered. "I am unable to enter your mind."

Her soul mate was initially taken aback by Jarlyn's comment. They had thought his mind block was in place only between the two of them. The hormone had given Koel more power than originally believed.

"The evolutionary change allowed me to inherit JoAnna's natural telepathic barrier, My Prime," Koel explained.

"What have you been able to do?" Jarlyn asked JoAnna.

She took a sip of tea and a bite from a pastry, before she answered the Prime Ruler. Let him squirm, she thought. After what he had put them through last night, she was in no mood to cater to his every question and desire.

"I was able to taste a memory from Tarsea Childers's childhood. I do not believe I could have done that previously."

"Fascinating," Jarlyn responded. "What else?"

JoAnna was tired of being treated like a carnival freak. "That is it for now. Regardless of the genetic enhancement, I did not want to overtax my brain and start to bleed. Why did you call me in this morning? After last night, I thought you would have some consideration where I was concerned."

Jeryl Jarlyn was taken aback by JoAnna's directness and tone. He may have forgotten what he had done the previous night, but she had not. JoAnna felt she had barely touched the surface of what she was capable of with her enhanced powers. She was prepared to play a life or death game of chicken if she had to.

Her uncle placed his tea cup on the table. Aware the Prime Ruler was unable to continue, Prime Adholm took over the explanation of why they were here. "There is an animal being held for a brutal murder. We do not have anyone who witnessed the crime, only several people who saw him in the vicinity."

"Our normal mind control telepathic interrogators have been unable to get a confession or catch him in a lie." The Prime Ruler had recovered his senses. "Neither your uncle nor I were able to catch the memory of the murder. He is obsessed with women; we were unable to get beyond his graphic thoughts on that subject. Our hope is you would have better success."

"Me?" JoAnna asked in disbelief. "If both of you were unable to break through to find the truth, why would you expect I would be able to? You have used your telepathic gifts your whole lives. I was unaware of my abilities until I came to the Troyk universe."

"You are a strong telepath and now you have enhanced capabilities," Jeryl Jarlyn answered. "I would rather have concrete proof before I make a ruling regarding this crime."

This was the Jeryl Jarlyn she knew and begrudgingly had started to respect, not the amoral bastard from last night. She knew little of Troyk's justice system, although she had heard stories about how they dealt with the guilty once a verdict was reached. JoAnna had the ability to bring justice for whomever the perpetrator cut down.

"Will he be restrained?" The closest JoAnna got to a criminal was going to traffic court. She was way out of her league.

"He will be properly bound and we will have palace guards in attendance. I assume you will want your soul mate present." Jeryl Jarlyn certainly got that right.

"She does not go anywhere without me," Koel added for good measure.

"As you wish," the Prime Ruler responded. "JoAnna, after the attack against you last night, I took the action I thought would best protect you in the future."

Once again, JoAnna was baffled by the Prime Ruler's behavior. His moral compass was broken if he thought what he had done was for her benefit. She would have to deal with these feelings later, she had a more pressing matter to deal with.

Although JoAnna would be surrounded by guards and her soul mate, she was petrified about entering the mind of a possible killer. She had slept with the lights on for a week after she had watched *Psycho*. Her sojourns into the thoughts of others were harmless parlor tricks, compared to what she was about to face.

The fear reflecting off his soul mate disturbed Koel, as they made their way from Jeryl Jarlyn's residence to the small prison located in The Palace's basement. Very few citizens knew of its existence. His cousin Starc had spent a few hours there after he and Shirl had sheltered Chartail Adholm. It was used as a holding cell before sentences could be arrived at and executed. A small warehouse outside of town was where convicted felons resided until the Prime

Council could come up with a new policy related to how convicted prisoners were to be handled.

The scandal related to feeding the Nightshade vampires convicted murderers and the existence of children in the penal world resulted in no long-term solutions for their criminal element. Past Troyk policies had brought about a world with very little crime. This could possibly change, if decisions were not made soon. Koel did not like having his soul mate involved in any aspect of their judicial system.

"You can still change your mind about the interview with the prisoner," Koel communicated to his soul mate through their closed channel. *"You had such a strong reaction to merely a terrible taste last night. I cannot imagine what entering the mind of a possible deranged killer will do to you."* He did not want to candy coat what JoAnna would face. The Troyk people had advanced medical technology for every part of the body except the brain. Even though they were a telepathic race, they knew very little about the complex organ.

"I don't know if I have the ability to back out now," JoAnna admitted. *"Besides, what better way to test my abilities."* Regardless of the brave face she presented, he could sense her apprehension. He knew she was petrified of what she was about to do.

The temperature dropped, as soon as they entered the basement prison. He could feel JoAnna shiver, as they made their way deeper into the room. If the chill was not bad enough, there was a strong smell of disinfectant. Koel could only imagine the living conditions the men and women, who temporarily resided here suffered. He placed his arm around JoAnna's shoulders and brought her into the warmth of his body.

They were led to a makeshift conference room in the middle of the basement. Two armed guards stood outside the cordoned off space. The guard who had led them from Jarlyn's residence had a short whispered conversation with the taller of the two sentries. Communal pathways could only be used if the information shared could be broadcast to a large audience.

"I am joining you." Solfa made a sudden appearance. Koel was grateful for her involvement in what was about to happen. She was a brilliant strategist and would quickly abort the interview if she felt JoAnna was in danger. He also did not miss JoAnna becoming a lighter shade of pale in response to Solfa being present. Although Koel was glad Solfa was here, his soul mate did not share the sentiment.

They entered the room and Koel was shocked to see the prisoner was no more than a boy. He could not be more than seventeen years old. No wonder the Prime Ruler said he was obsessed with women, most boys his age were. The suspect was chained to the chair, as well as the ground. Unless he had superhuman strength, the prisoner did not present a physical threat.

"Traves Choaks, you are being detained for the murder of Sharla Klepper." Solfa got straight to business, casting her cold stare at the boy before them. "JoAnna Carlson is a mind control telepath, who will assist me in this interrogation. She has the ability to enter your mind, whether you agree to her entry or not."

Koel watched, as the boy's eyes left Solfa and lit onto his soul mate. There was something wrong with the way he looked at JoAnna. He had an uneasy feeling about the look and the danger the prisoner presented to his soul mate. Koel had seen sexual hunger before, this was something different. The boy shifted in the chair, trying to get closer to JoAnna.

"Hold off entering his brain for the time being." Koel communicated through the warrior channel, allowing both Solfa and JoAnna to hear his order. *"Solfa, were any of the mind control telepaths who were part of the earlier interrogations women?"*

Solfa reached for the file on the table and reviewed its contents. After she finished reading what had been documented, she went through it again. *"All the people who have been involved in questioning the prisoner have been men. Why do you ask?"*

Koel struggled to translate a feeling he had into words in order to explain the vibe coming off Traves Choaks. *"I need to know what telepathic abilities the prisoner has and how brutal the murder was. Plus, have there been any unsolved similar crimes that have not been communicated through the communal pathways? What telepathic powers did the victim or victims possess?"* Koel noted JoAnna had been looking at him from the time they entered the room, not making eye contact with the prisoner. *"JoAnna, keep your focus on me. Under no circumstances do you look directly at the prisoner."*

"I need to further debrief my associates," Solfa announced to the other officials in the room. She obviously wanted answers to Koel's questions and some of her own. "Koel and JoAnna, we will meet in my office."

They exited the room and hurried to the third floor where Solfa conducted business. As they made their way up from the basement, Solfa barked orders to her staff through the communal pathways for every bit of information available on the case. Koel contacted Candy and requested she join them. He needed to know everything he could about her premonitions related to JoAnna. Something did not feel right.

"What is going on, Koel?" Solfa asked as soon as Candy arrived. They had worked together long enough for Solfa to respect his instincts.

Koel wiped the sweat from his brow, as he tried to make sense of the array of thoughts that assaulted his mind. When he thought he had a fully coherent storyline to tell everyone, more nuances of what he feared was occurring came to light. He needed to get a grip and construct a lucid explanation for the three women before him.

"This may sound insane, but have you heard stories about succubus? I am not referring to the stories of females who feed on the life force of others. There is a particular legend related to a male telepathic being who could steal the gifts of a female mind control telepath and leave her a hollow shell. Legend tells us you can identify these creatures by a flash of yellow light emitted from their eyes."

"I believe they are called incubus, if they are male," JoAnna commented. He could not help but give her a questioning look. "I loved the series *Lost Girl* and read some of the lore on the subject. They are more into sexual energy, then pulling telepathic power."

Solfa turned a light shade of green and quickly picked up one of the files on her desk. She shuffled through the papers until she found what she looked for. "The victim had her head bashed in and there was very little brain matter. They explained it away by documenting there had been a rodent infestation in the area."

"Gross," Candy and JoAnna said in unison. If the conversation was not so serious, Koel would have laughed at the girls having the same reaction to a bunch of rats living off whatever they could eat.

"Jeryl Jarlyn has never had issues sentencing people to death or the penal colony without a shred of evidence," Koel informed the group. "Now he personally interviews a suspected felon. He cannot reach inside his mind, so he asks JoAnna to do it. I swear, I saw a flash of yellow for an instant."

"It does not make sense, Koel." JoAnna sounded as frustrated as he felt. "Why would he blackmail us into making love and go through the evolutionary change, just to have me fall victim to this male incubus. By the way, I do not believe in such creatures, regardless of the entertainment value they provide on television."

"I do not know," Koel admitted. "It is just a feeling I have. Something is off about this whole situation. We need to take the threat seriously, even if the prisoner is not what I fear he is. Candy, have you been able to pick up anything?"

"Nothing concrete. I have had feelings that something bad would happen, but my anxiety level has reached critical this time around. It is all directed at Jo Jo."

Every instinct Koel had cried out for him to take his soul mate and leave this world. Perhaps he should take JoAnna and join his cousin in the penal colony. There she would be safe and they would work with Benko Jarlyn to overthrow his father. The Prime Ruler seemed to have set his sights on destroying his soul mate and Koel was not going to let it happen. However, it was questionable whether they would be allowed to walk out of The Palace.

Chapter 17

⌒

JoAnna gripped her soul mate's hand, as she attempted to enter Traves Choaks's mind. If he was the creature Koel thought he was, the boy presented a threat to her. She needed to face him where she had control, not being overtaken in some dark alley one day in the future. Not only was she a fifth-generation mind control telepath, but she was a mated one. With everything she could gather about telepathic strength, she was almost invincible. Now would be the best time to confront the beast within the boy or discover he was harmless. Either way, she was not going to live her life in fear, always looking over her shoulder.

She had a natural ability to block other mind control telepaths from her mind, which was reinforced by the same gift manifesting itself in her soul mate. Together, she prayed they would be able to counter anything thrown at them. JoAnna felt Candy's presence behind her, it reassured her she was well protected.

The boy's stare unnerved her. JoAnna nearly came out of her chair when Candy thrust a knife into the table. "You keep looking at my friend in that manner, I will put the dagger's partner in your chest." Traves Choaks did not even blink at Candy's threat. The sick grin on his face only got larger.

JoAnna needed to concentrate on the boy and ignore all the distractions. The pounding of her heart made it difficult for her to focus. It was almost deafening, as it beat a rapid rate.

"Solfa, please start asking him questions," JoAnna requested. She needed the prisoner to focus on something other than her. Solfa's glare usually was enough to scare the living daylights out of anyone. JoAnna was intimidated by the

woman who sat next to her. Unfortunately, it did not appear Traves Choaks had the same reaction.

"Tell me about your relationship with Sharla Klepper," Solfa said. "Did she turn down the repulsive thought of having sex with you? How badly did you want to hurt Sharla?"

Traves Choaks continued to stare at JoAnna, rather than respond to Solfa's taunts. His silence was unnerving. She felt as if something was trying to break through her natural telepathic shield. The sensation was not dissimilar to the start of a pressure headache. She decided it was wise to break eye contact with the boy and shifted her gaze over to Solfa. Perhaps if she concentrated on Traves Choaks, she could enter his mind without staring directly at him.

Solfa continued to drill questions at the prisoner, while JoAnna tried to project herself into the boy's mind. She caught glimpses here and there, but nothing concrete. It was like a bad movie, flashing on parts of a woman's anatomy, like a strobe light effect. Jeryl Jarlyn had mentioned he had only been able to pick up the thoughts of girls when he tried to enter Choak's mind.

The boy's continued silence added more tension in the room. Solfa's voice kept getting louder as she fired question after question at him. Traves's only reaction was to stare at JoAnna.

JoAnna reached beside her, she grasped Koel's hand. No one had mentioned soul mates became stronger with physical contact, but at this point, she was willing to try anything. Besides, it comforted her touching him. Koel tightened his grip on her hand, communicating he was there to support her. JoAnna knew he was opposed to her trying to enter Traves Choaks's mind.

"Try and project your mind into his, Koel." JoAnna was willing to try anything to break through the boy's initial layer of thoughts. Perhaps the soul mate link between them would enhance the gifts she already possessed.

JoAnna felt an all-consuming kiss between Traves Choaks and another person she could not identify. She sensed the pull of energy from the unknown woman powered the young man. It was unclear what type of power he was drawing from her. JoAnna needed to go deeper into the memory. With the precision of a surgeon, she focused in order to determine what the energy consisted of. She entered the vortex of the power, almost like something out of *The Outer Limits*.

"We are done here." Koel's voice penetrated her mind, as she felt her body being lifted from the chair. They were out the door before JoAnna was able to identify where she was. "What were you thinking? The bastard was draining you of energy right in front of us!"

None of this made any sense to JoAnna. "No, that isn't possible. He would need to have physical contact with me, like the kiss we experienced." JoAnna was still a little dazed from the experience. She was not sure how she knew what she communicated was true, JoAnna just knew it.

Koel placed her on her own two feet. JoAnna grabbed the door frame for balance, a bit shaky after her experience. It had all been so surreal and she struggled to come back to reality. When she closed her eyes, she could still see the boy staring at her with insanity in his gaze.

"Jo Jo," Candy said, "I felt you drift away. All my premonitions have been physical, but this one was more metaphysical. It is hard to describe. You were being drained of your telepathic ability, I am sure of it."

JoAnna started to spin, while the world stood still. She had heard acquaintances talk of vertigo attacks, but until this moment, she had never experienced one. It took all her effort to walk a straight line. "I am going to be sick," JoAnna said, as she put out her hand and placed it against the wall.

Hands grabbed her waist and pushed her through an open door. JoAnna fell to her knees, as Candy grabbed a waste basket and placed it in front of her. As the world continued to spin, JoAnna emptied her stomach.

Koel stood helpless, as his soul mate retched into the container Candy had placed before her. He had felt waves of nausea, as he had carried JoAnna out of the interrogation room. It was clear he had a mild case of whatever had impacted her.

He had not entered Traves Choaks's brain, chosen to unite minds with his soul mate instead. It was fortunate he had, since Koel had been able to feel the attack on her mind. As soon as he had felt JoAnna's diminished capabilities, Koel severed the connection his soul mate had with Traves. To play it safe, he also removed her physically from the incubus's presence. There was no longer any doubt what he now dealt with.

"Get in here and close the door," Candy ordered, as Solfa entered the room. "We need to elevate her feet and let the vertigo spell run its course. If you have something similar to an antihistamine, we should give it to her."

"Med-tech to room B108 in The Palace immediately," Solfa communicated through a communal pathway. He was not sure if a med-tech could help JoAnna, but it did not hurt to have her looked at. He never should have allowed her to enter that psychopath's mind.

"Tell Jeryl Jarlyn we saw the bastard kill the girl," Koel said. As far as he was concerned, whoever that girl Traves Choaks had kissed had ended up dead. The monster would pay for at least one murder.

"We can't be sure of that." JoAnna sounded weak and her voice was shaky. It was clear she was still in the grasp of the vertigo attack. Candy readjusted his soul mate's feet, making sure they were higher than her head.

"Yes, I can," Koel responded back to JoAnna. "The freak is guilty as far as I am concerned. I saw him take the last breath from that girl, as he took her telepathic abilities. Although I was linked in through you, I felt him drain her."

"I will document the results of the interview accordingly," Solfa commented. "We should be able to get a conviction and execute a sentence. Although I was horrified by our policy related to the Nightshade universe, I cannot imagine a more fitting fate for Traves Choaks to suffer. Let him get drained by a vampire, as he drained those poor girls. There have to be a dozen open homicides with similar particulars."

"Jeryl Jarlyn would never get away with sending another convicted murderer to the Nightshade universe," Candy said.

"Traves Choaks is too dangerous to house in our world. I will advise our Prime Ruler he does not have to worry about this animal any longer. Shirl will open a portal and only a few of us will know where he ended up."

"What if he asks?" Candy inquired.

"Gatherers have been combing parallel dimensions for dissidents," Koel said. "We merely have to let Jeryl Jarlyn know we abandoned the prisoner on a deserted world. I imagine our new allies in the Nightshade universe would be quite happy to relieve us of a deranged criminal who represents a danger to JoAnna."

"It's not right," JoAnna mumbled. Koel watched as his soul mate worked to sit up. She was still very shaky and ended up laying back down.

"Where is the med-tech?" Koel took her pulse. It was thready, scarcely perceptible. If help did not arrive soon, he would find a med-tech kit and take care of his soul mate himself.

Soon after Koel had that thought, a female med-tech arrived. She took JoAnna's vitals and packed up her kit. "There is nothing I can do here. She will recover from the equilibrium imbalance shortly and will be fine."

Candy appeared to be as unsatisfied with the lack of care given JoAnna as he was. "Don't you have an Antivert?"

"I do not understand what you are asking for. Your friend will be fine. There is nothing I can do for her." Obviously, the woman had other places to go and did not want to be delayed with a female who suffered a dizzy spell.

Candy tried to stop her from leaving, but Koel stymied Candy's efforts. "Let her go. If JoAnna does not feel better soon, we can have Shirl head to Ginkgo Terra and pick up the medications you mentioned."

"I feel so stupid," JoAnna said, as she once again tried to sit. This time her complexion had color and she successfully sat. Candy pulled over a chair and helped JoAnna to her feet and then into the chair. Although JoAnna had only been at the orphanage a short period of time, Candy treated her like she would Alex and Shirl. It was a relief how these telepathically superior women were looking out for his soul mate.

JoAnna placed her elbow on the desk next to her and balanced her head on it. Koel did not like the way her complexion was once again paling. Fortunately, this time around, JoAnna did not have the green tint she had earlier.

"Take her home," Solfa ordered. "I will report to Jeryl Jarlyn. As soon as I have the go ahead, I will communicate through the warrior link our plans to escort the prisoner to the Nightshade universe."

Solfa left the room, as Koel checked on the condition of his soul mate. He took her into his arms. "Let us get out of here. I will take you to the Childers's residence. Knowing Leenea, she will have some herbal remedy to help you."

Koel exited The Palace with his soul mate. His mind was racing with concerns related to why Jeryl Jarlyn had involved JoAnna in Traves Choaks interrogation and the upcoming trip to the Nightshade universe. He glanced at Candy, whose face reflected the worry Koel was dealing with. His soul mate was still in mortal danger and there was nothing he could do about it.

Chapter 18

~

JoAnna stretched out, as she woke from her nap. Her body was still fatigued from her vertigo attack. Koel had carried her home and quickly left, rather than remaining with her. He had muttered about not trusting himself and that she needed rest. They had not made love since the initial night they had been forced together. She realized a tremendous amount of events had occurred, but she still yearned to touch and be with her soul mate.

"It is about time you woke," a voice came from the shadows. She reached for the lamp on the nightstand and turned on the light. As her eyes adjusted to the brightness, there stood Traves Choaks. The boy was naked, his member erect.

"How did you escape?" The inane question was the first thing that popped into JoAnna's mind. She quickly communicated to her soul mate through the warrior channel, where all his friends would also hear she was in danger. *"Traves Choaks broke into the house and is in my bedroom."*

"I am a mind control telepath," Traves answered. "All I needed was to be alone with a weak minded guard to claim my freedom. These lower beings cannot judge me. My abilities place me on a different plane, one you belong on. I had never felt power that compares with yours."

A sick feeling descended upon her. "Did you harm anyone in this house?" JoAnna knew it had been empty when Koel brought her home. Communications through the warrior channel confirmed everyone was safe and accounted for.

"Distract him anyway you can," Koel communicated through the warrior channel. *"Do not let him kiss you and drain your power. Prevent him from creating a link with your mind, since he had been able to partially drain you previously. Someone will be there*

128

shortly." JoAnna had no intention of letting the psycho before her anywhere near her mouth. Unfortunately, Koel had removed her outer garments when he placed her on the bed. She only had a bra and panties on. JoAnna was any teenager's wet dream.

She rose partially, she leaned on her elbow, presenting Traves a better view of her full breasts. "Jeryl Jarlyn did not know what to do with you," JoAnna said. "He brought me in, hoping I would be able to break through your barriers. You are very powerful, I could barely make out anything because of the complexity of your mind. I am new to my telepathic gifts, I could learn a lot from you."

Traves Choaks had been looking at her breasts, but as soon as she bowed to his superiority, his gaze returned to her face. "I can teach you all sorts of things and in return I want to fuck you."

JoAnna was startled by his choice of words. No one in her acquaintance had ever been so crass. She did not believe the word existed in this realm, since it was an acronym on Earth. It was imperative she shake off his adolescent behavior and appear to be turned on by what he said.

"We can share power and our bodies," JoAnna said. "Jeryl Jarlyn is old and has no designated successor. The mind control telepathic government took power because they felt superior to the common people. They will not even see us coming." JoAnna tried to embody all the powerful female villains from campy films she had seen over the years. The boy was so over the top, she figured he would be turned on by her behavior.

"You are wearing too many clothes," Traves complained.

"Foreplay," JoAnna answered. "You want to build to the climax. I can teach you to savor a woman's body and extend your own orgasm." That statement stopped Traves cold. She imagined he was guilty of premature ejaculation in the past. That assumed he even had sex with a partner. JoAnna rolled over onto her back and raised an arm, inviting the boy to her bed. Where the hell was Koel?

The youthful enthusiasm of a seventeen-year-old boy preparing for sex should be bottled. It would power cities for months. There was no grace in the way he moved, unlike the feline grace Koel possessed. One moment he stood over her, the next he was on top of her. One of his grubby hands reached out and grabbed her right breast. There was no finesse in his touch, only inexperienced fumbling.

129

JoAnna had expected he would try to remove her panties and get right to the sex part of their relationship. She had miscalculated, Traves went straight to her mouth. It was impossible to shift her body, in order to protect herself from him placing his lips on hers. The all-consuming kiss of telepathic power she had seen in his mind was what Traves truly wanted. She did not have to enter his brain to figure that out. She had been played.

He took her lips, as if he planned to punish her for her involvement in his incarceration. Travis invaded her mouth with the battle techniques of Attila the Hun. If she survived this assault, her lips would be bruised and raw. She heard conversations within the warrior channel, but nothing to make her hope she would be rescued in time.

His mouth was rough, but it was not sexual. Traves prepared to transfer energy, not have sex. JoAnna could once again feel something coming at the barriers in her head. She had no idea how the walls in her mind were erected to begin with, so she was unsure how to reinforce them against his attack.

Something broke, she felt a stab of pain in her head. Thoughts that were not her own invaded her mind. She thought of her experience in the portal with Darden. Flashes of memories occurred when she entered a mind, not when someone entered hers. Was she somehow reversing the pull of Traves's gift?

JoAnna was pulled from her thoughts when Traves slapped her in the face. Even his slap was inept, surprising more than hurting her. "Stop whatever you are doing. I am the master of telepathic power, not you." He immediately brought his mouth back to hers. Oddly, he had broken the kiss to orally communicate, rather than telepathically convey his orders.

It was time to turn the tables. Whatever he was doing, Traves was failing. He had attacked women to steal their powers and now he had run into someone more powerful than he was. JoAnna grabbed his head with both her hands and deepened the kiss. Her powerful legs wrapped around his weaker limbs. She once again thought of the female heroine from *Lost Girl*. This time she was the succubus.

JoAnna used suction, caused by her breath, taking in Traves's power. He struggled, but she was superior in both physical and telepathic strength. She saw the atrocities the boy was guilty of. JoAnna only wanted to drain him enough to make him helpless to escape. The last thing she wanted was to bring any aspect of his insanity into her mind.

Words were shouted in her head, but she ignored them, as she continued to drain Traves. The power she gained was obscene and so seductive. She understood how movie vampires were helpless to stop from draining their victims. JoAnna could easily see how she could be considered a psychic vampire.

Traves's weight was pulled off her, as Koel brought her into his arms. She had temporarily fought releasing her victim, but relented as soon as she realized her soul mate had arrived.

"Koel, her eyes are glowing yellow." JoAnna somehow knew Tarsea referred to her. She struggled to mentally release Traves's mind, even though JoAnna was now free of his body. It felt as if the conversation that took place around her was in another dimension, alien to hers.

"I saw Traves Choaks eyes flash yellow for an instant when we were at The Palace," Koel said. "It must have to do with the transfer of telepathic power. Obviously, JoAnna got the better of him. Thank the Supreme Being, the Prime Ruler forced us to have sex. The kid did not stand a chance against a mated female telepath."

"Jo Jo, you have to come back to us," Alex cried. She could hear and sense her old friend, but she could not see her. JoAnna tried to release her hold on Traves Choaks's mind, but was unable to. It was as if she was in another dimension from her friends, with only the shell of her body still in their plane.

Someone grabbed her hand and placed something cold in it. A crystal. Moments passed and nothing happened. JoAnna was still caught in the stream she had created between herself and her victim. A second and third stone were added to her palm and capable hands closed her fingers around the crystals.

"Blue lace agate, amethyst, and rose quartz are calming stones. You need to concentrate on the power of the crystals and release your mind from whatever is controlling it." JoAnna tried to do as Shirl suggested. "Let the healing energy wash over your body."

Shirl made it sound so easy. JoAnna concentrated on the fist which held the crystals. All her effort was geared to tightening her grip on the stones. Slowly she felt her mind releasing its hold on what was feeding it. Her vision cleared and she could see Alex and Shirl in front of her.

"Thank God," Alex said. "Welcome back, Jo Jo. Your eyes are back to normal. Whatever held you captive, the crystals did the trick in releasing you."

JoAnna looked around the room and saw Koel and Tarsea leaning over a body. She rose to see what type of shape Traves Choaks was in. Her feet were a little wobbly, so JoAnna used Shirl as a crutch. She looked down at the boy's face and let out a blood curdling scream.

Koel could understand JoAnna's horrified reaction to Traves Choaks's appearance. The boy's frontal cranial bone had weakened and his upper forehead concaved back into his head. Brain matter started to leak from the damaged skull. It was obvious to Koel why Traves had taken a bat to his victims' skulls, to mask what had happened to their brains.

His soul mate had done this. She had stolen telepathic abilities from her victim and destroyed his brain in the process. It was an act of self-defense, but the magnitude of her strength was frightening. He could not fathom what JoAnna would become, nor his role in her heightened abilities.

"We need to get him out of here," Starc commented. "The last thing we want is to explain his condition to the authorities. Solfa has already communicated she would see to the disposal of Traves Choaks. I say we still take him to the Nightshade universe as planned. By some miracle, the freak is still breathing. He still holds value where the vampires are concerned."

Koel did not like his cousin's choice of words to describe the boy. His soul mate now possessed the power that might have driven Traves Choaks mad. He feared JoAnna was not ready for the amount of energy she now possessed.

"Agreed, you should deliver him to the Nightshade universe. I will stay behind and take care of JoAnna." His soul mate had calmed and based on the look on her face, she was not happy.

"I am coming with you," JoAnna said. "Do you think for one moment I will be able to sleep at night, fearing this monster will return from wherever you send him?"

His soul mate had a point, but the Nightshade universe had the ability to create nightmares for anyone unfortunate to venture to that parallel dimension. "Starc will make sure Traves is not breathing before he returns to the Troyk universe." Koel looked at the fallen boy. "I do not believe he will live long either way."

"Regardless," JoAnna stated, "I am going. The stories I have heard of that universe may put the issues I deal with in this universe into perspective."

"We are not going to enter through the natural portal into Yorik's hive," Shirl advised. "Drake should still be with Lorenz and Afton. I want to check on her anyway, so this trip is killing two birds with one stone."

Koel was continually stumped at the things Shirl and her friends said, with the exception of JoAnna. Whatever sayings the other girls learned, JoAnna either was not exposed to them or she did not use them. If it was not her use of contractions, one would never know JoAnna had not grown up in the Troyk universe.

"Let us go while Traves still holds value," Tarsea said. "Alex, would it do any good to ask you to stay behind?"

"You don't have to ask me twice," Alex answered. "I have no desire to enter the Nightshade universe again or to see Drake. Why that vampire believes he has a claim to my baby is beyond my comprehension. Although Benko Jarlyn struck a deal with Drake to see me, I don't feel obligated to make any additional trips."

JoAnna's preoccupation with the boy and her growing powers was evident when she did not make a comment about the vampire Drake believing Alex's unborn daughter was his soul mate. Stranger things had been known to happen, as far as Koel was concerned, but his main concern was the well-being of his own soul mate.

"We should do it then," Tarsea said. He took Alex into his arms and kissed her. Koel finally understood his friend's obsession with Alexandra, since her entry into their world. Nothing would have made him happier than to do exactly the same thing to JoAnna. However, now was not the time for them to become intimate.

Starc and Tarsea gingerly picked up Traves. His cousin grabbed the boy's shoulders, while Tarsea got his feet. Shirl's amethyst started to glow and a portal opened. A forced portal had a smaller air density than a natural one. The energy to produce such an event horizon was excessive, but Shirl's powers allowed her to open one with little effort.

One by one, his friends entered the portal, until JoAnna and Koel were the only ones remaining in the room. "You can still back out of going," Koel told her. "Starc would not lie about Traves's death. I am sure Alex would love your company while her soul mate is in the Nightshade universe."

"No, I want to go. I need to see this to the end. Besides, I heard all about the Nightshade universe and I am curious about what a real vampire looks like. Any red-blooded American woman has some type of fascination with fictional vampires. I have certainly read my fair share of paranormal romances featuring a vampire as the hero."

"Just be prepared for what you are about to see," Koel warned her. "Drake and Lorenz were made by the original vampire, thus they appear human. The other creatures are in various stages of decomposition. There is nothing sexy about them. They are dangerous because they are starving for blood."

"Shirl did not bat an eye returning to that world. I am sure I will be fine."

Koel took his soul mate's hand and was prepared to walk her through the event horizon before it collapsed. She had been through so much in the last two days, he was not sure how much more she would be able to take. Entering the Nightshade universe was certainly not his idea of having JoAnna take it easy. One never knew what would be on the other side of the portal.

Chapter 19

~

The Nightshade Universe

JoAnna felt a chill as soon as she exited the portal. What else would you expect when you entered a universe populated by vampires? Part of her had wished she had taken Koel's recommendation to stay behind, but she needed to see Traves Choaks dealt with. The images she pulled from his brain would haunt her the rest of her life.

The first person JoAnna saw was a blond man, fashionably dressed with a beautiful deep tan. He could not possibly be a vampire. The man was probably the handsomest creature she had ever laid eyes on. His hands were clasped on a raven haired woman who was as striking as he was.

"Welcome to my home," the vision said. "My name is Lorenz and this is my soul mate Afton. I have alerted Drake to your presence. He will join us shortly."

"I thought you said Lorenz was a vampire," JoAnna communicated to her soul mate. *"He looks like he could give George Hamilton a run for his money. That is some tan he has."*

"You look taken aback," the ethereal beauty who stood by Lorenz said. "I figure you were expecting wan, starving creatures." The girl considered her words and continued. "Actually, that was exactly what I was until I made love to Lorenz. We are evolving into something, I am just not sure what. I can harvest the energy of the sun, as Shirl does the powers contained within crystals." The girl went over and hugged her friend. "As the sun's energy is depleted from my body, I will lose the tan."

"We have an offering," Koel said. "Fortunately, he will not last much longer. His blood should not have been impacted by his injury."

Lorenz knelt and placed two fingers on Traves's neck to feel for his pulse. "His death is near. Afton and I no longer require blood, but the offering is sorely needed and I thank you." Lorenz snapped his fingers and two vampires came forward to take the body.

JoAnna was momentarily shocked by the condition of the creatures who approached Traves. They looked like the vampire version of the zombies from Michael Jackson's *Thriller* video. Her desire to see the boy take his last breath overcame her initial reaction. "He needs to be dealt with here, so we can witness his demise. The boy is responsible for the murder and mutilation of a number of women from our world."

"As you wish," Lorenz quickly responded. He turned to address a pair of vampires. "Feed your hungry cells."

The two monsters bared their elongated teeth and fell upon Traves Choakes. One bit into his neck, while the other sunk his teeth into the boy's femur artery. She could hear bones crushed, as the vampires fed. Under normal circumstances, JoAnna would have looked away. His body fought the vampire's attack and he made sounds like an injured animal. Her mind recalled the violence he inflicted on those poor women. Traves got exactly what he deserved. If someone thought her moral compass was now defective, so be it.

A dark, pale, gorgeous man entered the room and watched the two vampires finish off their prisoner. He went over, took Shirl's hand, and kissed it. The stunning vampire did not seem at all put off by Shirl's soul mate who stood right next to her. This creature had to be Drake.

The two vampires drained Traves of every drop of blood they could recover from him. Starc declared that the boy was dead and the two vampires removed the body from their presence. JoAnna did not care how they disposed of the corpse. Traves Choaks was no longer a danger to anyone, particularly to her.

"I sense extreme power, and it is not from you, my love," the black haired vampire dropped Shirl's hand and made his way to her. She would be lying if she did not admit her heart skipped a beat or two as Drake approached. The vampire reached to touch her, but Koel grabbed his forehand, stopping him cold.

"You can trifle with Shirl all you want, that is Starc's problem," Koel advised the vampire. "This one is my soul mate and she is off limits to you."

Drake stepped back, a grin on his face. "A mate worthy of such a powerful woman. My congratulations, Koel. I sense you have more capabilities since the last time we met. Alexandra is not among you, I hope the meal our men just enjoyed is not the reason why."

"My wife and daughter are fine, and it is none of your concern." Tarsea stepped from the shadows to confront the cocky vampire. JoAnna had to admit, Drake was certainly charming. Only a deadly creature would be so blatantly cavalier with these three Troyk warriors. JoAnna was certainly happy he was on their side.

"Oh, you have finally made an honest woman out of the chameleon," Drake said. "I believe that is what they call it where she was born and raised."

"We will eventually have a ceremony," Tarsea started to backpedal. "Our bond was forged the moment we touched. A bond my daughter will one day share with another Troyk male. I do not know how you have manipulated Benko Jarlyn, but as soon as he reneges on whatever deal you two came up with, my daughter is off limits to you."

JoAnna was so engrossed with the discussion, she did not notice Afton approach. "Let the boys continue their pissing contest. We should talk before you leave my world. I sense there is much within you that is crying to come out."

Afton took her hand and led JoAnna to a small sitting area, not far from where the men continued to throw barbs at each other. Just short of their destination, lovely rugs covered the stone floors of the keep. The furniture was a rich burgundy satin. JoAnna did not know if she had ever sat in such a comfortable love seat. Shirl joined them, sitting next to JoAnna.

"I am so glad you have come to my world and hope you will come often," Afton said. "We three have incredible power, abilities that seem to grow with time. Shirl has been on her journey longer and already has the scars to prove it." JoAnna had witnessed firsthand Shirl's telepathic strength. It was a relief to JoAnna she was not alone in dealing with what was happening to her. "I am alone in this world and hope you will return to Nightshade regularly. My soul mate is incredibly supportive, but it is not the same as having girl friends who have experienced the same issues."

Suddenly, JoAnna had problems swallowing. "I pulled the telepathic power from that boy and left but a husk. It was so easy. Every day I seem to get more powerful and it scares me to death."

JoAnna was amazed by the stress released from her body with the confession. Somehow Afton knew what JoAnna needed. Perhaps she suffered from feelings that needed to be voiced as well.

Shirl put her arm around JoAnna's shoulder. "Jo Jo, that child was a killer with no conscience. We look at him and see a boy, but inside he was a monster. There was a man who hurt Alex, I had no qualms bringing him here to allow Drake to administer justice for his unborn soul mate. We do what we have to do to survive and make the Troyk universe a place where we want to raise our children."

"I suppose I have it easy, I just killed blood lusting vampires," Afton shared. All three women looked at each other and laughed. Somehow their lives had turned into B-horror and science fiction movies. None of their former friends on Earth would believe any of the tales they could share of their lives in these parallel dimensions.

"It is nice to meet you, Afton," JoAnna said. "Since your soul mate is no longer a vampire, why do you stay in this terrible place? There are so many worlds you can live in and not have these monsters baying at your door." She had certainly seen her fair share of bad films, JoAnna used melodramatic speech from her younger years of watching them with her parents.

"Lorenz has four blood brothers. Until they have found their soul mates, we will continue to reside in this world. Helpless victims are caught in portals and brought into this universe every day. It is my duty, with my enhanced powers, to help as many as I can. I wish I could help them all, but in some instances my hands are tied."

JoAnna did not miss Afton look in the direction of a small redheaded woman on the other side of the room. She instantly thought of Alex, they were so similar in stature. However, unlike Alex, that girl did not blend into the shadows. Too bad for her.

"We should head back before the men's friendly jabs turn into something more physical," Shirl said. "I promise to check on you regularly and send as many people you rescue home."

JoAnna entered the portal Shirl opened, walking alongside her soul mate. She had indirectly taken a life. Although she shared what she had done and her concerns, JoAnna had barely touched the surface of how worried she was about her ability to control her ever growing powers.

Chapter 20

〜

The Troyk Universe

It had been the second time she had ventured to a parallel universe, but it still amazed JoAnna she had actually visited another dimension. Although she had not brought up returning temporarily to Earth to see her father, JoAnna knew there was little involved in making the trip. The only issue was what to tell her father about where she had been. It would be difficult to tell him she planned to live the rest of her life in another realm of existence.

JoAnna exited the portal beside Koel. It troubled her they had not had sex since the first time they came together. Her friends managed to steal away to have relations with their soul mates, while Koel seemed overly concerned about her physical well-being. What kind of man was he? JoAnna knew she should be thrilled with such a considerate mate, when all she wanted to do was jump Koel and have her way with him.

"Shirl and Alex," JoAnna communicated through their closed link channel. Although Candy was not physically there, JoAnna knew her friend would pick up what she was broadcasting. *"Would you mind disappearing again with your men and leaving the house for me and Koel?"*

JoAnna did not miss the smiles that crossed each of their faces. They did not have to telepathically share they would honor her request. There were two apartments and the safe house her friends and their soul mates could use. Zane and Leenea Childers managed to steal away when one of their children wanted the house to themselves.

"I am hungry," Alex said. The announcement was not news to anyone. Although Alex had not joined them in the Nightshade universe, she had not left the room. Her friend had a voracious appetite and it was the perfect ploy to start the mass exodus. "Why don't we head out for something to eat? Tolfer and Candy can join us, let's give the poor guy a break from always cooking."

"If it is all right with everyone, Koel and I will stay behind," JoAnna chimed in. "It has been a whirlwind kind of day and I would just like to get some more rest."

Koel looked at her with concern, he swallowed her cover story. She was mentally drained, so whatever he picked up from their link, supported her claim. What he did not realize was that there was only one thing that would revive her. He appeared to barely notice his friends leaving the room and heading out for a meal.

The ever considerate soul mate of hers started to exit the room as well. "Where are you going?" JoAnna inquired. "I don't want you to leave. Your place is beside me, giving me the strength I need to deal with everything that is happening."

"I will only exhaust you," Koel admitted. "My body craves yours so much, I can barely control myself being in the same room with you." There was an edge to his voice, which reflected the fragile control Koel had been able to maintain. JoAnna knew he was at his breaking point and she was willing to let him fracture, as long as they did it together.

"For some reason you are under the misconception I need to rest, rather than work out all the frustrations this world has created. I am certainly not a sexual succubus, but I know being with you again can only revive my weakened soul."

Koel approached her and took possession of her mouth. A sudden vision of Traves Choaks and his attempt to suck her dry flashed within her mind. Her soul mate picked up the vision and released her lips.

"Don't let him take this from us," JoAnna pleaded. "I am not sure how long memories of what he tried to do will surface, but your kiss is nothing like what happened between me and the boy. His was a weapon, while your lips make love to me. We can and will move past this. Don't back off when I have an episode."

Koel's eyes examined her face, while she felt his essence check the link which connected them. He slightly nodded his head and returned his luscious lips to hers. JoAnna needed to concentrate on the man who possessed her heart, not the maniac who tried to take her gift.

She raised her arms and brought her hands into his thick, dark blond hair. It was just the right length to allow her to wrap her fingers around the wisps, which stubbornly tried to curl at the ends. He had not cut his hair since she first saw him on Earth. She would have to stop him before he made the tragic error of cutting it again.

Her soul mate's hands rummaged all over her back, shoulders, and her hips. He finally brought them to the bottom of her tunic and in unison removed the shift from her body. Rather than returning his lips to hers, he started to nuzzle her neck. He executed a combination of brushing and kissing her delicate skin with his lips. The result was magical. It felt so damn good after everything she had suffered.

Koel navigated her to the bed and made quick work of removing her leggings, as she got ahold of and removed his tunic. In her mind, she considered getting on her feet, removing his leggings, and exploring his anatomy with her own lips and tongue. However, her body wanted her soul mate inside her too much to further delay retrieving what she craved. She literally burned for him. Her body was creating its own natural aphrodisiac.

Whether it was the soul mate link or his own need, Koel entered her with one powerful thrust. JoAnna cried out with pure joy. They no longer had the specter of Jeryl Jarlyn over them. Their coming together was a natural reaction to the chemistry which existed between the two from the time they were born.

JoAnna shifted her hips and brought her knees closer to Koel's waist. Her adjustment brought Koel in deeper. He touched her physically and mentally where no man had ventured. For an insane minute, she imagined Koel was her own James T. Kirk.

Koel continued to enter and exit her body, as they both became slick with sweat. Nature's natural lubricant was working its magic both internally and externally. They operated as a perfectly oiled machine, no human frailties entered the picture.

Everything was almost perfect, except for the chatter from the communal pathways. How could she enjoy the pure perfection of what was happening to her with all the whining and annoying stories being shared? JoAnna had a natural barrier to protect herself against someone entering her mind. Why could she not shut herself off to the pathways that interrupted what she and

Koel had together? JoAnna concentrated and turned off the noise in her head, as she would shut off a radio.

Koel stopped in the middle of his latest penetration into her eager body and looked at her in concern. "What is it, Koel?"

"The pathways have shut off in my mind," Koel said. He was clearly alarmed by the silence within his own mind.

A grin crossed JoAnna's face. "I wanted our time together to be free of the intrusion of others. Because of the bond between us, my turning off the conversations in my mind carried over to yours. Now, back to work, baby, we have not finished yet."

A wicked expression lit Koel's face, before he lowered his forehead to hers and drove into her one last time. They fractured together, as they both climaxed. The rapture she had just experienced far exceeded what had occurred the first time they were together. JoAnna imagined their love making would only become more intense as they spent time together.

"I do not want to move," Koel whispered in her ear, "even to shower. Whatever you want, just ask it, but do not demand I move."

JoAnna laughed. Things had been perfect between them. Rising to shower, to eat, or for whatever reason, would break the euphoria she was currently in. Obviously, Koel felt the same way. "I would have to do you serious harm if you even suggested we do anything other than hold each other."

Everything was perfect. JoAnna had never been more physically and emotionally happy in her life. For however long she could, she wanted to hold on to what they had. Unfortunately, she figured it would not be as long as she wished.

What was the banging that interrupted his well-deserved sleep? Koel had never slept so deeply. He woke in a daze. His soul mate nestled next to him, also struggled to rejoin the world.

The door opened and Starc entered. "Why have you not been responding to us? We have been trying to contact you for twenty minutes. Shirl and I have been ordered to take JoAnna and Prime Adholm to the penal colony."

Koel still struggled to break the hold sleep still had on him. He had to be dreaming, his cousin just said they were ordered to the prison world. JoAnna muttered something into his neck.

"What is wrong with the two of you? Get up and meet us in the common room in ten minutes." Starc finished barking orders and left the room, slamming the door behind him.

The fog slowly left his mind, as Koel realized Starc's presence was very real and for some reason they had been ordered to take his soul mate and her uncle to a world no one returned from. Had Jeryl Jarlyn finally lost his grasp on reality?

Koel shook JoAnna, he needed her to come back to full consciousness. She had turned off all the pathways into their minds. He had never felt so helpless in his life. Something major had occurred and Koel was ignorant about what happened.

"JoAnna, you need to wake. Restore the communal and warrior pathways to our minds. While we slept, an order was given to send you and Prime Adholm to the penal colony. We need to know what is going on."

JoAnna shot up in bed. Her complexion had lost all color. She brought her head to her knees and placed her arms around her head. Slowly the chatter from different pathways reentered his mind. A sense of normality returned to Koel. He had never realized how accustomed he was to having so many people connected to him. For a short period, it was nice spending time literally alone with JoAnna, but he needed to rejoin his world.

Koel kissed his soul mate and rose to take a quick shower. He would meet with Starc and the others as JoAnna prepared. It would have been faster if they shared the shower, but Koel knew he would end up making love to her again and not meet the desired time frame Starc had set for their meeting.

The warrior link was focused on the logistics of the trip, not what had triggered the sentence. Koel did not want to interrupt the progress they made. He would ask his cousin all the questions which had plagued his mind since Starc entered JoAnna's bedroom.

Koel stepped into the common room, still towel drying his wet hair. Tolfer must have cooked up some quick bites while he and JoAnna slept. He grabbed a couple and popped them into his mouth before he started questioning his cousin.

"Why have JoAnna and her uncle been sentenced to the penal world? There have been no arrests, no hearings, nothing," Koel said.

"You got it wrong. JoAnna and Prime Adholm have been granted a visitation with Chartail in the penal world," Starc advised his cousin. "The rescue of Candy and Tolfer showed the Prime Ruler people would be able to enter the penal colony and leave without releasing any of the prisoners. Solfa will also accompany us to get intelligence for Jeryl Jarlyn."

Koel could feel himself pale. Benko Jarlyn was in the penal world. Although Solfa was aware Benko was alive and last living on Earth, she had never been in the position of being cross-examined by Jeryl Jarlyn about his son. All sorts of issues started to enter Koel's mind about the trip they were about to make to reunite a father with his daughter.

"Do you think Solfa would recognized Benko?" Koel asked. "We will not be able to warn them about our arrival. Fortunately, it will be daylight, so we do not have to worry about Drake visiting with Benko. I imagine there will be additional Crystal Telepathic Guards who will accompany us to protect Prime Adholm. I just hope Darden hides himself, as soon as he recognizes who is coming through the portal."

So many things could go wrong. Koel did not have time to deal with all the possibilities. If events went badly, there were various worlds Darden or Shirl could take them until forces were ready to mount an attack to bring Benko Jarlyn to power. Koel just hoped it did not come to that.

JoAnna walked into the common room and then directly into the kitchen. He imagined she planned to prepare herself some coffee. They had both woken in a fog. The latest disaster to befall them had jolted him wide awake. She quickly returned with two mugs, handed him one, and joined him on the couch.

"So, I finally get to meet my cousin Chartail." JoAnna must have listened through the warrior channel, as she showered and dressed. "From everything I have heard about her, she sounds like an emotionally strong woman. She would have to be, considering all she has been through. At least her father has finally come through for her. When I first met him, he was shattered by what he did to his only child. I cannot imagine my adoptive parents ever deserting me like that."

"We better head on out," Starc announced. "Prime Adholm continually pleaded with the Prime Ruler to allow him to visit Chartail since Candy returned from that world. Now that Jarlyn has given in, The Prime is anxious to see his daughter."

"Were there any inquiries into Traves Choaks?" JoAnna asked.

"None," Starc answered. "Jeryl Jarlyn appears to be happy to be rid of the problem. We still do not know if he set up JoAnna or genuinely believed she would be able to break through his mind without any injury to herself."

"Yet again, JoAnna's destination has been communicated through the communal pathways. There is still the earlier attack on her we have not been able to solve. I have asked for a contingent of guards to escort us to the portal. Solfa also has to research if Traves had any family. We do not want any upset siblings coming after us." Koel was not going to take any chances with his soul mate's life.

When he returned from the penal world, finding who fired that laser shot at JoAnna would be his first priority. There was still someone out there who wished to do harm to his soul mate. Koel only hoped it was a single individual and not a band of rebels who viewed her in the same light as Jeryl Jarlyn.

Chapter 21

The Troyk Penal Colony World

JoAnna was not sure what she had expected in the Troyk penal colony world, but not the rudimentary huts, which made up the village her cousin lived in. There were children living in what she could only call squalor. When she returned to the Troyk universe, she would have a discussion with Jeryl Jarlyn about the horrible poor living conditions the prisoners had to live in. How had Candy ever survived here for weeks?

Very few people were in the village when they arrived. She figured the majority of the occupants of the settlement were out foraging or hunting for food. These people had to work for everything they had. A number of older women welcomed them and brought them refreshments. They must have thought they were prisoners sentenced their world, although no one asked about the armed guards who had accompanied them. JoAnna had imagined they would have recognized Shirl and the others who had helped save their lives during the earlier attack.

"Where is everyone?" JoAnna asked. "We are looking for Chartail Adholm, this is her father and I am her cousin." The two women who stayed behind with them did not seem surprised by her announcement. They must have recognized Prime Adholm, since he had held a position in the Troyk government for over twenty years. Most of the surviving inmates of this world had been dissidents against the government.

"They will return after they harvest fruit, chop wood, or hunt the animals we will have for dinner," one of the women answered. "Ours is a constant battle to survive. Except for the children, there is no time to relax and take it easy."

JoAnna had no idea what she had done to offend the woman, but the hostility in her voice had been clear. She would have no idea of her relationship with the Prime Ruler. JoAnna had thought they would be welcomed with open arms, since they had brought much needed supplies

A striking blonde entered the encampment from JoAnna's left side. She immediately made a beeline for Shirl and Candy. The woman had to be Chartail. Prime Adholm had momentarily stepped behind one of the huts and had missed his daughter's entrance. Chartail glowed. This environment, as rustic as it was, certainly agreed with her.

"Chartail," Prime Adholm cried after he rejoined them. JoAnna saw she was momentarily taken aback by her father's presence. Once she recovered from the surprise, Chartail ran into her dad's arms. JoAnna felt a stab of pain in her heart, she missed her own father dreadfully.

"Benko and Darden, do not enter the camp. We have company. My father has arrived with a number of CT Guards. Starc, Shirl, Candy, Solfa, and Koel are among the group." JoAnna heard Chartail's warning through the warrior channel, loud and clear.

JoAnna looked up to see Cassie Jarlyn walk in her direction. The girl stopped dead in her tracks as soon as she saw JoAnna. A variety of looks passed over Cassie's face, until an expression of total boredom replaced the more dramatic of the expressions.

"Who are you guys?" Cassie asked. She eyed the area where the natural portal existed. "Are you new prisoners sent because you oppose the current Troyk ruler?" JoAnna was relieved the girl had asked the right question. No one would imagine she was anyone other than a child of a dissident born in this world.

"My name is JoAnna Carlson," she answered. "We have been allowed to visit my cousin Chartail."

"We?" the girl asked inquisitively.

"I am Prime Adholm, Chartail's father." The Prime Representative still had not released his daughter. JoAnna had not seen this side of the man before, he seemed so loving.

Cassie alternated between glaring at Chartail and Prime Adholm. "Will you take her back to the Troyk universe with you?" There was a hopeful tone to her voice. Perhaps Cassie was jealous of Chartail's beauty and feared Darden would prefer her. That seemed highly unlikely, since the two were soul mates. Regardless, there was some kind of tension between the two women.

"I wish that was possible," Prime Adholm answered. "For now, I just have to be content visiting with Chartail. We will come often, we will bring supplies with us. Let my niece JoAnna know what you would like and she will make sure we bring it on our next visit."

Prime Adholm's directions gave JoAnna the perfect opportunity to steer Cassie away from the group and talk to her alone. "Why don't you show me around and you can share with me whatever you would like brought on our next trip."

JoAnna and Cassie left the camp and walked along the lake shore. The sun was shining, causing the water to shimmer. It was such an idyllic scene, compared to the chaos she imagined normally was present in the village. JoAnna hoped the lake had fish in it, which would feed the people in the village. On a hot day, she imagined the water would be refreshing.

"I thought you came here to see Chartail," Cassie said. "Why are you not worshiping at her feet like the rest of them?" Boy, she had nailed Cassie's jealousy of Chartail right on the head.

JoAnna knew she would not be able to reason the girl out of her feelings about Chartail. Those would have to wither with time. Alex had told JoAnna about her initial negative impressions about Chartail, which were quickly replaced with gratitude after she stood up against a man who had been stalking her. For now, JoAnna knew she needed to focus on Cassie and her needs.

"What is really bothering you, Cassie? You are obviously here by choice, although some modern conveniences would be a tremendous help."

"I have waited so long to be with Darden," Cassie confessed. "When he came here to live, I thought we would finally be together. But, no! We kiss and all, but he won't go beyond that. It's not like I'm under eighteen anymore." The normally chatty girl dumped her body on the sand and sulked.

With everything she had been through with Koel, JoAnna could understand how Cassie felt. She wondered if Darden held off having sex with her for the same reasons her soul mate had. JoAnna joined Cassie on the sand and took her hand. Cassie turned and JoAnna could see the tears in her eyes.

"Are you a mind control telepath?" The girl looked suddenly frightened and merely nodded her head. "I thought so. How powerful are you?"

"Too powerful," Cassie whispered. "I see how the villagers look at Chartail in fear because of her gifts, I don't want them to be afraid of me."

"I thought Chartail did not have mind control telepathic abilities," JoAnna said.

"The baby transferred his or her power to her for the time being. As soon as the child is born, she will no longer be burdened with the abilities. I wish I could rid myself of them as well."

A thousand thoughts flew through JoAnna's mind. Chartail had been through so much, she hoped the child was conceived in a non-violent act. Her stomach started to churn just thinking about it. JoAnna needed to spend some time alone with her cousin before they returned to the Troyk universe.

"Cassie, in this world they know you are Benko Jarlyn's daughter. They have to know you have power. You need to learn to control it, not hide it. If you unleash the power without training, you may end up doing something you will never be able to live with. Darden probably senses that and is fearful of providing you further enhanced telepathic abilities the first time you make love. Fear is uncontrollable if you can't see or measure what you are up against. Chartail is a very brave woman. If you go to her for help, together with your soul mate and your father, you will mature into an incredible woman."

Cassie's eyes seemed to get a spark in them and she embraced JoAnna. "You need to come back and visit often. I have had no one to talk to and I have been so alone. It is funny how you can be surrounded by people and feel so isolated."

"Let's head back to the village. We are supposed to be strangers. If we are gone too long, they will start to suspect something."

They walked the short distance back to the village. Cassie was back to the vocal child she had ridden to Sedona with. For the time being, the issues that had been troubling Cassie were forgotten. JoAnna made a mental note of all the things Cassie wanted them to bring from the Troyk universe on their next visit.

When they returned, the CT Guards, Solfa, and Prime Adholm were gone. "What happened?" JoAnna asked Chartail, who appeared to be awaiting their return.

"My father was overwhelmed by seeing me again and how I was living. He got over excited and Solfa determined it was best Shirl return him to the Troyk universe and return for you after they get my father medical assistance."

Cassie stood beside them, rocking on her feet. She was like a puppy, with too much energy. "I need to find Darden," Cassie finally said. "Chartail, I want to talk with you later." The girl leaned in and gave JoAnna and then Chartail a kiss before she ran off.

"What did you say to her?" Chartail asked. She looked like someone who had just opened a birthday present and got exactly what she wanted. "I have tried to develop a relationship with her, but it has been next to impossible. Cassie takes everything I try to do the wrong way."

"I don't know what things would have been like in the Troyk universe, but being a teenager on Earth was no picnic. At eighteen you have many of the responsibilities of an adult, but very little experience to properly function as one. To add insult to injury, Cassie is burdened with powers which terrify her. Can we take a walk?"

Chartail looked around the village and finally nodded. Rather than returning to the beach, they headed toward the forest on the far side of the encampment. It was warming and the wooded trail offered relief as well as protection from the sun.

"Cassie tells me you are pregnant and have developed mind control telepathic abilities." JoAnna put it all out there at once. From this point on, she could somewhat relax as they talked.

JoAnna was not sure what type of reaction she was going to get from Chartail, but she had not expected laughter. "I can see you grew up with Alex, Shirl, and Candy. Those three do not hold back. Yes, I am pregnant with my soul mate's child. And before you ask, it is Benko Jarlyn's."

The tables had certainly turned, JoAnna was overwhelmed with the news. She had not been aware Benko Jarlyn was now residing in the penal world, until Chartail had provided the earlier warning through the warrior link. It made sense for him to leave the Earth realm after JoAnna entered the Troyk universe. There would have been too many questions about Benko. She imagined Jeryl Jarlyn's gatherers were scouring Arizona, looking for his son.

"At first the power terrified me. I had been bitter about how I was treated as a child and came to despise the ability. Then I realized, it was not the telepathic gift, but how the possessor used it. Benko spent most of his adult life on Ginkgo Terra and only leveraged it for self-defense purposes. An occasional gatherer would find him and Benko had to deal with convincing the crystal telepath he was not the person he sought."

A woman shouted some distance behind them. JoAnna and Chartail stopped walking and tried to determine what was going on. Candy and Koel ran toward them. "Get down," Candy shouted and launched herself at Chartail, driving her to the ground. A spear came flying in JoAnna's direction. Had Koel not tackled her, the weapon would have landed in her chest.

⌒〇

Chartail hit the ground hard, with Candy landing on her with little grace. She was not sure what had happened, but she knew of Candy's talents, she imagined the warrior woman of Troyk legends had saved her life. It made sense not to move until Candy got off her and advised it was safe to get up. There were various people shouting around her, the loudest of which was her soul mate.

"Find the bastard who threw that damn spear," Benko Jarlyn ordered, "Secure the area. Keep Chartail and JoAnna down until we know it is safe. I want to know what the hell is going on."

"The immediate danger has passed," Clarke informed Benko. "Whoever threw the spear is no longer in the vicinity. He may have doubled back to the village or gone deeper into the woods. It is one of our spears."

Chartail knew the weapon had been either stolen or one of the villagers had attacked her and JoAnna. Since no one knew who JoAnna was, Chartail was the likely target. Thank goodness Candy had been part of the Troyk party who had accompanied her cousin to the penal world.

Candy rolled off her and Benko offered Chartail his hand to assist her in getting back on her feet. Her savior brushed off dirt and leaves from her tunic and leggings, as Chartail righted herself. "Thank you, Candy."

"Frankly, I do not know who the intended target was," Candy admitted. "Most of my visions have been related to JoAnna. She was introduced as your cousin when we arrived. There may be someone here who had a score to settle with Prime Adholm. All the CT Guards left with your uncle. I stayed around to guard JoAnna. Feelings kept nagging me that something was going to happen."

She turned to see her cousin clutching onto her soul mate. Koel tried to calm JoAnna. Chartail was between the attacker and his prey, she had to be dealt with in order for him to get to JoAnna. Candy had brought her down because Chartail was in immediate danger.

"Feelings or not," Benko said, "I want both women guarded until JoAnna exits this world and protection to continue for Chartail until the culprit is caught." Her soul mate finally took her in his arms.

Chartail was getting used to Benko being a leader first and a soul mate second. It was something she would have to come to terms with if their relationship was going to work. She had been a spoiled brat most of her life, not unlike Cassie. He had a world to ultimately govern and she was destined to be by his side, supporting his path in life.

"It was probably one of the stray lunatics who still wander through the forest," Chartail said. She did not want to burden Benko with worry related to her safety. The poor man had enough on his shoulders.

"There is also the possibility word spread to another village on the outskirts, where all telepathic usage has been outlawed." Benko was in his element, he used his superior intelligence. "Knowing we have people with mind control telepathic powers may have put them on the offensive. Either way, we need to strengthen our troops. I want Darden to start visiting worlds where they sent dissidents and bring those willing to fight here. They can act as reinforcements until we are ready to make our move."

Koel came alongside Benko and the two started to plan their next steps. Darden soon joined them. Chartail waited for her cousin to catch up with her, she too had been temporarily abandoned by her soul mate.

"Are you all right?" she asked JoAnna.

"I have had someone try to kill me with a laser blast, suck my telepathic abilities from my skull, and now tried to skewer me with a spear. I'm just peachy!"

"And we don't know what the Prime Ruler has planned for you," Candy added.

"Oh yes, let's not forget about Jeryl Jarlyn. Chartail, do you know that monster blackmailed Koel to make love to me with his sister's life? One minute I think I am in the most remarkable dream of my existence, the next I am in a nightmare."

"Things have not been easy for any of us for some time," Chartail admitted. "I doubt we will see matters improve until Benko is back in the Troyk universe and has liberated his people. We have a long and hard road ahead of us."

"Jo Jo has been able to link into our private channel, Chartail," Candy said. "We still do not know what it represents, since so far only you, Alex, Shirl, Jo

Jo, and I have been able to enter. We are unaware of any Troyk legends related to a channel populated with a select number of women. There has to be some significance behind it. Someone needs to study the old legends. Alex likes that type of crap, I will have her start researching when we return."

"In the meantime, Candy, you need to become JoAnna's shadow," Chartail said. "I know you have been assigned to Shirl, but that particular woman does not need someone to protect her. She is probably the most powerful being in any universe. JoAnna's weapon is her mind. I am sure it is impressive, but it has its limitations when someone is out to kill her."

Why these women all of a sudden looked to her as their leader, was beyond Chartail's comprehension. Shirl and Candy had both saved her life, yet they abdicated leadership to her. Surprisingly, it was a natural role for her to play.

As they made their way into the village, there was a commotion around the center gathering place. Several people held a struggling man. Benko, Koel, and Darden went to investigate. Chartail's eyes immediately sought to find Cassie. To her relief, the girl was safely with a group of young women preparing dinner. They had temporarily abandoned their task to watch the confrontation.

Candy placed herself in front of JoAnna and Chartail. JoAnna placed her hand on Candy's shoulder. *"They may need me,"* JoAnna communicated through the channel the three women shared.

"It is too dangerous. Besides, Benko has the ability to use mind control telepathic techniques." Candy responded through the same pathway.

"Benko and Cassie live in this world. The community is already freaked out about Chartail's new gifts. I will be leaving through the portal and will not represent a threat to them."

JoAnna stepped around Candy, but Chartail grabbed her hand before she got any further. "You do not have to do this."

The woman who Chartail knew would one day become her friend smiled and said, "Yes, I do."

Koel could not believe his eyes as JoAnna approached. The last time he glanced in her direction, she was safely behind Candy. Whatever his soul mate had planned, Koel knew he was not going to like it.

"The man endangered my life, as well as Chartail's," JoAnna announced. "I can assist in the interrogation of the suspect." Koel wished he could disagree with what she had stated, but to his utter horror, he could not. JoAnna was the right choice to cross-examine the man. They did not want to scare the populace of this village with the powers either Benko or Cassie possessed. Even Koel was unsure of the extent of their gifts.

Clarke, the head of Benko's guard, came forward to meet JoAnna. "We caught him returning a couple of the spears he had borrowed to dispose of the two of you. The idiot could have abandoned them in the woods, but I imagined he feared we would need them if the village was attacked." The man's regard for JoAnna surprised Koel. He imagined being identified as Prime Adholm's niece gave them an idea of her power, as well as the fact her parents were dissidents.

His soul mate approached the prisoner. Koel took his place behind her, placing his hands on her bare neck. If she was going to enter the man's mind, Koel would accompany her. Starc was able to navigate the portals through Shirl's telepathic powers, Koel was going to see if he could do the same.

Koel knew the instant JoAnna entered the man's mind. He saw flashes of memories belonging to the prisoner, first in the Troyk universe and then in the penal colony. JoAnna navigated thru thoughts to find what she was looking for. As a parasite, Koel continued along the threads of her mind control talents.

"The thought is right there, JoAnna," he communicated through the soul mate link. Connected in this way, he had naturally transmitted the thought, as if he was thinking to himself. The sensation was incredible. They were truly one in this regard. "He had fought the mind control telepaths in the Troyk universe, had to endure living with the portal guardians, only to have his mind manipulated by a pregnant woman. When he saw Prime Adholm and his niece enter his world, this man knew he had to take action." Koel said the last part aloud, so the rest of the group would know why the prisoner did what he did.

"You see how they can steal from your mind," the prisoner yelled. "I tried to save us all from them manipulating us."

"What would you have done, Abbout?" Benko Jarlyn asked, "Would Cassie and I be your next victims? There may be others in the village who hide their true talents because of what they fought."

"Chartail first used her latent talent against me," Clarke shared with the group, "but she has worked hard to control her abilities. Our hopes are dependent on Benko Jarlyn overtaking his father, but Benko is a mind control telepath as well. The powers are among us, as is the crystal telepathic gift. It is a blessing that can be used in a productive manner."

Koel knew Clarke held a lot of respect within the community. Murmurs of agreement were shared among the people gathered around. The man ceased his struggles, realizing he had lost his battle to sway the crowd.

"What do we do with him?" Darden asked. "He may attempt to hurt you, Cassie, or Chartail again. We cannot run the risk of him harming anyone and we cannot trust his word not to attack again."

"Take him back to the Troyk universe," someone from the crowd yelled.

"He knows too much about this world and Benko Jarlyn." Koel knew they could not take Abbout back with them. His crimes were grave, but sending him to the Nightshade universe was too extreme. Since he was not a mind control telepath, taking him to Ginkgo Terra would be a death sentence. "In the past we have sent dissidents to the Standish universe. The world has recovered from an ice age, once again inhabitable for humans. It is a tough existence, but Abbout existed here, so I imagine he would be able to live there with few issues."

Benko Jarlyn approached the prisoner. "Would that be acceptable to you? You present a threat to my family, I cannot afford to give you leniency."

"Yes," the man said. "I should have trusted in you in the flesh, as I had when you were a dream to our cause. My apologies to your mate and her cousin. I regret my actions and accept my fate."

Darden stood near the natural portal and partially entered it, setting the frequencies within to open a wormhole to the Standish universe. "A settlement is not far from the portal. Share with them as much as you like." After Darden's instructions, Abbout entered the portal.

Shirl would return shortly to take them back to the Troyk universe. Koel could still feel fragments of what it had been like to be of one mind with his soul mate. It had been an incredible experience, one he hoped they would share again.

JoAnna and his abilities continued to evolve, which made her more of a target. They had foiled one attempt, but more seemed to be mounting. There was still someone in the Troyk universe who had attempted to kill her. Koel doubted dealing with him would be as easy as it had been with Abbout.

Chapter 22

~

The Troyk Universe

The smidgens of the euphoria JoAnna felt from joining minds with Koel was lost as soon as they exited the portal. A squadron of palace guards were waiting for them. JoAnna doubted they were there strictly present for her safety.

"We have orders to bring Miss Carlson to see Jeryl Jarlyn," one of the guards informed them. "The audience is to be private. No one else is to accompany us. There is another contingent of guards at the trail head. They will arrest anyone who interferes with our delivering Miss Carlson to Jeryl Jarlyn."

JoAnna believed she was finally going to discover what the Prime Ruler had planned. Why else would he require they meet alone? The uncertainty of her situation caused her sleepless nights. Only physical or mental exhaustion guaranteed her any rest.

Broken communication related to Koel's rage at Jarlyn's demand distracted her thoughts. Some fragment of their earlier mental connection must still exist. She and Koel had to choose their battles, this was not the time.

"Don't fight this, Koel," JoAnna shared through the warrior link. *"Candy, do you sense anything related to me or Koel?"* She didn't have Candy's abilities, but JoAnna did not feel at ease where Koel and Jeryl Jarlyn were concerned. Until she made The Prime Ruler realize Koel enhanced her powers, she feared he would look at her soul mate as being dispensable. JoAnna could not share these impressions with Koel, his pride would not allow him to back down in his role of protecting her.

"Frankly, there are so many abstract impressions I am getting, I cannot decipher a particular threat."

They were so far up the mountain, the chance of the others having heard Candy was slight, but at least the guards were not privy to their discussion. JoAnna had hoped for a more specific warning, in order for her to better manage Koel. He had an arrogance about him that would only agitate the one man they needed to be careful around.

JoAnna needed to better understand the legends of soul mates to reinforce the need to have Koel near her constantly. Candy would not be able to help in this manner, but perhaps Tarah would, since she was a mind control telepath. Who would be more likely to dive into stories of legends, than someone who carried the trait? Once they got closer to town, JoAnna would be able to contact Tarah and get the information she desperately needed.

Because of Candy's role in the CT Guard, she was allowed to walk beside JoAnna. Shirl, Starc, and Koel were forced to make their way down the mountain several yards behind them. JoAnna felt as if she was walking to her own execution.

They were half way down the mountain when the communal pathways started to invade her mind. Since the warrior link was stronger than any of the other pathways, with the exception of the soul mate channel, JoAnna knew she could now contact Tarah. She was anxious to see how close fables came to the truth.

"Tarah, I am being escorted to The Palace to meet with Jeryl Jarlyn. Can you tell me any of the legends related to mind control telepathic soul mates?" JoAnna could only hope Tarah would have been as inquisitive as she would have been to learn these stories. Their lives might end up being dependent on it.

"There are not many that are in the books we read as children," Tarah admitted. *"When I was in college, I found an ancient text in the archives which told about a fifth-generation mated female mind control telepath. She was able to join as one with her soul mate and dive deep into another's mind. So deep, she could not only read the person's past and present, but his future intent as well. It was really quite fascinating."*

Koel and JoAnna had already accomplished the joining as one, but had not delved deeper into Abbout's mind, other than to determine his guilt for the current crime he had committed. *"Was there anything else?"*

"If legends are correct, a fifth-generation mind control telepath who has mated will be able to get past the half-truth defense. Her soul mate is not required for that to occur, according to what I read."

The last part JoAnna could work around. After all, they were only stories and JoAnna and Koel were the real thing.

"Thanks, Tarah. I will let you know if I need anything else. If you remember any other stories, I would be interested in hearing them."

"I know where to find the book. Tomorrow I will head to the Starling Province and see if I can check out the manuscript and bring it back for you to read."

When they reached the outskirts of the city, Tarsea was there to meet them. He called Koel over to talk with him and her soul mate reluctantly agreed. JoAnna continued to walk toward The Palace, thankful Tarsea had interfered. She was not sure if Alex had asked him or if Tarsea realized he needed to rescue his friend before he did something they would all regret.

As usual, they entered The Palace without going through security checkpoints. Candy continued to walk beside her, no one had separated them yet. When they stood before Jeryl Jarlyn's study, they were instructed only JoAnna could enter. Nothing good ever was communicated when they met in his private lair.

JoAnna took a deep breath and entered the room, expecting the worst. She stopped dead in her tracks when she saw Jeryl Jarlyn behind his desk with a blood soaked handkerchief in one of his hands. His left hand was closed in a fist, but yellow light was visible.

She got a hold of her senses and ran to see if she could help Jeryl Jarlyn. His fist was hot to the touch, no doubt from the energy emitted from the stone. "Jeryl, you need to release the crystal before you do any more harm to yourself."

"I could not enter that little brat's mind, but you were able to," Jarlyn admitted. "The crystal will give me more power, which will enable me to be as powerful as you."

If Jeryl Jarlyn wanted to win a pissing contest, why did he force Koel and her to have sex? Their mating would only make her that much stronger. JoAnna continued to have issues reading Jarlyn and his motives.

"If Benko has a child, she would be a fifth-generation telepath, like you are. The power my grandchild would possess would be obscene." JoAnna was not sure if the Prime Ruler talked to her or himself. It was irrelevant, she needed Jeryl Jarlyn to release the crystal before he started to hemorrhage or worse have a stroke.

"Show me the beautiful crystal you are holding," JoAnna said. "I love when you tell me the properties of the crystals in your collection. When I see Shirl, I can almost match her knowledge of these magnificent stones."

"This one is so pretty, but powerful." The Prime Ruler opened his hand and showed her the glowing crystal. She had only seen crystals behave that way when they opened a portal.

"May I?" JoAnna asked. After the Prime Ruler nodded, JoAnna gingerly touched the crystal with the tip of one of her fingers, to make sure she would not burn herself. Although the rock was hot, it was not scalding. As soon as JoAnna picked up the yellow stone, it no longer beamed out light. "How do you make it glow?"

"Only the most powerful among us can do that. It is how the Prime Ruler can establish dominance in his realm." JoAnna had heard Shirl and Candy question what the Prime Ruler did with all the crystals, now she knew. It was also a dangerous topic to continue discussing. The Prime Ruler was truly losing his mind and until Benko took control from him, the man was extremely dangerous. No one in this world would dare stand up to Jeryl Jarlyn. His control was absolute and deadly.

"You wanted to see me, sir?" JoAnna did not want to do anything to threaten him.

The Prime Ruler looked at JoAnna for several moments with a blank expression on his face. It was as if he had turned off. She was about to touch him, when his head jerked and he had his faculties once again.

"While you were visiting Chartail in the penal world, several dissidents were returned. I would like you to interview them. They are locked in the basement cells, you can interrogate them in the morning. We can all use some sleep."

The Prime Ruler rose and left the room, not saying another word to JoAnna. She did not have the opportunity to tell the Prime Ruler Koel should help her interview the prisoners. Hopefully, Solfa would also be present. Considering how much she feared the head of intelligence when she first arrived, JoAnna liked having her around when they were at The Palace. Solfa did an excellent job of running interference.

When JoAnna exited the Prime Ruler's study, two guards were there to meet her. She attempted to walk around them, but they detained her. "The

Prime Ruler has set up rooms for you to occupy. He does not want you endangered walking the streets of Aster Province."

"Candy is capable of protecting me," JoAnna countered. "We reside in the same residence."

"Miss Phillips has been escorted from The Palace and ordered to return to her home. As I already stated, rooms have been prepared for you."

JoAnna considered using mind control telepathy on the guards to convince them they did not properly understand their orders. However, the compulsion would not last long. Once they returned to their regular duties or dealt with a commanding officer, both would realize she had manipulated their brains. She doubted she would even make it out of The Palace. She was a prisoner and there was nothing she could do about it.

JoAnna did not get any sleep the night before. Koel continued to argue with her through their shared link about having given in too easily to the Prime Ruler and then dealing with his failed attempts at joining her. It got to the point she wanted to ring his neck.

A change of clothing was provided to her from the most expensive store in Aster Province. The toiletries in the washroom were of the highest quality. She was in a gilded cage, but a cage, regardless how nice it was.

When she exited her quarters, she was guided to the Prime Ruler's greeting rooms to share breakfast with him. JoAnna was tired, angry, and had a caffeine headache by the time she joined him. She quickly poured herself a cup of coffee and had several sips before she addressed her jailer.

"Jeryl, I cannot stay here," JoAnna said. "Once the mating link opened, if I do not have regular contact with my soul mate, it feels like I have regressed in power. Koel seems to be able to balance and enhance my telepathic abilities." She was not totally lying, her lack of sleep and their arguments had tapped her physically and mentally.

The Prime Ruler's eyes roamed her face, down her body, and then made eye contact with her once again. "You do look a bit fatigued. Your mental barrier feels weaker this morning, although still impenetrable. I had merely your safety in mind when I requested you stay the night."

JoAnna choked on the coffee she had just swallowed. If what she experienced last night was a suggestion, she feared what an order would feel like. She continued to cough, trying to deal with the liquid that went down the wrong way. It did not surprise her the Prime Ruler sat like a statue, as she continued to get control of herself. Finally, after taking several sips of water, JoAnna had stopped hacking.

"If I am going to be of any use today, I will need Koel by my side." JoAnna took a bite of the danish she had placed on her plate. There were other items available, but JoAnna always chose what she was familiar with. Since the Troyk people took the best from the worlds they explored, she figured the unidentifiable items were delicious. One day she should request a doggy bag and try the other items with Alex. That girl could sure eat!

"He has been sent for, even before you requested it. My apologies for last night. I was eager to have you interview the men we have captured and did not want to delay."

It was well known the Prime Ruler was paranoid of the dissidents who had left their world. There had been numerous attacks made on his life, although they had all occurred from within the Troyk universe. Every entry through the portal into this world was investigated by CT Guards. Gatherers traveled between worlds looking for people who escaped and could present a future threat. Plots to unseat him had been constant since he took control, even by his own son. JoAnna could not imagine living that way.

"Three prisoners were brought back from the Standish universe. We believe they originated from this world and present a danger to the order we have established here." It took all her control to swallow what was in her mouth, without spitting it out or having it go down the wrong way.

"Three people have been brought back from the Standish universe to be questioned. If Abbout is among them, we are so screwed." JoAnna finished her communication through the warrior link and took another bite of her pastry as if her world was not being ripped apart at the seams.

⌒๑

After her breakfast with the Prime Ruler, JoAnna was led to the third floor to help conduct the interview. Solfa would join them, as well as Koel. The frightening part was a second mind control telepath would join them. He was an up and comer in the intelligence community and appeared to be totally faithful to the Prime Ruler.

JoAnna was the first to arrive in the room and her stomach rolled as soon as her eyes met Abbout's. She noted the surprise on his face when she entered the room. He was bound to the chair and the floor with chains.

There were two other men restrained next to Abbout. JoAnna had no clue if Koel and his friends had been involved in getting them out of the Troyk universe. She started to regret having had breakfast.

"My name is JoAnna Carlson and I will be one of the two mind control telepaths involved in questioning you." It was her way of warning Abbout another would be able to determine if he was lying or not. JoAnna had no way of knowing if Abbout was proficient at answering questions with half-truths. If the same questions were asked a variety of ways numerous times, most people would slip up somewhere along the line.

Solfa was the next to enter the room. She glared at each of the prisoners and JoAnna could sense the fear this woman instilled in their minds. JoAnna herself had been a victim of the same intimidation.

The head of intelligence reviewed the folders on the desk. JoAnna prayed Koel would be the next one to enter the room. Perhaps together they could project the mental barrier they now both possessed to Abbout. Hopefully, the man across the table from her worked on his cover story, reviewing it in his mind again and again.

To her utter relief, her soul mate was the next to join them. As if he was a schooled actor, Koel did not react to seeing Abbout. He sat next to JoAnna and took her hand. A sensation of warmth and safety washed over her. She did not let down her guard, but she relaxed enough to let her shoulders come down from her ears. If she was on Earth, she would have made an appointment for a deep tissue massage.

A young, good looking man entered and took the chair on the other side of Solfa. He seemed at ease with himself and a threat to their very lives. Sensing her unease, Koel squeezed her hand.

"My name is Solfa Theflar and I will conduct this interview. I will be aided by two mind control telepaths: JoAnna Carlson and Rupheart Stollar. The other gentleman is one of my intelligence operatives." Koel once again squeezed her hand, warning her not to react. "We believe you are all from the Troyk universe and at one time were dissidents against our government. The other residents in the Standish universe had papers that proved they had legally migrated from our world and paid a crystal telepath to transport them. Why anyone chooses to live in that world is beyond me, but that is not why we are here today."

Rupheart Stollar took his opportunity to take over the interview and impress Solfa. The man had a lot to learn about impressing a superior, who happened to be a woman. "What are your names and why were you in the Standish universe? You, go first." He pointed to Abbout. Their time had just run out.

JoAnna entered Abbout's mind, with Koel's consciousness in tow. If she would read thoughts, perhaps she could manufacture them. A story planted in his mind by a mind control telepath should ring true.

"I was disillusioned by the Troyk government twenty-two years ago, just after Benko Jarlyn failed to overthrow his tyrannical father. Through the black market, I paid a crystal telepath to take me to another world where I could find peace. He sent me to the Standish universe. I worked myself to death trying to survive in that world." Abbout said the words aloud, as JoAnna placed them in his mind. As far as Abbout was concerned, it was a true memory.

"He is telling the truth," Rupheart said. "We might as well cut him loose and have him returned to that hell hole. His past political beliefs have not changed and he should not be allowed to stay in our harmonious world."

JoAnna was relieved when Abbout was released and a group of CT Guards accompanying Shirl arrived to escort the prisoner to the portal. The other two men were interviewed and their stories confirmed. They had legally migrated to the other world, but were not carrying the necessary paperwork to prove their claims.

Both men spoke highly of the Troyk universe and the trials they experienced in the Standish universe. To JoAnna's surprise, they were offered the opportunity to stay in the Troyk universe and both declined the offer. They did not state so, but they preferred the hard life in the Standish universe, over the mind control influences of the Troyk universe.

She had used her power in a new way and she had fooled a fellow mind control telepath. The immediate danger was over, but JoAnna knew she could not rest easy. This world presented one challenge after another. She needed to traverse this universe carefully, otherwise she would find herself tripped up. No matter how many items she concentrated on, she still could not forget about the laser shot that almost killed her.

Chapter 23

JoAnna felt like she had been through the wringer. These people traveled from world to world, as if they were going across town. Her life was threatened, not because of who she was, but because she was a powerful mind control telepath. She just needed a little normalcy, a little "me" time.

"I would like to do some shopping." JoAnna laughed at the pained expression on Koel's face. "Why don't you go back to your normal routine? Shirl, Starc, and Candy are accompanying Abbout back to the Standish universe. I doubt I am going to be in any danger as I walk from shop to shop in broad daylight."

She could see the indecision on Koel's face. It was unrealistic to be under guard twenty-four hours a day. JoAnna could not live her life like this.

"I'll get something naughty to wear tonight," she whispered in Koel's ear. The flirtation had an immediate effect on her soul mate. JoAnna could feel a certain part of his anatomy stiffen with her comment. "I want to start living in your apartment. You should head over there and get rid of anything you don't want me to see. There will be a palace guard with me until I am delivered to our place." Having referred to Koel's residence that way had a nice ring to it.

"I will give your bodyguard the address. Do you think you can find something in red, like the dress you wore the first time I saw you?" Koel's usual icy blue eyes were several shades lighter from the heat he generated internally.

When she traveled back to Earth to see her father, JoAnna would have to bring the red dress back with her. Maybe she would start a new fashion trend in this universe. Troyk evening wear relied on exposing the woman's body, not necessarily showing it off to its advantage. The little red number did a job on Koel, no doubt about that.

Koel gave her a goodbye kiss to tide her over until this evening. The contact had not been enough, she had a voracious appetite for this man. He telepathically communicated his address to her guard and then took off.

JoAnna's bodyguard walked behind her, as she started toward the dress shop she wanted to hit first. His positioning gave him a better vantage point to identify any threat present. Because of his proximity, she felt she was being stalked.

They were barely halfway to their destination, when a laser shot was fired and JoAnna was dragged down by her guard. As she lay on the ground, she felt blood seeping onto her back from the dead man on top of her. Several more shots were fired and screams were heard all around.

She struggled to get the dead weight off her and seek shelter. JoAnna was just about to call out to Koel, when her head was lifted and then pounded into the ground. She was so stunned, JoAnna did not call out for help. The voices and static from all the pathways quieted in her head. The body was rolled off her and she was lifted into someone's arms. This was not a lover's caress, but a determined madman's rough handling. He leaned her against a wall and drove her head into the stone structure.

"You make a sound or struggle, I will end you right here and now." She nearly gagged at the smell of onions he had on his breath. JoAnna was not going to do anything to provoke the madman before her. She nodded her understanding and did not provide any resistance as they walked into the delivery entrance adjacent to the alley they were in. Unlike Traves Choaks, this man was large and foreboding. He looked like any number of bouncers she had seen standing in front of bars in the past.

Her assailant pulled out another crystal weapon and killed the two clerks who were in the wrong place at the wrong time. He dragged her in front of a number of conveyances used to deliver large appliances. JoAnna was tied up, gagged, and pushed into one of the cargo holders. When she struggled against what was being done to her, her captor punched her hard several times.

The box she was forced into gave her very little room to move. It was not long before JoAnna felt she was being relocated. She was tied in such a fashion she was unable to make any noise alerting anyone to her presence. The streets quieted; she could hear only the sound of the wheels as it was dragged against the cement.

Although she tried to use a number of the closed pathways to alert Koel and her friends to what had happened, JoAnna was still not connecting. She did not know if it was the injury to her head or the enclosure she was in.

Suddenly, JoAnna noticed light did not penetrate the container. Was oxygen entering her prison or was she consuming the little breathable air she had? JoAnna started to panic. When did damage start to occur in the brain when it did not get enough oxygen? Was it three minutes? She needed to calm down and use her telepathic abilities to slow her heart and respiration rates.

She started to get light-headed. JoAnna was not sure if it was because of what she was doing or the container was running out of air. She made one more attempt to contact Koel through their telepathic link before she lost consciousness.

⌒〇

Koel had not gotten far when he heard laser fire. The communal pathways immediately reacted to the incident and he picked up the start of communication from JoAnna, before it was cut off. He started to run in the direction of where the incident had occurred.

Four bodies were on the ground, including JoAnna's guard. He had been shot in the back. There was no sign of his soul mate. Chaos was all around him. The palace guards attempted to restore order, as well as process the crime scene. One of their own had been killed and they were taking this crime seriously.

Solfa approached, after she concluded her discussion with one of the officials. "Several eyewitnesses saw the palace guard shot and fall on a woman. The shooter let off five more shots, emptying two crystal weapons. People scattered in response to the lasers. We feel JoAnna was the target and the additional shots were used to mask his getaway. There were several conveyances on the street he could have used to cart JoAnna away. The fact her body is not here is a good sign."

Koel looked around and noticed a number of delivery carts were being searched by palace guards. How many were pushed out of the general area before the street was shut down? There would have been no other way to move JoAnna without witnesses.

"This was not planned," Koel told Solfa. "He would have had no idea JoAnna was going shopping. The bastard must have been following her for days, waiting for an opportunity. He saw an opening and thought quickly on the fly. I do not like how he was able to think on his feet."

A palace guard approached him and Solfa. "We have found two bodies in the store to your right. The name of the store will be communicated through the communal pathways with your approval."

"Do it," Solfa quickly answered. "I want a physical inspection of every visible conveyance and scour the location of every reported sighting. No one will have time off until JoAnna Carlson is found. I want the CT Guards involved as well."

"Understood, I will make it happen." The guard took off as he communicated through the communal pathways JoAnna's description, as well as the name of the store. People were instructed to report any detections of their delivery carts.

The chatter in the communal pathways was too active to make sense of what was communicated. Koel had to work past his personal feelings for JoAnna if he was going to function. His soul mate depended on him to rescue her.

"Let us head to my office," Solfa suggested. "We are only in the way of the guards trying to do their job. All the buildings are being searched in case he did not cart her away. As soon as she is able, JoAnna will communicate to you. Based on experiences with Alex, the soul mate channel is the first pathway to mend itself."

Koel reluctantly agreed, he was only a distraction to the men and women who investigated the shootings and the kidnapping of his soul mate. It had to be the same person who had fired at them several days ago. All evidence made it appear this was the job of a single man. If there was a silver lining, at least they were not dealing with a revolutionary group.

When they got to Solfa's office, Candy was awaiting their arrival. She immediately came into Koel's arms. "I am so sorry. The attack was primarily on the guard, I did not see it coming. Shirl, Alex, and I keep trying to reach JoAnna through our pathway, but have been unsuccessful. We have to wait until she comes to or the pathways mend."

Koel knew his friends were doing all they could. Now it was a waiting game. He had never felt so helpless in his life. Every moment that passed without hearing from JoAnna was time lost in finding her. It was doubtful they had much time.

JoAnna slowly woke, she found herself bound and lying on a hard floor. At least she was out of the box and no longer gagged. She shifted her position to get a better look at her surroundings. There were no windows to help identify where she was or sounds from the outside. The room was bare, except for some plumbing. Perhaps she was in some kind of laundry facility. Numerous drains were situated every several yards, supporting her initial assessment.

She heard a door behind her open and JoAnna shifted to see who entered. The same man who had killed her guard and kidnapped her strolled in. He did not try to hide his face, which was not a good sign. If he wore a mask or some other means to prevent her from identifying him later, it would have meant she had a chance of getting out of this alive.

"I have to use the bathroom," JoAnna said.

"Soil yourself, I do not care. I can just hose down this place later."

Thankfully, she did not have to go, it had been a ploy to see if he would unbind her. Did she dare use her mind control abilities? Odds were he did not have a doubt regarding what he planned. The man already had a minimum of three deaths to his credit.

JoAnna once again tried to use the soul mate channel. Everything she had heard about that particular pathway would indicate it would be the first one to heal. She needed to stay alive long enough to allow it to mend to contact Koel.

"What do you want?" JoAnna asked.

"I want to deliver you brain dead to the Prime Ruler," her kidnapper answered. "It will be a warning to all mind control telepathic practitioners that none of you are safe. As long as the government continues to manipulate their citizens, they will all walk the streets of Aster Province in fear."

A chill ran down JoAnna's spine at his words. This was all premeditated and she did not seem to have any means to sway him. There was such hatred in his voice. Hostage negotiators she saw on television always tried to open a dialog with the criminal.

"What is your name?" JoAnna thought of a variety of names she would like to call him, but she could not alienate him at this point. If she was able to keep him talking, she would buy herself more time.

"My name is irrelevant. The government sees me as insignificant since I do not have any special type of telepathic ability that would make me stand out. I am not a mind control or crystal telepath. Chartail understood what it was like to be invisible in this world, felt to hold no value."

"Chartail?"

"She was brilliant, as well as beautiful. Her plot to kill the Prime Ruler would have worked, had I not backed out."

JoAnna had heard about her cousin's plot against Jeryl Jarlyn and the co-conspirator who was responsible for the ultimate failure of the assassination attempt. Chartail preyed upon men who were attracted to her beauty and were easy to manipulate.

"You were the one who alerted The Palace to what was planned? Two guards and two of your team were killed. My cousin and another accomplice were sentenced to die in the Nightshade universe. Do you know what your cowardice exposed my cousin to in that horrific world? She was raped, drained, and brutalized."

"Shut up, bitch," he shouted. The bastard kicked her for good measure. JoAnna needed to placate him, not get him riled up with anger. "You do not know anything."

"I have been to the Troyk Penal Colony world and have seen my cousin." Although JoAnna knew she should not point fingers at him, he had been the reason her cousin was in the position she was now in. "You are responsible for her being there and what she has endured. She knows you betrayed her."

"You have seen Chartail?" Her captor appeared to still be in love with her cousin. JoAnna knew how she was going to buy additional time. Chartail was not present, but she was going to save JoAnna's life.

"The Prime Ruler granted Prime Adholm and me the ability to see my cousin. She is living with a group of dissidents from this world. I am sure you heard about Candy Phillips and Tolfer Childers's escape from that world. I went with Candy and our friend Shirl, who is a crystal telepath, to the penal universe."

"You know Shirl, the female crystal telepath who saved Chartail from the vampires in the Nightshade universe?" For a man who had stalked her for days, he did not appear to know a great deal about her friends. She seemed to have captivated him, he sat next to her.

"I grew up with Shirl and Candy in Ginkgo Terra. We were daughters of dissidents from this world. They are my closest friends in this or any parallel dimension. I can have Shirl take you to see Chartail."

The man seemed to consider what she dangled in front of him. JoAnna was his only avenue to see Chartail, if that was what he desired. She could only hope he wanted to reunite with her cousin, more than he wanted to harm her.

"I need to think," he said and left her, as he locked the door behind him.

JoAnna lay there, not having any other options. She had won round two of their little war. Now, she needed to come up with other arguments she could use to bait him to buy herself more time.

"JoAnna?" she heard Koel communicate through the soul mate channel.

Koel had finally connected with JoAnna, thank the Supreme Being. *"Can you describe where you are?"*

"I am in a windowless room, with a cement floor, and numerous drains. It may have been a laundry at one point?" It was wonderful hearing her voice through their soul mate link. Koel had been terrified he would never connect with her again. Now, he needed to find her so they would be physically reunited.

He communicated what JoAnna had shared through the warrior channel. Solfa, Tarsea, Starc, and Shirl were physically with him in Solfa's office. Candy was with the other CT Guards who investigated all the leads reported through the communal pathways.

"Drains could also mean an abandoned slaughterhouse, hydroponic gardens, dye manufactures, just to name a few," Tarsea added.

"Ask JoAnna what he looks like," Solfa suggested. "If we can identify who he is, we may be able to find her through where he works."

"JoAnna, try to transmit to me what he looks like. We are soul mates, if I can see through your mind, we may be able to identify the son of a bitch." Koel knew they had

untapped telepathic abilities they now needed to leverage if he had any hopes of rescuing her.

He closed his eyes and concentrated on his soul mate. Koel had been able to transmit his consciousness to JoAnna when they were in the same room, now he needed to do it through the soul mate link. She was a fifth-generation mind control telepath, capable of unknown power. He needed to believe all the stories he had heard were true.

Flashes of a face came through the channel, not unlike what they had originally seen when they entered Traves's mind. *"Concentrate, JoAnna. Relax and only think about what he looks like. Pretend you are painting a picture."*

JoAnna did not respond, but the images she sent were becoming clearer. He was able to make out a face of someone in his mid-twenties. The man had a broad nose and forehead. His eyes were set wide apart, with bushy eyebrows. Dull blue eyes and nondescript brown hair came to light as the picture continued to clear.

"Check with Tarsea, Koel," JoAnna communicated through the link, ending the pictorial transmission. *"He was involved in Chartail's conspiracy, the one who turned them in."*

Koel had an ability to sketch. He quickly drew the image he had pulled from JoAnna's mind. As soon as he was done, he handed it to Tarsea. If anyone could identify one of the men who hung around Chartail, it would be her former boyfriend at the time of the plot.

Tarsea looked at the drawing and Koel knew immediately he recognized the man he depicted. "That is Harewood Danvers. He worked at a meat packer operation on the outskirts of town. Everything fits, based on the little JoAnna was able to share."

"We will take it from here," Solfa informed them. "This abduction is too public to have our little group take down Danvers. He was also initially involved in the assassination attempt on Jeryl Jarlyn. The man has eluded us since we took down his accomplices."

Koel knew it was futile to argue with Solfa on this point. "Not a problem, but I am going with you. I am part of your intelligence network after all, as well as Tarsea. However, Candy needs to be present. Her foresight may come in useful."

Solfa nodded her consent. They quickly exited her office and started toward the abandoned warehouse Tarsea had mentioned. Coded communication was sent through the communal channels to alert the palace and CT guards of their destination.

"Hold on a little longer, JoAnna," Koel shared with her through the soul mate channel. *"We have identified your kidnapper and have a good idea where you are. You promised me a little red naughty outfit tonight and I plan to collect."*

❧

JoAnna's eyes were glued to the door Harewood Danvers had entered earlier. She prayed the door would open and Koel would walk through the entry, not Harewood. Her stomach was in knots waiting for a rescue, which might come too late.

The communal pathways were still active with discussions related to the attack, but no mention of any operation to rescue her. She had not expected public conversations on that topic, it would spell her immediate death if Danvers was anywhere nearby. The warrior channel, however, was active with Koel, Tarsea, and Candy communicating. She figured Shirl and Starc were nearby, but not actively involved in the planning of her rescue, so they did not communicate through the pathway.

How many episodes of television dramas had she seen where the police thought they had the right location, only to come up short? The victim had been moved or they were wrong in their assessment. Why didn't the Troyk universe have squad cars they could leverage just for such an occasion? The small amount of pollution they would emit could not possibly cause the general population harm.

The door opened and JoAnna's heart sank when she saw Harewood Danvers. *"Koel, he's back, hurry!"* JoAnna had to lure him into conversation long enough to give the authorities time to get to her. "So, did you decide to let me take you to see Chartail? Shirl will do whatever I ask of her."

"I figure I can get Shirl to take me to see Chartail, I do not need you to be involved. Your worthless brain will make a much louder statement." JoAnna for the first time noticed he was grasping a thick pipe.

Her rescuers were not going to get here in time. JoAnna needed to rescue herself. She looked Harewood in the eyes and concentrated on shutting down his ability to walk. Movement was a function of the brain as it communicated to the rest of the body. In anatomy class she remembered it was the primary motor cortex which controlled movement. She would focus on that part of the brain.

To her amazement Harewood stumbled. She needed to continue to concentrate on stopping the motor cortex from firing neurons. Regardless of the struggle Harewood was experiencing, JoAnna could not let up.

"What are you doing?" Danvers cried, his speech somewhat slurred. Her continued attack on his brain had caused him to have a small stroke.

"Two more minutes, JoAnna," Koel communicated, *"hold him back two more minutes. We are almost there."*

JoAnna intensified her attack on Harewood Danvers's mind. She did not care if she left him a vegetable, which was what he had planned to do to her. There was a kind of poetic justice to all this. He fell to his feet and had a seizure.

It was less than the two minutes Koel had projected when the first of the palace guards rushed into the room. Her soul mate was the fifth man to enter, but the first to come directly to her. Koel took her into his arms, as Tarsea cut the ropes that restrained her movement.

A med-tech entered and went immediately to Danvers, who was still seizing. "He does not get medical attention until his victim is seen to," Solfa instructed. "I do not want any other med-techs to enter the crime scene." Alex's cousin may have just driven the last nail in Harewood's coffin.

"The contusion on her head is nasty, but I can take care of it," the med-tech reported. JoAnna relaxed as the small machine healed her head wound from the inside out. In a matter of minutes, the gash was no longer a factor. The med-tech examined the rest of her body and identified the damage Harewood's punches caused. "There is some internal bleeding, which we will see to next. The bruises on the surface of the skin will go away in time. There is nothing I can do about that."

"Thank you," JoAnna said. The headache she had earlier was no longer a factor. She had ignored the pain and concentrated on what she needed to do to survive and stop Harewood Danvers.

The med-tech did not seem anxious to finish with her and attend to the fallen man. "One of the people he killed today was a friend of mine. My duty is to heal, but I also take orders from the government. I will stay here and monitor your progress until I am ordered to see to the prisoner. There is always the possibility I may have missed something in my tentative examination of your injuries."

JoAnna smiled. "He did punch me a number of times." She did not miss Koel swear under his breath. He squeezed her hand a little harder. "I was a bit out of it, you may want to examine my whole body one more time. Take it nice and slow, we do not want you to miss anything."

"The Prime Ruler wants the prisoner brought to The Palace for a public trial tomorrow morning," Solfa reported. "He wants immediate justice for the people who violently died today at the hands of Harewood Danvers. Jeryl Jarlyn has advised medical attention can be given to the prisoner once he is incarcerated."

"You should be able to stand now," the med-tech advised.

Koel helped her to her feet. Considering what had been done to her by Harewood Danvers, JoAnna felt great. There was only one thing she wanted now and no one was going to stand in her way of obtaining it, not even the Prime Ruler.

Chapter 24

~

Koel held his soul mate as if his life depended on it. After everything she had been through today, JoAnna was bursting with energy. He could feel the extreme power through their link; it fueled his own mentally exhausted psyche. Throughout her kidnapping, he ran on pure adrenaline. Normally when he ran in that manner, he quickly crashed. Not this time. His body craved hers, and not just for fuel. Once more he needed to consider her state, rather than his own needs. She needed to rest mentally, come to terms with everything that had happened.

"Let's get out of here, head to your apartment." JoAnna used their closed channel, not wanting to advertise their plans. Her need for him appeared to be as powerful as his. *"The thought of being with you got me through this. When I thought all was lost, the memory of your embrace lifted my spirits. All I need is you to be inside me."*

Any thoughts of needing to let her rest were nullified with JoAnna's request. They both desperately needed to forget the emotional stress they had just been through and let the sexual physical release cleanse their souls. Everything except what they had together did not exist.

Koel took her hand, and they left the dank prison she had been held in. He wanted to get home as quickly as possible, but he took the long way through the park. The purple blooming flowers and shrubs always renewed him and he hoped they would do the same for her. She tightened her grip on his hand and brought herself closer to his body as they walked through nature's balm. He heard her breathe deeper, inhaling the healing floral aroma.

When they arrived at his apartment, he opened the door and turned on the lights. Although he had lived here for two years, the space was bare of any decorations or personal items. "I guess you can make this place your own. Nothing ever seemed right on the walls. Maybe I was just waiting for you to make it a home."

"How much money do you earn, Koel? It's going to take a lot of work." He could hear the laughter in her voice.

"That will not be a problem. Although it appears I never work, I am quite good at choosing what commodities to buy. If you would like, you can bring some of your favorite things from Ginkgo Terra."

Koel went to the bar and pulled out two glasses. He figured they could both use a drink to help them wind down. JoAnna had other ideas, as she launched herself on top of him. She kissed him, as if starving for his taste.

JoAnna released his lips. "That is just a sample. Where is your bedroom?" Koel tilted his head slightly to the right, answering her inquiry. "Give me time to shower and prepare myself."

What a fool he was! He should have known the first thing she would want to do was clean up and remove the clothing drenched in her late guard's blood. Koel figured he would throw those garments away and have one of the girls bring her a change of clothes before they headed to Harewood's trial tomorrow morning.

He was a little ripe himself. Koel did not want to join his pristine soul mate in this condition. While she showered in the master bath, he cleaned-up in the guest washroom.

After he showered, he knocked on his bedroom door. *"Come in,"* JoAnna replied, using their channel. He shook his head and chuckled. At least she no longer shouted through closed doors.

When he saw JoAnna, he stopped in his tracks. She wore a deep red cami and barely there panties. The outfit emphasized her full breasts and small waist. His mouth started to water, yearning to take her nipples into his mouth.

Koel never brought women here; he knew she had not found the outfit in one of his dresser drawers. "How?"

"It is very convenient having a crystal telepath as a friend. She generally does not portal travel between locations within the Troyk universe, but she made an exception this time. You wanted red lingerie."

JoAnna had been stunning in the black lingerie she wore the first time they were together, but red was definitely her color. He was so hard, it was painful. It was doubtful he would have any control or finesse this evening.

He saw the bruises on her delicate face and body. "Do they hurt?" he asked, as he lightly brushed his fingers along her black and blue discolored skin. Momentarily, Koel stepped back to give her space in case his touch caused her discomfort. He wanted to strangle the life out of the bastard with his bare hands.

"No," JoAnna answered. "The med-tech healed me, the broken blood vessels are not very pretty, but they are not painful."

Her gaze was stirring a fire already blazing. "I hope that beautiful outfit was not expensive, because I am going to tear it to shreds."

JoAnna did not give him the opportunity to come to her, as she once again launched herself toward him. He caught her as she made contact with his upper body. She wrapped her arms around his neck, her legs around his waist, and plastered her lips on his.

True to his statement, Koel grabbed the back of her sheer top and easily ripped it from her body. JoAnna let out a little cry of surprise, but continued to kiss him. The panties she wore required a little tug and they were history.

Fortunately, when he was done with his shower, Koel only put on a pair of boxers. Their skin on skin contact was incredible. The heat they were generating was causing each of them to sweat. He was surprised the moisture on their bodies did not sizzle.

Koel brought JoAnna down on the mattress and took one of her breasts into his mouth. Her heels attempted to push down his underwear. He released her waist and removed the barrier she wanted gone. As he sucked her nipple a little harder, JoAnna let a moan escape, which was music to his ears.

Impatient, JoAnna grabbed his rod and directed him to the entry of her moistened folds. Not wanting to disappoint, he entered her with one massive thrust.

She cried out as he drove deeply inside her. "Deeper," she screamed, JoAnna adjusted her legs, allowing him to do as she requested. He drew out of her and thrust again. She met his rhythm as he continued to drive and withdraw. Friction and tension continued to build to a pitch he had never experienced.

As he continued to drive into her, Koel could feel JoAnna's presence in his mind. She was not controlling him, but experiencing his enjoyment of the act, as well as her own. Koel concentrated on entering her mind, as his body continued to work toward nirvana.

⚮

JoAnna lost herself in Koel, body and soul, forgetting everything that had occurred. If only for several perfect moments, the events of today no longer plagued her. She felt the utter enjoyment he was feeling within his mind, while she felt him trying to enter hers, to share the same type of experience. Nothing compared to being of one mind and body. Just as he connected with her brain, their bodies fractured. It was beyond anything words could describe.

Koel rolled onto his side, taking her with him. He had not exited her body or her mind. They lay together as one, both too exhausted to let go. Once they had found the right spots to occupy within each other, it was hard to break the connection. No place was as safe or as comforting as what they found together. Her friends were not mind control telepaths, they would never experience what she had with Koel.

"I am not moving again, they can bring us food." Koel did not communicate through their link, but mind to mind while he was situated in hers. It was as if it were her thought, but she knew it had come from Koel.

She wasn't used to this much intimacy, it frightened her. She had lost both birth parents and her adoptive mother, plus her father was in another dimension. After what she experienced with Koel, she did not know if she would survive losing him too.

"Release your hold," she asked. He immediately complied.

Koel looked into her eyes and then placed his forehead against hers. He knew what she had been feeling and respected her decision without argument or condemnation. There was a peace in knowing Koel would know everything, not requiring her to explain.

"We have some things to get used to," Koel commented. "There is no instruction manual on how to be mind control soul mates. If I pick up something you do not want to discuss when you allow me into your mind, just tell me. I will do my best to respect your privacy. There is not a whole lot you can hide from me when we are one."

"So much for planning a surprise party for you." Humor seemed like the best way to cut through the intimate tension.

Koel continued to run his hands up and down her body. He was making her all hot and bothered again. When he brought his hands to her inner thighs, she almost jumped.

"Are you trying to distract me?" JoAnna asked. Actually, he could distract her like this anytime. He was doing all sorts of tantalizing things with his talented hands. She leaned back and enjoyed the sensations he was eliciting from her body. He was a master musician and she was the fine-tuned instrument he was playing.

"I can continue if you wish or we can grab a bite and get some rest before tomorrow."

"You're too damn considerate," Joanna complained. "Right now, I plan on taking the ride of my life. If I cannot keep my eyes open tomorrow during the trial, all the better."

Tonight she was going to exhaust her body and nullify her mind using Koel. Tomorrow she would have to deal with the horrible things that occurred today. JoAnna was petrified of what would happen at the trial. She planned on continuing the one thing that would not have her dwell on that fact. Her soul mate certainly seemed ready to oblige her.

Chapter 25

The courtyard in front of The Palace was packed with angry people. Their world was generally a safe and violence-free universe. What had happened yesterday rocked their community. They wanted blood and the culprit sentenced to the Nightshade universe. JoAnna thought of the angry French citizens, who stood before the guillotine and cheered as the aristocracy were beheaded. It was a testament to how frenzied the people were.

Harewood Danvers was bound to a post on a dais, which was quickly constructed for the morning's event. They must have worked all night to build the apparatus. Although Danvers struggled against the bindings, it appeared his left side was weaker than his right, evidence he had a stroke. She stood next to Jeryl Jarlyn, who was waiting to address the angry crowd.

When she was taken earlier to The Prime Ruler's greeting room for breakfast, the old man embraced her. He had not asked her a single question about what had transpired. It was clear he had already made up his mind about Danvers's guilt.

JoAnna could not condemn herself for the injury she inflicted on her kidnapper. Her ability had been the only weapon available to her, and she used it to its greatest advantage. She had been forced to draw on a power she had not realized the magnitude of.

Jeryl Jarlyn rose to a roar of applauds. His right hand was in a fist, grasping one of his many crystals. JoAnna noted a slight yellow light emitted from the cracks in his hand.

"Troyk citizens, an atrocity occurred on our streets. Our friends and loved ones were cut down in the prime of their lives, violating our once peaceful and tranquil home. I realize there are some among you who are opposed to my government, but what happened yesterday is not an answer to your concerns. This man killed five of our own, murdering them just to cover his other crime. The animal in front of you kidnapped and harmed one of our returning children."

Jeryl Jarlyn extended his hand, JoAnna joined him. "Look what this beast did to our beautiful daughter." The Prime Ruler pushed back the hair she had used to shelter her facial bruises from prying eyes. He raised her tunic slightly to expose the bruises near her left kidney. "This young woman has done nothing other than stop a man who had attacked, killed, and mutilated women. She has returned from Ginkgo Terra to a Troyk universe I no longer recognize."

Jeryl Jarlyn did not know what ultimately happened to Traves. He certainly was ignorant of what she had done to him. JoAnna doubted the Prime Ruler would have phrased what he communicated to the crowd any differently had he known.

The crowd screamed their support of Jeryl Jarlyn. JoAnna did not know if it was an authentic response or influenced by the crystal in his hand. Almost everything Jeryl shared with the audience was true and persuasive. He did not need the power of the crystal to sway the people before them.

"There was an attempt on my life earlier this year. Our misguided child, Chartail Adholm, was behind the plot. I have recently allowed her father and Chartail's cousin to visit the young woman in our penal colony, an off-world dimension now basically populated by dissidents and their children. I no longer send criminals to that world because of those young ones. My greatest hope is one day we can bring those people home."

A roar of support overcame the crowd. Jeryl Jarlyn raised his free hand to the populace. Loud shouts continued to call for Harewood Danvers to be sentenced to the Nightshade universe.

"This man was one of Chartail's henchmen, who planned for my death. I promised you, my people, I would not send anyone to the Nightshade universe again. Our children in the penal colony cannot be subjected to such an animal. Do you want this monster in our universe?"

More voices from the audience called for the death of Danvers. The crowd was in a frenzy, screaming for justice for the people who were murdered. Jarlyn pulled a dagger from his belt, turned to the prisoner, and rammed it into his chest.

JoAnna still held hands with Jeryl Jarlyn and stared in disbelief, shocked by what she had just witnessed. It was so surreal. The crowd had quieted, taking in all that occurred. Slowly the mob started to cheer. After JoAnna internalized what had happened, she screamed. Her cries were silenced by the crowd. The Prime Ruler released her hand and Koel took her into his arms.

"Get me out of here," JoAnna pleaded. She used their soul mate link, since the crowd still roared.

As Koel led her off the platform, JoAnna turned to see Harewood Danvers, with a dagger jutting out of his chest. She had watched Traves consumed by vampires, but witnessing the Prime Ruler thrust a knife into Danvers was more than she could take.

"I want to go home," JoAnna added, *"back to Ginkgo Terra."*

Koel had been horrified by Jeryl Jarlyn's public execution of Harewood Danvers. He could not fault the action, it was something he would have done himself when he found JoAnna bound and battered. It had been the madness in Jarlyn's eyes before he plunged the dagger into Danvers's chest that troubled Koel.

Since entering the Troyk universe, his soul mate had been subjected to one violent action after another. When she asked to go back to Ginkgo Terra, Koel could not deny her request. He would stay with her as long as he could function with the headaches the atmosphere would create.

"Shirl, I need you to open a portal to JoAnna's home in Ginkgo Terra. We will meet you at the Childers's residence."

The crowd parted as Koel and JoAnna made their way from The Palace. The communal pathways and the verbal remarks coming from the crowd supported JoAnna and were concerned for her. He had not heard a single negative comment along the way.

They continued through the streets toward their destination, holding hands, but did not share any thoughts. Koel imagined JoAnna was physically and emotionally exhausted after last night and her latest ordeal. Harewood Danvers would have killed her, had JoAnna not taken control of the monster's mind. Yet again, her life had been threatened.

When they arrived, Alex hugged JoAnna. Her friend closely examined the bruises on her face. "How is your head? I have some of the herbal beverage to help mend your injuries."

"I am fine, Alex," JoAnna responded. "The med-tech took care of my injuries last night. It's time I go home for a little while. I just cannot take any more." Koel knew his soul mate was nearing her breaking point.

Alex stepped back and nodded. She offered no arguments to talk JoAnna into staying. How could she ask her to stay in a world where she was in constant danger?

Shirl and Starc entered. Like Alex, Shirl went directly to JoAnna and hugged her. Although she had been healed internally, the bruises on her face were quite alarming. Leenea Childers herded them into the common room and gave JoAnna an icebag to reduce the swelling. Koel felt he should have thought of that last night, rather than having sex with his soul mate.

"I will open a portal for you to the exact location Darden had earlier," Shirl informed him and his soul mate. "Have you considered the power you both share will include protecting Koel against the atmosphere that killed our parents? Alex, Candy, and I cannot make Earth our home, but you both could possibly."

"If Koel can withstand the headaches, you should stay on Earth until we bring Benko Jarlyn back to the Troyk universe," Starc added. Koel never imagined he would live any other place than Aster Province.

Alex started to cry. "I found you again, only to lose you."

JoAnna took Alex in her arms. "I just want to see my dad and get some rest. My real mother and father fought for something and lost. I would like to see their vision realized. This world was where I was born and where I ultimately want to live."

"I will check on you every day to make sure Koel is all right," Shirl promised.

"What will happen if Jeryl Jarlyn asks for me?"

"We will tell him the truth," Starc said. "You have had a very tough couple of days. Your reaction to what happened today should indicate to him you need time away from the intrigues of our world. Ginkgo Terra in many ways is still your home."

"I don't want to endanger any of you," JoAnna cried. "I just can't stay here for the time being."

"Every one of us have wanted to go home, Jo Jo," Alex said. "We grew up on Earth. Candy, Shirl, and I have been able to support each other through our challenges in this world. You have a father who raised you and I know you miss him dreadfully. We will be here when you return."

"Open the portal, before I change my mind," JoAnna sobbed. "I am not going to say goodbye, since I will be back."

His soul mate watched as the air before her started to shimmer. They once again entered a portal which would take them to another universe. Koel did not care which world they resided in, as long as they were together.

Chapter 26

⁓

Ginkgo Terra

JoAnna exited the portal into an alcove off the hotel's main lobby. Koel was right beside her. She came into his arms before they exited into a public area.

"Thank you for coming with me," JoAnna said.

"You are my life, my soul mate," Koel answered. He kissed her with a passion she would never tire of. "I will stay with you as long as I can. If we cannot be together on Earth or the Troyk universe, there are other places we can consider. Perhaps Shirl is right and your mind control immunity to this world's atmosphere will protect me as well."

They exited the alcove and walked through the lobby toward the elevators. Her father's suite was on the twentieth floor. She had a condo several miles away, but wanted to stay with her father for the duration of their visit.

She knocked on the door and her father opened it almost immediately. Before he could react, JoAnna launched herself into his arms.

"JoAnna, where the hell have you been?" her father asked. "You have worried me to death. Blake keeps calling demanding to know where you have gone. He can be a persistent bastard. I guess he has had second thoughts about breaking up with you." She realized the exact moment her father noticed Koel.

"Dad, I have a lot to tell you. This is Koel, he is a big part of the incredible story. Can we come in?"

Her father looked momentarily stunned, surprised by his rudeness. "Yes, of course." He stepped away from the door and allowed his daughter to enter. He extended his hand when Koel approached. "Matthew Carlson." Koel shook his hand. If not for his strange clothing, he could have been any of the countless boys and men she had brought home over the years.

"Daddy, you are not going to believe it, but I have been to where my birth mother was from. It is a parallel dimension to our own." JoAnna stopped, she expected her father to call a psychiatrist.

"I know," her father answered. "A few years back, I was aware of a millionaire from Scottsdale keeping tabs on you. I went and confronted the man. His name was Ben Clark and he told me an unbelievable story. When I did not believe him, a young man named Darden took me to where the portal existed in Sedona, Arizona. I knew eventually you would find your way back to where you were born and I would never see you again."

"Daddy," JoAnna cried, "I would never leave you forever! A lot happened in the Troyk universe, but the most important part is Koel. He is literally my soul mate. We are connected with our bodies, souls, and minds. He helped save my life yesterday. Had it not been for Koel, I would have been in a lot worse shape than just these bruises. We will be staying here for a little while, if that is all right with you."

"Nothing would make me happier. It will give me time to hear your stories and get to know your soul mate." JoAnna had no intention of telling her father everything, she did not want him to worry when she eventually returned to the Troyk universe. There was unfinished business which needed to be addressed. In the meantime, she would recharge her energy before she returned.

Koel stood in front of the wall of glass and watched the thunderstorm roll across the body of water. Thunderstorms were rare in the Troyk universe, never had he imagined such an incredible view this force of nature presented. He would miss this when he returned home. There was no urgency in returning, since he had not experienced a single headache in the three days he had been here. As promised, Shirl arrived daily to see if he needed to leave Ginkgo Terra. She did not stay long, since she feared her migraines would return.

"You are captivated by the storm, like most men are glued to television watching football." JoAnna approached and he immediately brought her into his arms. "I hate to break up your fun, but security called about two men asking to see me. He said they were wearing Shakespearian clothing."

"I do not get it," Koel replied.

"Tunics and leggings. It appears we have a couple of Jeryl Jarlyn's gatherers looking for me. I told the front desk that they can allow them upstairs."

"This cannot be good," Koel mumbled under his breath. It had been so tranquil being with his soul mate here. All threats to her life and Benko's revolution were temporarily forgotten in Ginkgo Terra. "Shirl must have shared where we can be found. I hope he did not threaten her."

"I doubt it. Jeryl fears the power Shirl possesses, although he does not know the extent of her strength. If it was something alarming, Shirl would have warned us."

There was a knock on the door and JoAnna let the gatherers in. Koel was curious to find out what they wanted. He was surprised to see Cianan was one of the two men.

"Relax, everyone is fine," Cianan shared through the warrior link. "Our Prime Ruler has requested you return home. He has discovered new intelligence and wishes to discuss it with JoAnna." A second crystal telepath gatherer stood near the door. He was not introduced nor did he contribute to the conversation. Koel figured the unidentified man was in training under Cianan's tutelage.

"What type of intelligence?" JoAnna asked. "I do not know if I am ready to return to the Troyk universe. It has been very nice not having my mind assaulted by the communal pathways, not to mention two psychopaths I got up close and personal with."

"Your friends miss you JoAnna and we need a Koel's tactical mind to review the finishing touches on our campaign to bring Benko home." For the benefit of the unnamed crystal telepath Cianan verbalized, "Our Prime Ruler is anxious to continue your training. He has missed you greatly and, if I may say, has been in an exceptionally bad mood since you have been gone."

"Well, we certainly cannot have that, can we?" JoAnna walked to the windows and watched the storm come closer to shore. "I need to say goodbye to my father and do a couple of other things before I return. Have Shirl come tomorrow for me."

"The Prime Ruler will be pleased. Shirl has been powering a crystal to open a temporary portal to bring you home," Cianan said that last part for the benefit of the other crystal telepath. Since Shirl was a mated female crystal telepath, she could open a temporary portal with little effort. "We will go now. I will see you soon."

Koel escorted the two men to the door and then returned to her side. Together they watched the show the lightning was presenting over the Gulf of Mexico. It was a magnificent sight. He was going to miss this world.

"You do not have to return as commanded," Koel advised her.

"We can return here at any time. Besides, I am curious about what the Prime Ruler is up to. From what Cianan said, it would appear his time ruling the Troyk universe is reaching its end. I would like to see Benko unseat his father. One minute I think Jeryl truly cares for me and the next he throws me to the wolves."

Since accompanying JoAnna to Ginkgo Terra, she started to use Earth expressions he was unfamiliar with. Koel, however, understood what JoAnna was saying. Did Jeryl Jarlyn see her as a long lost daughter, a sacrifice to be offered, or an enemy to be eliminated?

Chapter 27

⁓

JoAnna was still shell-shocked after her audience with Jeryl Jarlyn. Her barrier and superb acting abilities hid her reaction to the questions he asked her. She needed to talk to her friends immediately. Due to the number of loyal followers in the warrior channel, she could not use that link. Not everyone who could join in the pathway knew all their secrets.

People had started gathering at the Childers's household when JoAnna arrived. Koel would be meeting her there. She stupidly sent him off to run errands, while she met with Jeryl Jarlyn. JoAnna immediately went into the common room and poured herself a drink.

"This can't be good," Alex commented when she saw JoAnna.

"No, it's not," JoAnna replied. "Let's wait for everyone to arrive. Give me a couple of moments to compose myself." She took a sip of whatever alcohol she had poured. It burned as it made its way down her throat. Her body immediately started to relax, as the liquor circulated through her system.

"I will help Tolfer in the kitchen." Alex quickly exited the common room, giving JoAnna the space she wanted. As people arrived, the little redhead directed them to the kitchen until JoAnna was ready to meet with them.

When Koel arrived, JoAnna swallowed the remainder of her drink and instructed everyone to join her in the common room. All eyes were on her, waiting for her to drop whatever bomb she was going to let loose.

"The Prime Ruler wanted to meet with me because he knew I had met Cassie Clark. He somehow found out she is his granddaughter and is demanding to know her whereabouts."

Her statement was initially met with silence. Eventually, a variety of colorful words were echoed. JoAnna was not surprised by the reactions she got to her news, they were all similar to hers.

"So, it begins," Alex said.

Her oldest friend was right on. This was either the start of a new beginning or the first step to their destruction. JoAnna walked into the warm embrace of her soul mate. They would see whatever fate had planned for them together.

The End

Enjoy the beginning of 'Nightshade'
Book One: The Nightshade Saga

Prologue

The Nightshade Universe

He was older than dirt, Drake thought after the lovely blonde who stood before him asked his age. How do you explain the unexplainable? Drake's existence defied nature.

This was one of the rare occasions he wished he was something other than what he was. His kind was a blight on any world they inhabited. A mistake, never intended to exist in this or any other universe.

At the beginning of time, as worlds fractured across dimensions, a division went terribly wrong. A sentient energy was forged rather than coming to life organically. The oddity traveled between worlds, leaving holes of negative matter in its wake. These frequency pathways between universes were never intended to exist.

As the energy mass traveled, it drew on the life-force of living particles. When it came across man, it claimed its first victim as a shell to occupy.

After settling into the primitive brain and physiology, it evolved from draining a being's life-force to drinking the fluid carrying the elements needed to regenerate the fragile biological cells, allowing the body to physically continue.

Thus, the first vampire came to be.

Drake had been one of the first men the vampire converted. For eons Drake traveled with this creature, living off the blood of others. Over time they converted worthy victims to join their family. Since women had the ability to reproduce, they only changed the male of the species. As a sense of ennui set in, more of the sacrificed were changed into vampires. The newly made helped to relieve the boredom of immortality.

The vampires grew weary of being intergalactic nomads. Eventually they settled in the Nightshade universe. Satisfied within their own world, the knowledge to manipulate matter to travel between universes was lost. Thus, only the original retained the ability.

There had been so many world divisions since his making, Drake had no idea which world had been his birthplace. It was best not to think along those lines. The ones he left behind had long been in their graves. Their progeny would no longer have known he ever existed. His life was now tied to his creator. The entity seemed content to stay in the Nightshade universe, while Drake had nowhere else to go.

The numerous portals leading to the Nightshade universe provided enough unfortunate beings pulled into their world to offer ample sustenance. Blood was plentiful in those early days. The maker was comfortable living off the unlimited supply of blood, until a woman came through one of the portals and life as they knew it changed.

She had a type of power over his creator Drake had never witnessed before. Her presence seemed to relieve the constant hunger the entity suffered. The master referred to her as his soul mate.

Through their bonding, the master thought he would transform into whatever nature had originally planned. They would venture off together, sometimes disappearing for weeks. Finally, one day the master left through a portal with the woman, never to be seen or heard from again.

After his departure, various legends related to their destined pairing began to be told. Over time, most vampires chose to ignore and ultimately forgot those stories. However, in Drake's darkest times, the thought of one day finding his own soul mate made him persevere.

Over several millennia the numerous portals started to close, until only three were active in the Nightshade universe. The vampire population had become so large, and the blood sources so scarce, most were shadows of what they once were.

Now blood frenzied creatures, they slowly wasted away. No amount of blood could regenerate those beings back into what they once were. Only the vampires who had been created by the master, had been spared the horrible thirst. Their bodies were as they were when they were first transformed. Drake held on to what little humanity he had left, waiting for his soul mate to become reality. Through her, Drake could finally transform from the parasite he was.

The woman in front of him was someone else's soul mate. She had the ability to navigate portals using her telepathic abilities and a crystal. The woman, Shirl, had entered their world and was now being held captive. Drake took the opportunity to offer his protection, capitalizing on the opportunity to spend time with the beauty. He had abused his role as a guest within the Venture Hive, to possess the woman for whatever time he could have with her.

Drake manipulated the telepathic bond that tied Shirl to her soul mate. Until he was forced to give her up, he would hold on to her with every fiber of his being. She was as close as he had ever come to finding his own soul mate.

What little happiness he currently had would be cut short when the daughter of the Venture Hive's master was exchanged for Shirl. Everything would be lost if Afton returned to the Nightshade universe.

Coming Soon: Feral Nightshade
                 Book 2: Nightshade Saga

About the Author

When Evelyn Lederman retired from her career as an insurance executive, she cheerfully anticipated the freedom to finally spend as much time reading as she'd always wanted. The twist in her story came when as-yet unwritten characters started cropping up in her thoughts, asking her to tell their stories. Now, she spends her days in Florida on the beach… with her laptop.

'The Chameleon Soul Mate', 'The Crystal Telepath', and 'The Warrior Woman' are the first three books in her paranormal sci-fi romance series,

Worlds Apart. 'Nightshade' is the first book in her new series, The Nightshade Saga.

Keep up to date with her at EvelynLederman.com or on Facebook. Contact her at evelynlauthor@gmail.com

www.ingramcontent.com/pod-product-compliance
Lightning Source LLC
Chambersburg PA
CBHW071603180626
46819CB00002B/108